"Your aunt gave you that house because she knew you loved it. She wanted you to remember the good times you had. The last thing she'd want is for all the happy memories to be overshadowed by what happened to her," Bruce said.

Lila made figure eights in her coffee with a spoon. "Are you saying that I should pack up everything and just move right in?"

"What I'm saying is that maybe you should at least go and take a look at the place."

Lila tossed her brown hair over her shoulder. "I don't know. It's all too freaky—going to the place where she was murdered."

"Confronting your fear might be exactly what you need."

Lila's fingers played nervously with the buttons of her cashmere cardigan. Her voice was heavy. "This is going to sound crazy, but what if we go to the house today, and the murderer is there? You know what they say—a murderer always returns to the scene of the crime."

Bruce gave Lila's hand a loving squeeze. "Don't worry so much," he said reassuringly. "I won't let anything happen to you."

The *valley* has never been so *sweet*!

Having left Sweet Valley High School behind them, Jessica and Elizabeth Wakefield have begun a new stage in their lives, attending the most popular university around – Sweet Valley University!

Join them and all their friends for fun, frolics and frights on *and* off campus. How can you resist not to?

Ask your bookseller for any titles you may have missed. The Sweet Valley University series is published by Bantam Books.

1. COLLEGE GIRLS
2. LOVE, LIES AND JESSICA WAKEFIELD
3. WHAT YOUR PARENTS DON'T KNOW
4. ANYTHING FOR LOVE
5. A MARRIED WOMAN
6. THE LOVE OF HER LIFE
7. GOOD-BYE TO LOVE
8. HOME FOR CHRISTMAS
9. SORORITY SCANDAL
10. NO MEANS NO
11. TAKE BACK THE NIGHT
12. COLLEGE CRUISE
13. SS HEARTBREAK
14. SHIPBOARD WEDDING
15. BEHIND CLOSED DOORS
16. THE OTHER WOMAN
17. DEADLY ATTRACTION

THRILLER: WANTED FOR MURDER
THRILLER: HE'S WATCHING YOU
THRILLER: KISS OF THE VAMPIRE
THRILLER: THE HOUSE OF DEATH

SWEET VALLEY UNIVERSITY®

THRILLER EDITION

The House of Death

Written by
Laurie John

Created by
FRANCINE PASCAL

BANTAM BOOKS
NEW YORK · TORONTO · LONDON · SYDNEY · AUCKLAND

To Adam Christopher Rose

THE HOUSE OF DEATH
A BANTAM BOOK : 0 553 50442 8

Originally published in U.S.A. by Bantam Books

First publication in Great Britain

PRINTING HISTORY
Bantam edition published 1996

The trademarks "Sweet Valley" and "Sweet Valley University"
are owned by Francine Pascal and are used under license by
Bantam Books and Transworld Publishers Ltd.

Conceived by Francine Pascal

Produced by Daniel Weiss Associates, Inc,
33 West 17th Street, New York, NY 10011

Bantam Books are published by Transworld Publishers Ltd,
61–63 Uxbridge Road, Ealing, London W5 5SA,
in Australia by Transworld Publishers (Australia) Pty Ltd,
15–25 Helles Avenue, Moorebank, NSW 2170,
and in New Zealand by Transworld Publishers (NZ) Ltd,
3 William Pickering Drive, Albany, Auckland.

Printed and bound in Great Britain by
Cox & Wyman Ltd, Reading, Berkshire.

Chapter One

"Shall we proceed?" Mr. Ethan Ambercrombe took a seat behind his enormous mahogany desk. He pushed back his horn-rimmed glasses and reached into a file drawer, pulling out a large yellow envelope.

"I think we're ready," Grace Fowler answered, her voice cracking. She squeezed the hand of her husband, George, who was sitting on her right, and turned to her daughter, Lila, who was sitting on her left.

Mr. Ambercrombe, the lawyer, folded his hands neatly on the top of his desk. "Before I read the will, I just want to offer you my deepest sympathies. Katherine's murder was a horrible tragedy. She was a wonderful gourmet chef and a bright, vibrant person. I consider myself extremely fortunate to have known her."

"Thank you," George Fowler said with a polite nod.

Lila tossed her chestnut brown hair over her shoulder and shifted uncomfortably in the burgundy leather chair. *Let's just get this over with,* she thought grimly. Aunt Katherine had been buried only yesterday, and here they were the very next day, sitting in a lawyer's office, waiting to divide up all her possessions. Lila's stomach churned in disgust.

Mr. Ambercrombe broke the seal on the envelope sitting on his desk and emptied its contents onto the desktop. There was a small box, a book, and a packet of papers.

Lila sank her fingernails deep into the soft, smooth leather. She bit the inside of her cheek, focusing her attention on the identically bound law books that stood in neat rows on Mr. Ambercrombe's bookshelves. Next to the bookshelves was a white marble pedestal with a circle of four lions carved into the top. An old globe was carefully balanced on the heads of the lions. Lila looked at the colored patches marking different countries. *I'd rather be anywhere else in the world than here,* she thought. "And now, the will." Mr. Ambercrombe picked up the thick packet of papers and read aloud:

> I, Katherine S. Cage, being of sound mind and body, bequeath to my lovely sister Grace three items. The first is a gold engraved pocket watch that once belonged to our dear father. The second is a journal of my favorite recipes, which I collected during

2

my culinary travels—I hope you enjoy it as much as I did. And the third and final item is my most treasured possession—the diamond that Chester gave me for our twenty-fifth anniversary.

Lila ran a finger over the hem of her slate gray skirt. She remembered the diamond, even though she had seen it only once, many years ago. In her mind's eye, she remembered it was shaped like a teardrop and was about the same size as a walnut in its shell. It weighed about thirty carats. Lila's mother had told her that it was one of the largest pink diamonds in the world.

Lila remembered when Aunt Katherine had let her hold it for a moment in the palm of her hand. She remembered moving it slowly as she watched the colors shift, the light shimmering like a thousand dancing fires.

Mr. Ambercrombe handed the pocket watch and the book to Mrs. Fowler. Grace Fowler held the items gingerly, as if they would melt under her touch.

George smoothed back the hair that was graying around his temples. "I assume the diamond is being stored in a vault for safekeeping."

Mr. Ambercrombe took off his glasses and laid them on the desk. His hazel eyes narrowed. "I'm sorry to tell you this, but the diamond was never recovered."

Lila's parents looked at each other. "What exactly

do you mean, Mr. Ambercrombe?" Mr. Fowler asked.

Deep lines creased the lawyer's forehead. "I know this must be a terrible shock in light of all that's happened," he said delicately. "The diamond was one of the few pieces the police suspect the murderer stole. Please be assured that if the jewel does turn up, it will be handed over directly to you."

Smeared mascara darkened Grace Fowler's eyes. "Poor Katherine," she cried.

Waves of nausea began to wash over Lila. *Who would do such a thing?* she wondered in horror. *Who would kill a wonderful person for a stupid diamond?*

"Shall I continue?" Mr. Ambercrombe asked.

"Please do," George said wearily.

Mr. Ambercrombe put on his reading glasses, then resumed where he left off. *"The balance of my estate, including my house in Sweet Valley and all its contents, shall be given to my darling niece, Lila."*

The words tore through Lila like a jolt of electricity. She looked at Mr. Ambercrombe, then at her parents, then back at Mr. Ambercrombe. "There must be some mistake. . . ."

"There's no mistake, my dear," Mr. Ambercrombe assured her. "Katherine made her wishes quite clear to me. She always wanted you to have the majority of her estate. She loved you like a daughter."

Lila bolted out of her chair. "But I don't want it! I don't want anything to do with that house!" A sour feeling was beginning to rise up to her throat. "I don't need any more money!"

"Aunt Katherine wanted you to have it. You should try to respect her wishes," Grace said softly.

"I can't do it," Lila said, backing away. Tears streamed down her cheeks. "I can't live in the same house where my aunt was murdered."

"How about another one for the road?" Elizabeth Wakefield smiled coyly as she wrapped her arms around Tom Watts's tanned neck. It was well after midnight, and the only sound that could be heard outside Dickenson Hall was the faint chirping of crickets and the rustle of tree branches swaying in the wind.

"You bet," Tom answered, putting his hands on Elizabeth's slim waist. With one smooth motion he hoisted her onto the front steps. Tom stared dreamily into her blue-green eyes, then pressed his lips against hers in a long and lingering kiss.

Elizabeth smiled languidly. "If you keep this up, I'm going to stay out here all night," she said with a giggle.

Tom caressed her silky blond ponytail. "I wouldn't mind at all."

"But I can't," she said with a groan. "It's getting late. Besides, we both have a lot of work to do at WSVU tomorrow."

"Don't remind me," Tom said glumly. He gave her one last kiss before turning down the path. "Call me tomorrow for breakfast."

Elizabeth blew him a kiss and waved good-bye as she watched Tom retreat into the darkness.

Longing tugged at her heart. Even though Tom only lived on the other side of campus, it was always hard for Elizabeth to let him go.

Elizabeth opened the door to room 28 and stepped into the darkness. "Are you here, Jess?" she called in a hushed whisper. Elizabeth listened for her twin sister's deep-throated snore, but the room was completely silent.

"I should've known better." Elizabeth grunted, hanging up her mini backpack on the coatrack by the door. Jessica was never home around midnight and probably wouldn't be back for a few more hours. Elizabeth hated coming home to a dark room and told her sister to leave the light on before she went out. Obviously Jessica hadn't been listening. "What else is new?" Elizabeth muttered to herself.

Marching bravely into the shadows, Elizabeth reached blindly for the lamp that was somewhere on the opposite side of the room. Just as she was about to touch the light switch, Elizabeth's foot landed on something small and hard. She slid across the floor and began to lose her balance. Her hands clawed wildly at the air, searching in vain for something to break her fall. Elizabeth landed painfully on her side.

"Ow!" she moaned. Elizabeth stood up slowly, her hip throbbing. She switched on the light. The hard, slippery culprit at her feet was a small wooden hairbrush.

It was Jessica's.

"What is a hairbrush doing in the middle of the

floor?" Elizabeth gave it a hard, swift kick toward her sister's side, and it slid under Jessica's rarely used desk. Elizabeth's jaw clenched as she looked around the room. It looked as if it had been hit by a mortar shell. The only items hanging in Jessica's closet were empty hangers; every piece of clothing she owned was in a pile outside the closet door. Bras were hanging from doorknobs and chairs. The contents of Jessica's makeup kit littered every available surface.

"This time she's gone way too far," Elizabeth said, her eyes smoldering. She took out her favorite pj's, the cream-colored ones with little brown puppies all over them. They were right where she always kept them, in the second drawer of her bureau, neatly folded. Elizabeth didn't expect Jessica to be as neat as she was—it was too much to ask. But she did expect her to at least keep their room from looking like a battlefield.

Don't let her get to you, a little voice whispered in Elizabeth's ear. *She's not worth getting all stressed out over.* Pulling the covers up to her chin, Elizabeth nestled in her pillow and focused her mind on more pleasant thoughts. It was almost one o'clock in the morning when she began to feel the sweetness of sleep overtaking her, drifting like a soft, warm cloud on a sunny afternoon.

Then she heard sounds coming from the hallway outside her door.

"You're kidding!" a voice shouted, followed by shrieks of laughter.

Elizabeth groaned and rolled over.

7

Several male voices mingled, their words becoming clearer as they walked down the hallway. Hysterical laughs erupted. Elizabeth knew that this could only mean one thing.

Jessica was back.

Someone banged against the door and suddenly it opened, filling the room with harsh yellow light. Bodies tumbled in and someone let out a deep, hearty laugh.

"SHHHHH!" Jessica hushed loudly. Her attempt at quieting them degenerated into a fit of giggles.

This is just great, Elizabeth thought grimly. She lay still, careful not to flinch at any sudden noises. Through slitted eyes she watched as five members of the Sweet Valley University soccer team made themselves comfortable on the floor of their room. *Jessica will kick them out,* Elizabeth hoped. She breathed heavily through her nose, inhaling with a light snore and exhaling with a low whistle. *She won't let them stay if she thinks I'm asleep.*

"I think Liz has some in her desk," Jessica said loudly. She clicked on Elizabeth's desk lamp and looked through the drawers.

A snore caught in Elizabeth's throat. Her body went rigid as she fought the urge to jump out of bed and demand to know what Jessica was up to.

"I found them," Jessica said triumphantly, holding up a deck of playing cards.

Good, now you can leave. Elizabeth resumed her heavy breathing, hoping Jessica and her posse would continue the party elsewhere.

But instead of leading everyone back out into the hall, Jessica took a seat on the floor. "Brad, did you bring the poker chips?"

"Yup," he said. The other soccer players whistled and cheered, obviously unfazed by the fact that there was a sleeping person in the room.

Elizabeth's blood had reached its boiling point. *There's no way they're going to play poker in my room.* In a fury, Elizabeth threw off the covers and sprang out of bed. "WHAT DO YOU THINK YOU'RE DOING?" she shouted.

Everyone stopped. They stared at her with blank expressions, as if she was a professor who'd asked them a question they didn't know the answer to. One by one their eyes fixed on Elizabeth's doggie pajamas.

"Who's the animal lover?" Brad asked Jessica.

They snickered at her. Elizabeth's face turned a deep, embarrassed red. She wrapped herself in a fluffy pink bathrobe, but somehow that didn't seem much better.

"Liz, I didn't know you were awake." Jessica's lips twitched as she tried to suppress a smile.

Elizabeth angrily folded her arms across her chest. "Did you actually think I'd be able to sleep through this racket?"

Jessica shrugged as she started to deal out the cards. "I'm sorry. We'll be more quiet." She pointed to each guy in the circle. "Liz, this is Brad, Tory, Sullivan, Buddy, and Tex." They nodded dully in Elizabeth's direction. "Guys, this is my mother—I mean *sister*—Liz."

Tex tugged at the visor of his baseball cap. "Nice to meet you, ma'am," he drawled. "Do you want to join our game?"

Elizabeth tapped her foot impatiently. "What I want is for all of you to get out of my room! Do you have any idea what time it is?" She crossed to the other side of the room, making her way around the soccer players and piles of clothes. She yanked open the door, but it only moved halfway. In a huff Elizabeth removed a shoe that was wedged under the door and tried again.

Jessica sullenly tossed the remainder of the cards in the middle of the pile. "I guess you'd better go," she said dejectedly.

They stood up and slowly skulked out the door. "Tell your sister to lighten up a bit—it'll do her some good," Sullivan said in a low voice.

Tory and Buddy each gave Jessica a kiss on the cheek. "We're going to stop by Sigma house to see what's going on," Buddy said. "Do you want to come?"

Jessica shook her head. "I'd better stay."

Brad dumped the pile of poker chips in her hands. "Give me a call when you don't have a curfew."

Jessica pouted as she watched them leave. "I'm really sorry!" she said.

Tex was the last one to mosey out the door, and Elizabeth slammed it firmly behind him, turning

10

the lock. She glared at her sister. "It completely amazes me that you apologized to those guys, but you won't even think about saying sorry to me."

Jessica scowled. "Don't start with me, Liz," she said, throwing herself onto the bed. "Thanks to you, my social life is over."

Bruce Patman grabbed a little glass jug filled with maple syrup and poured it over his strawberry waffles. He looked like he had just rolled out of bed, with his brown, tousled hair sticking up in every direction. Bruce was dressed in an old pair of sweatpants and a white T-shirt that emphasized his well-developed muscles. His dark, worried eyes gazed at Lila, who was sitting on the other side of the cafeteria table. She was unusually quiet this morning, seemingly preoccupied by the clouds of cream in her coffee cup.

"So, how did you sleep?" he asked, taking the first bite of waffle.

Lila tore open a packet of sugar and stirred it into her coffee. "Not very well. I kept dreaming about the house."

Bruce reached across the table and touched her lightly on the hand. There were dark circles under Lila's bloodshot eyes. She had been through so much in the last few days. "What are you going to do, Li?"

Lila's pale hand touched her long, slender throat. She opened her mouth to speak, but no words came.

Bruce frowned. "Are you sure you don't want

something to eat?" He speared a piece of waffle. "How about a bite? It's really good."

"No, thanks," Lila answered softly. She took a sip of coffee. "I wish my aunt hadn't willed the house to me. All I want to do is forget this whole thing, and I can't because I have her stupid house to worry about now."

Bruce wiped his mouth with a napkin. "I know this must be hard for you, considering that your aunt was murdered," he said delicately. "But tell me something—would you feel differently about the house if she died of natural causes?"

"Of course I would," Lila answered, looking directly into his eyes. "I loved that house when I was growing up."

Bruce nibbled on a piece of bacon. "See, that's my point. Your aunt gave you that house because she knew you loved it. She wanted you to remember the good times you had. The last thing she'd want is for all the happy memories to be overshadowed by what happened."

Lila made figure eights in her coffee with a spoon. "Are you saying that I should pack up everything and just move right in?"

"What I'm saying is that maybe you should at least go and take a look at the place," he said.

Lila tossed her hair over her shoulder. "I don't know. It's all just too freaky—going to the place where she was murdered."

"Confronting your fear might be exactly what you need." Bruce took another bite of waffle.

"I'll tell you what. If you want, I'll meet you at the house around three o'clock, after my Sigma meeting."

Lila's fingers played nervously with the buttons of her cashmere cardigan. Her voice was heavy. "This is going to sound crazy, but what if we go to the house today and the murderer is there? You know what they say—a murderer always returns to the scene of the crime."

Bruce gave Lila's hand a loving squeeze. "Don't worry so much," he said reassuringly. "I won't let anything happen to you."

Chapter Two

"What is this?" Jessica asked, tossing her book bag onto the floor. Posted on the back of the door was a sheet of paper that looked suspiciously like a list of rules.

"What does it look like?" Elizabeth asked flatly, not looking up from the book of poetry she was reading.

Jessica ran her fingers through her golden blond hair. The wrap skirt she was wearing opened a bit along the side to show off her bronze legs. "I can't believe you're still flipped out about last night."

Elizabeth snapped her book shut and put it on the shelf above her desk. "Last night isn't the only thing that's bugging me. I'm sick of practically breaking my neck every time I walk in here because you always leave your stuff all over the place."

Jessica rolled her eyes and plopped down onto the couch. "You're exaggerating."

"Am I?" Elizabeth's voice was edgy. "What about the time you shoved a box of leftover pizza under your bed and it took us three weeks to figure out where the smell was coming from?"

Jessica studied her cuticles, pretending not to hear what Elizabeth was saying.

"Or when you threw your hot curling iron on a pile of clothes and nearly burned down the dorm?"

She sure knows how to hold a grudge, Jessica thought. "What are you getting at, Liz?"

Elizabeth took the list of rules off the door and handed them to her twin. She hooked her thumbs on the belt loops of her baggy jeans. "Things have got to change, Jess. You're not the only person living in this room."

Jessica sighed and snatched the list from her sister's fingers.

RULES FOR ROOM 28

1. *Each person's mess must be confined to her side of the room.*
2. *No guys in the room after 11 P.M.*
3. *If one person wants to do something that affects the life of the other, permission must be granted.*
4. *Roommates should always treat each other with consideration and respect.*

Jessica handed the list back to Elizabeth. She covered her mouth to stifle a fake yawn. "Where

15

did you get the rules? *The Miss Manners Book of College Living?*"

Elizabeth posted the list back on the door with four thumbtacks. "I'd appreciate it if you took this a bit more seriously."

"Let's get one thing straight, Liz," Jessica said, swinging her tanned legs over the arm of the couch. "I came to college to get away from rules. It wouldn't hurt you to lighten up a little bit."

"And it wouldn't hurt you to clean up for once," Elizabeth shot back. She stood with her hands planted firmly on her hips, looking utterly defiant. "Whether you like it or not, Jessica, there're going to be a few changes around here."

Lila drove up the winding road, on her way to Aunt Katherine's mansion. The right side of the road was protected by a thin guardrail, and beyond that was a rocky cliff and the crashing waves of the Pacific. Lila gripped the steering wheel tightly in her hands and tried not to look over the edge.

Just as she reached the highest point of the cliff Aunt Katherine's house came into view. Warm sunlight reflected off the creamy exterior and red-tiled roof of the Spanish-style mansion. It looked so inviting from the road—no one ever would have guessed what horrible things had happened inside.

"Here we are," Lila said under her breath as she turned into the steep drive. She stopped the car in front of the garage and turned off the engine.

There it was, standing before her in all its magnificence, with its curving arches and great open veranda. It was a wonderful house. Lila eyed it with a mixture of fright and curiosity, as if waiting for it to divulge all its secrets. She wished the house could speak to her—to tell her what had happened on the horrible night Aunt Katherine had died. But instead it remained in stoic silence, the mystery guarded safely within its walls.

"Hurry up and get here, Bruce." Her palms were moist. Lila's eyes rested on a window on the side of the house. The blinds were drawn, and the lower pane of glass was lifted about an inch. Air was seeping through the crack, moving the blinds back and forth. *Was that the window the murderer pried open to get into the house?* Lila wondered anxiously. *Did the murderer leave it open so he could return?*

Lila's breathing was shallow. "Where are you, Bruce?" she asked aloud, her voice touched with urgency. She imagined he was still at Sigma house, gabbing with his buddies, completely unaware of the time. Agitation gnawed at her insides. "Thanks for being so dependable."

Suddenly Lila felt a strange sensation on the back of her neck, as if someone were watching her. Instinctively she reached over and locked the door on the passenger's side, then checked to make sure the back doors were also locked.

Unable to wait a second longer, Lila grabbed her car phone. "You'd better be on your way, Bruce," she said shakily as she dialed the number.

Perspiration beaded on her forehead, and

Lila opened the window a crack for some air.

"What's going on?" Lila screamed. The car phone went flying, landing on the floor of the passenger's side. Her heart raced as she struggled to free herself from the seat belt that held her down. Lila shoved open the car door and stumbled outside.

But no one was there.

The speed limit was forty miles per hour. Bruce took his eyes off the curvy mountain for a minute to look down at the dashboard. The orange needle on the speedometer was quickly approaching sixty. "Slow down, Patman," Bruce told himself. He gently let his foot off the gas and the needle started to fall. *Who cares if you're a little late, as long as you get there in one piece?* The corners of Bruce's mouth turned up in a smirk. *Lila cares, that's who.*

"I'm sorry I'm late," Bruce said aloud, practicing what he was going to say to Lila as soon as he arrived. "The Sigma meeting went longer than I expected, but what was I supposed to do? I'm the president of the fraternity—I *had* to stick around."

Bruce steered the Jeep around a sharp corner, not entirely pleased with his excuse. Even though it was the truth, it lacked the drama necessary to win Lila's sympathy. "I would've been here sooner," Bruce said, trying a different tack. "But a family of grizzly bears was blocking the mountain road. They wouldn't let me pass until I fed them raw steaks."

The fire-engine-red Jeep climbed higher, and Bruce's ears popped as he gained altitude. He al-

18

ternated his gaze from the road ahead to the vast expanse of blue ocean below. All it would take was the slightest skid—maybe even a few inches—to send a car careening over the edge into oblivion.

"I'm late because—" Bruce paused. He turned his head back to the road just in time to see a car stopped directly in front of him. His immediate reaction was to slam on the brakes, causing the back end of the Jeep to swerve to the right. It came to a halt just inches from an old Chevy Nova.

The dusty blue car was practically in the middle of the road. An elderly lady with white hair was leaning against it, supporting herself with one hand and waving at Bruce with the other. He could see that her back tire was flat.

Bruce groaned as he unbuckled his seat belt. There was no way he could leave her there. If a truck came up over the hill and didn't see her—Bruce hated to think of what could happen. Still, he thought of Lila, waiting at the mansion, ready to kill him.

"Maybe this is just the excuse I need," he said, picking up the car phone. Bruce dialed the number to Lila's car phone, but there was only a busy signal. *At least she's talking to someone. That should keep her busy until I get there.*

Bruce stepped out of the Jeep and walked over to the elderly woman.

"Do you need some help, ma'am?" he asked pleasantly.

The woman smiled and pointed to the sagging back tire. "There was some glass in the road, but by the time I saw it, it was too late. By the way, my name is Bernadette, but you can call me Bernie."

Bruce nodded politely. "Do you have a spare, Bernie?"

Bernie waved a set of keys in front of him. "In the trunk. There's a jack, too. Oh, dear, I hope the tire is still good." She walked slowly toward Bruce, keeping one hand on the car. "You're an awfully nice young man to stop and help me."

Bruce lifted the rug in the back of the trunk and quickly unbolted the spare tire. He wondered if Lila was still talking on the phone or if she was sitting in her car cursing at him. "Looks like your tire's good, Bernie," Bruce said, giving the spare a solid bounce against the pavement.

"Oh, that's wonderful," Bernie answered, clapping. "What did you say your name is?"

"Bruce," he answered as he loosened the lug nuts.

"Bruce—now there's a handsome name," she said, her blue eyes gleaming. "I once knew a Bruce. He was tall and had thick, dark hair. Kind of like yours—"

"Is that right?"

"And he had this smile that could light up a whole room without his even trying. We met just after the war. He used to take me dancing. Every Saturday night we'd go to a ballroom with an orchestra that played the most wonderful music."

"You might want to move away from the car, Bernie, just in case the jack slips," he said, securing the jack under the car.

Bernie moved away. Her eyes were distant, lost somewhere in the 1940s. "I used to wear a red dress with a full skirt, and every time Bruce spun me around it twirled!" Bernie giggled.

Bruce jacked up the car and began removing the nuts. He worked as fast as he possibly could. "This will be done in no time. We'll have you back on the road in a jiffy!"

"You should have seen us out there on the dance floor. Out there, we didn't have a care in the world." Bernie demonstrated for Bruce by doing a wobbly kick.

"Be careful," Bruce warned. He took off the flat tire and replaced it with the spare. In just a few minutes he'd be done and on his way to Lila.

Bernie regained her balance. "Is there a special young lady in your life?"

A nervous smile crossed Bruce's face. "As a matter of fact, there is—and she's expecting me right now."

"I should've known he'd be late," Lila muttered to herself. The heels of her leather sandals snapped angrily against the driveway as she paced back and forth. She yanked off her blue silk hair band and ran an impatient hand through her long brown hair. Ten minutes late, she could understand. Twenty was pushing it. But forty minutes was absolutely inexcusable.

"I don't know why I let him talk me into coming here in the first place," she said through bared teeth. The whole situation was stressing her out. Lila couldn't wait to see Bruce's car pull up in the driveway so that she could let him have it.

The clouds shifted and blocked the sun's rays. The strong wind bent the boughs of the trees that were clustered just beyond the garage. Lila stopped and listened to the rustle of the leaves. It sounded faintly like voices, a chorus of voices calling to her.

"It's just the leaves," she said nervously to herself, trying to forget the gravestones behind the house. Aunt Katherine and the rest of Lila's ancestors were buried in the family plot, only a few yards from the very spot where she was standing. *Come to us,* Lila thought she heard them calling. *Come join us.*

The clouds passed, and Lila felt the warmth return to her skin. The sunlight filled her with a strange sense of peace and contentment, warming her from the inside out. Her shoulders relaxed.

Don't be afraid, a gentle voice inside her head kept repeating. The voice reminded her of Aunt Katherine.

As if waking from a dream, Lila suddenly realized that she was standing on the porch. A reddish brown door appeared in front of her, its brass door knocker staring at her in silence. Lila's head was throbbing. Secrets were waiting for her behind that door. *Come inside.*

Lila entered the house and closed the door behind her. She stood in the foyer for a moment and leaned with her back against the door. It closed solidly behind her.

The foyer was dark and silent. The heavy red brocade drapes were drawn, letting in only an occasional sliver of sunlight. Lila stood completely still, her feet planted firmly on the hardwood floor, as if she were waiting for something to happen.

Is that you, Lila? a familiar voice whispered in her ear. Lila's heart started to pound. Her eyes darted around the room while her body remained frozen in place.

I'm up here.

The voice was coming from upstairs. A stray tear coursed down Lila's cheek as she climbed the stairs to the second floor. Memories came flooding back to her. Rainy afternoons spent baking cookies with Aunt Katherine. Holiday dinners. Singing while Uncle Chester played the piano.

Not here. In the attic.

Lila kept moving forward, past the bedrooms, past the mahogany armoire that stood in the hallway, toward the voice. Her heart pounded and an icy chill ran down her spine. Lila was terrified of where the voice was about to take her, but at the same time she couldn't stop herself.

Slowly she made the climb up the stairs to the attic door.

Chapter Three

"How about doing a story on body piercing and how it's affecting the students of SVU?" Tom asked. He walked across the floor at WSVU, the campus television station, and took a seat on the lumpy couch next to Elizabeth.

Elizabeth shook her head. "This is a college TV station, not a fashion magazine."

"I'm getting desperate—what can I say?" Tom shrugged his strong shoulders. "Is it my fault there hasn't been any hard news in the last two weeks?"

Elizabeth tapped a notepad thoughtfully with her pencil. "I was wondering if we should do a piece on the cafeteria. You know, a behind-the-scenes kind of thing."

Tom made a face. "I guarantee that if people knew what was going on back there, they'd never eat again." He picked at the spongy foam sticking out of a hole in the couch's armrest. "I know—we could interview that pizza delivery guy who's always around campus. I bet he's got a few interesting stories."

Elizabeth laughed. "Now you're *really* digging." She swung her legs around and put them across Tom's lap. Suddenly she felt something sharp jabbing her hip. "Ouch!"

"Are you okay?" Tom asked, his eyes filled with concern.

Elizabeth nodded as she shifted her weight to the other side of the couch. "Here's a news flash for you—WSVU Ace Reporter Impaled by Couch Spring. When are you going to get rid of this heap of junk?"

Tom's fingers stroked Elizabeth's hands. "I don't know, but if we don't come up with some interesting stories pretty quickly, we can kiss our meager funding good-bye."

Elizabeth sat up and pulled Tom's arms around her. "Speaking of kissing . . ." she said with a coy smile.

Tom pressed his forehead against hers. "Is there something you had in mind, Ms. Wakefield?"

Elizabeth nodded, biting her lip. She moved closer, until the tips of their noses barely touched. She could feel Tom's breath on her lips. Closing her eyes, Elizabeth was swept away as Tom's tender mouth came down on hers.

A deep rumbling started within her, gradually spreading throughout Elizabeth's entire body. It shook her very core as she trembled uncontrollably. Elizabeth leaned forward, pressing herself against

25

him. Tom responded to her touch instantly. Elizabeth was lost in the intensity, certain that this was the most incredible kiss of her life. The passion was enough to make the earth move beneath them.

Suddenly something fell off a shelf and slammed onto the floor. Tom and Elizabeth pulled apart, startled. One by one videocassettes were falling off the walls. An entire shelf collapsed. The black filing cabinet in the corner started to move from side to side. Tom's desk chair wheeled aimlessly across the room.

The vibrations were getting stronger. Elizabeth jumped to her feet and looked at Tom in horror.

"Oh, no!" she screamed. "It's an earthquake!"

Open the door.

Lila pressed her ear to the attic door. There was a faint tinkling of wind chimes coming from the other side. She touched the doorknob, the cold brass sending chills up her arm. Suddenly the floor lurched, rocking back and forth, and Lila pulled away, her blue eyes wide with fright.

"I'm sorry," Lila whispered to the air. "I'm afraid."

She was descending the attic stairs to the second floor when the house began to shake violently. Lila grabbed the handrail to steady herself.

"Don't be angry. Please don't be angry with me, Aunt Katherine," Lila whispered out loud.

Her knees weakened as she tried to make her way down the small staircase. As she went to take the next step the floor seemed to shift under her, and Lila's toe caught on the edge of the stair.

Before she had a chance to react, Lila was hurling through space, down to the bottom of the staircase. She fell onto the wooden floor, hot pain searing her body. She began to sob.

Please forgive me, Lila pleaded in silent terror. She reached for the windowsill and tried to make herself stand up. The wood vibrated beneath her fingertips. She leaned heavily against the window frame, her breathing coming in short gasps.

Aunt Katherine isn't doing this—it's an earthquake. Instinctively Lila moved away from the window, afraid of shattering glass. She had to get out of there. Fast.

Lila turned and headed for the enormous staircase leading to the first floor. The ground shook powerfully. Lila had images of the earth splitting open and swallowing the house whole, with her still inside.

Then she heard a loud *crack* just outside, in front of the house. It was a clean, dry sound, like splitting wood. Lila stood at the top of the stairs near the armoire and looked through the windows as a huge tree crashed through the front porch, blocking the front door. There was no escape.

Lila covered her mouth to stifle the scream that rose to her throat. She was trapped. The antique armoire that towered over Lila started to tilt. She turned just in time to see it come crashing down on her. "No . . ." she screamed.

Then everything went black.

*   *   *

"Aw, that was nothing," Bernie said when the shaking stopped.

Bruce shoved his hands in the pockets of his jeans so Bernie wouldn't see them trembling. His black T-shirt was damp with sweat.

Bernie laughed. "I don't even think that one qualifies as a real earthquake. It seemed more like a tremor to me."

Bruce nodded distractedly, one hand still gripping the door handle of Bernie's car. He took a timid step forward, assuring himself that the ground beneath him was solid. Few things terrified him more than an earthquake. As far as he was concerned, nothing made a person more vulnerable than feeling the earth moving out from underneath him.

Bruce looked up at the trees that covered the top of the cliff. A few of them had fallen from the quake. Somewhere beyond the thick forest Lila was alone, still waiting for him. Was she okay? The color drained from Bruce's face. If something happened to her, Bruce didn't think he'd ever forgive himself.

"Are you all right?" Bernie asked as she opened the car door and sat in the driver's seat. "You look like you've seen a ghost."

"I'm worried about my girlfriend."

Bernie pinched her small mouth in exasperation. "Then what are you waiting for? You should've been on the road five minutes ago."

Bruce scratched his head quizzically. "I can't

28

leave you here alone. What if there's an aftershock?"

She slammed the door and started the engine. "I can take care of myself. You were kind enough to help me change that tire, but you certainly don't have to stick around and look after me, thank you very much." Bernie took a pair of sunglasses off the visor and put them on. "Go and take good care of that sweet girl of yours. Now if you'll excuse me, I have some errands to run." She started the engine and turned the car around, heading back down the mountain.

A cloud of dust kicked up behind the Nova as Bernie drove away. Seconds later Bruce started the engine and the Jeep was roaring up the mountain.

I'll be there soon, Lila. Bruce's knuckles turned white as his hands clenched the steering wheel. The road turned and twisted unpredictably in front of the windshield as he climbed higher. Bruce dodged large rocks that littered the road— remnants from the earthquake. Thoughts of an avalanche surfaced in his mind, threatening to break his concentration. Bruce gritted his teeth and shoved the thought back, deep into the recesses of his brain.

A yellow, triangular road sign with a jagged arrow and the word DANGER! appeared up ahead. Sections of the guardrail were missing, shaken loose from the crumbling rock. Bruce's muscles contracted, and every nerve in his body was on edge. He pressed his foot down on the accelerator just as the road took a sharp turn.

That was when he saw the snakelike crack in the road.

"No!" Bruce shouted as he slammed on the brakes. The Jeep's tires skidded to a halt. Bruce pummeled the steering wheel ferociously with his fists. He'd never get to Lila now.

"Are you all right?" Tom asked, his arms still clinging tightly to Elizabeth's waist.

"I'm fine," she said as she glanced around the station. Videotapes were scattered on the floor. Papers and books had fallen off the desks and shelves. The filing cabinet had moved several inches, and its drawers were still open. Miraculously, the expensive production equipment remained untouched.

Elizabeth brushed back a strand of golden blond hair that had fallen in her face and tucked it into her ponytail. "Looks like we've got a story after all."

Tom's eyes widened. Elizabeth could see the gears turning in his mind. "Maybe we should grab a video camera and survey the damage. We could probably squeeze in a few interviews, too." Tom grabbed his camera, a videotape, and his battery pack. "Are you up for it?"

Elizabeth nodded. "This is just the break we've been looking for." She snagged the microphone and some cable. Her eyebrows furrowed as they always did when they were on the trail of a hot story.

They rushed out of the station into the bright sunlight. Students milled around outside the buildings just in case there were aftershocks. A few bicycles were knocked over, but everything else seemed to have held up pretty well, at least on the outside. From past experience Elizabeth knew that even though everything looked fine on the outside, there could still be a lot of damage on the inside.

They headed off toward Tom's dorm, taking a shortcut across the grassy green lawn of the quad.

As they neared the building Elizabeth heard the agitated, worried voices of students. She sensed tension in the air.

Tom cut through the crowd and moved to the front door, Elizabeth following closely behind. Just as he reached for the door handle a security guard blocked the entrance.

"You can't go in there," the burly guard said.

Tom flashed him a stubborn look. "I know you have to keep us outside as a standard procedure, but I only need to go in for a second."

The guard stared him down. "It's off limits," he said.

Just as Tom was about to argue, someone called to him. He turned around to see his roommate, Danny Wyatt, standing only a few feet away.

"Hey, Danny," Elizabeth said.

Tom walked over to where Danny was standing. "This guy's giving me real attitude," Tom said, pointing to the guard.

Danny's brown eyes looked tiredly at both of them. He was wearing shorts and a yellow tank top, the color contrasting with the darkness of his skin. "He's not trying to give you a hard time—

the place is really off limits. Of all the buildings on this campus, ours was the only one they didn't make quake-proof. The water pipes broke, and the whole dorm is flooded out."

"Oh, no," Elizabeth whispered under her breath.

The corners of Tom's mouth turned down into a harsh frown. He didn't say a word.

Danny looked at them solemnly. "It looks like we have to find somewhere else to live."

Bruce furiously kicked a rock into the crack, and it fell endlessly into the darkness below. He tried taking a step over it, but his stomach contracted into sickening spasms. It was just too wide. If the road had split only a few inches less, Bruce was sure he could have made it.

He looked up at his shiny new Jeep, the red paint glinting in the sunlight. Lila was so close, but he couldn't get to her. He imagined Lila hurt and bleeding, totally alone. *Don't overreact,* he told himself. *She's probably fine.* He wanted to believe it. But he had no real way of knowing.

Bruce reached for his car phone and dialed 911. Seconds later an operator answered.

"This is Bruce Patman," he said with a calm voice, even though his hands were shaking. "I'm up here on the Sweet Valley Summit. My girlfriend is alone on top of the cliff, and I can't get to her. I need someone to go to her house and make sure she's all right."

"Please repeat that, sir," the female operator

answered in a nasal voice. "Did you say your girl-friend is hurt?"

Bruce shifted restlessly in his seat. "I don't know for sure. I haven't seen her. I want someone to go and check."

"I'm sorry, sir. We're taking hundreds of calls right now, and our services are limited. I cannot dispatch an ambulance unless someone is actually hurt." There was a click, and the dial tone returned.

"Beautiful. Just beautiful!" Bruce slammed down the phone. He turned on the ignition and backed the Jeep down the steep hill. He couldn't leave Lila alone up there. He'd just have to figure out a way to get to her himself.

After rolling back several feet, Bruce stopped the Jeep. He yanked on the emergency brake, then gunned the engine. He gritted his teeth as he stared at the dark crack ahead. He continued to press down on the accelerator, and the engine roared. Bruce's heart pounded furiously, as though it were about to explode in his chest. "I'm coming for you, Lila."

In a split second he dropped the emergency brake and the tires squealed, leaving a patch of rubber on the road. Bruce pushed the accelerator all the way to the floor, and the Jeep zoomed up the hill at full speed. The engine roared in his ears. The crack loomed closer, and every muscle in Bruce's body tensed as he braced himself for impact.

Bruce gasped for air and closed his eyes. The Jeep hit a bump, but instead of keeping contact with the road, the front wheel seemed to hang in midair. Then the back wheels hit. For a few moments Bruce felt the eerie sensation of flying, as though the Jeep were cruising through the atmosphere. He opened his eyes to see nothing but calm blue sky in front of him. The road had disappeared.

Seconds later the Jeep landed heavily on the road. The back bumper scraped against the pavement as the back wheels touched down. Bruce looked in the rearview mirror to see the crack disappearing behind him. He made it.

With his foot still to the floor Bruce tore up to the top of the cliff, to the steep drive in front of the mansion. As he was pulling in he saw Lila's car sitting in front of the garage. No one was in it.

Then he noticed the tree that had crashed through the front porch, blocking the door.

Bruce ran out of the Jeep, leaving the door open and the engine running. "Lila!" he yelled at the top of his lungs. "Lila! Where are you?"

There was no answer.

Chapter Four

Bruce ran back to the Jeep and dialed 911 again.

As soon as he heard the phone pick up at the other end he started to speak. His words came out in short bursts as he tried to catch his breath. "This is Bruce Patman . . . I called a little while ago . . . my girlfriend is trapped . . . inside the house."

"Are you certain she's in there?" the same operator said in a flat voice. "We don't have time for nonemergencies."

Bruce gripped the phone tightly in his fingers. "There's no . . . no answer," he stammered. "I think she's hurt."

"But you don't know for sure . . ."

"Look—I need help!" he thundered into the receiver. "Send someone over here. Now!" Bruce gave her the exact address.

"I'll see what I can do, sir. But I can't guarantee anything. We're severely understaffed."

Bruce grunted in frustration and slammed the phone back on the seat. He got out of the Jeep and ran behind the house, looking for an unblocked entrance. Bruce tried to slide open the glass doors leading to the patio, but they were locked.

"Lila? It's me—are you okay?" he shouted through the glass. He listened closely, but no sounds came from the house.

I have to get inside. Bruce began to panic. He tried the door again. It wouldn't budge. Shading his eyes from the glare of the sun, Bruce peered through the window into the kitchen. Lila wasn't there. *She has to be somewhere in the house,* he reasoned. If she wasn't in her car or on the grounds, where else could she be? A thin, clear piece of glass was the only thing that kept him from finding out.

Bruce whipped around, in search of something heavy. In the corner of the patio he spotted a broken marble statue. While most of it had been smashed, a large piece of it was still intact. "Well, here goes nothing," he said as he picked up the piece and hurled it through the glass door.

The glass shattered violently, raining down like broken icicles. Bruce shielded his eyes from the flying shards of glass. He looked up to see a gaping hole through the door.

Bruce stepped inside, glass crunching under his feet. "Lila!" he called, his voice echoing through the silent kitchen.

He ran out through the hallway, peering into each room he passed. His thick, dark hair stuck to his damp forehead. "Lila! Where are you?" When he had covered the entire first floor, Bruce ran up the main staircase to the second floor.

"Lila!" he yelled, louder this time. He stopped and looked around the dark hallway. A few vases had smashed onto the floor, and lamps were overturned. Not too far from the top of the stairs an enormous armoire had fallen over.

Bruce wandered down the hall, looking into each bedroom. Had he missed her somehow? He walked around the armoire and opened the dark wooden door to the study. It was empty.

"Where is she?" Bruce said aloud. Fear and frustration gripped him, and he gave the armoire a hard kick. Suddenly Bruce's eyes bulged as he looked down at the toes of his sneakers.

They were covered with blood.

Bruce's stomach heaved. A stream of dark red blood trickled out from underneath the armoire. He looked down and saw a pale, slender hand resting right next to his foot.

"Oh, no! Lila!" Bruce's terrified scream echoed down the stairs.

He knelt and gripped the edge of the heavy armoire, his knuckles scraping the blood pooled on the hardwood floor. He took a deep breath, then tried to lift the enormous piece of furniture. A blue vein in Bruce's neck popped out as he strained against the weight. It lifted a few inches. He held it in place for several seconds, his arms shaking, before he had to let it drop again. He cried out as it fell back down, afraid to hurt her even more.

"Don't worry, Li. I'll get this thing off you." He watched her hand for some sign or movement, but it continued to rest limply on the floor. Bruce wiped the tears and sweat from his eyes.

Bruce moved around to the other side. He squatted down and took a firm hold of the wood. On the count of three he lifted it, again only a few inches off Lila's body. He teetered there, his face turning shades from dark red to purple. Tears rolled down his cheeks.

"Pull!" he wailed. Bruce's muscles throbbed under the weight. He couldn't let it fall on her again. A sudden burst of adrenaline shot through his body and the armoire gave way, moving up inch by inch. When it reached the point where Bruce could move underneath it, he leaned in with his shoulders and pushed all his weight against it. The armoire gained momentum and tipped over, crashing down the staircase. By the time it hit the bottom of the stairs, it looked like a pile of sticks.

Bruce's lungs struggled for air as he bent down to look at Lila. Her hair was matted and dark with blood. Lila's skin was frighteningly pale. He gently stroked her white cheek. His fingers held her wrist, searching for a pulse.

A siren screamed outside. Bruce ran over to the window to see an ambulance in the driveway. He waved at the paramedics and showed them the way inside.

Bruce lifted Lila's slack shoulders and held her

close to him. "It's going to be all right," he cried softly. He brushed her hair from her face and rocked her gently. "I'm with you now. You're safe." A tear fell from the tip of Bruce's nose onto Lila's cheek.

The first paramedic reached the top of the stairs. He was short and stocky and carrying a large first-aid kit. Bruce saw a look of alarm on his face when he saw Lila. "What happened?" he asked quickly.

"The armoire fell on her," Bruce mumbled.

The paramedic leaned over the banister. "Wayne—get the stretcher and some oxygen. Now!" He reached for her wrist. "Does she have a pulse?"

Bruce's eyes were glassy. "I don't know."

Two other paramedics ran up the stairs. "Please move back, sir," one of them said.

Bruce withdrew reluctantly. He stood by, helpless, as they began to work over her. *Please don't die, Lila. I need you.*

"She's got a faint pulse," the first paramedic said. They fixed an oxygen mask over her face and strapped her onto the stretcher.

"How long has she been like this?"

Bruce swallowed hard. "Since the quake. I guess it's been almost an hour."

They dressed her wounds and gave her an injection. Bruce looked away. *If only I had been here,* he thought guiltily.

They started to ease her down the stairs.

Bruce turned to the first paramedic. "Is she going to be all right?" he asked.

The paramedic looked at Bruce. Deep lines

creased his forehead. "To be honest, it doesn't look good."

Jessica squinted from the harsh fluorescent light of the hospital waiting room. The television perched high in the corner of the room was showing a news program with footage of the earthquake. Someone had turned the volume all the way down, and Jessica tried reading the newscaster's lips to figure out what she was saying. She wasn't really interested, but it was something to do to keep her mind off Lila.

Tom and Elizabeth were sitting on the gray couch opposite, whispering to each other. Bruce was in the corner by himself, his face buried in his hands. He had been that way for the last hour. Jessica suspected he'd become bored and dropped off to sleep. She resisted the temptation to throw a magazine at his head to find out.

Jessica walked over to the couch and took a seat next to her sister. Elizabeth reached over and gave Jessica's hand a reassuring squeeze. Jessica smiled wearily and squeezed back.

"Looks like Patman's all broken up," Jessica said, pointing to Bruce. "I didn't know he had it in him."

Elizabeth flashed her a disapproving glance. "How can you be so hard on the guy, Jess? His girlfriend is in the intensive-care unit!"

Jessica's lips puckered in disdain. "Come on, Liz, you know as well as I do that Bruce Patman doesn't care about anyone but himself. I bet he's

40

been sleeping in that corner over there the whole time." She stood. "I'm going to wake him up."

"Oh, no, you don't," Elizabeth protested, blocking Jessica with her arm. "Leave the poor guy alone. He's had a traumatic day."

"Like Lila hasn't . . ." she mumbled bitterly.

When they'd first entered the waiting room, Bruce was hysterical. Even though he spoke nothing but gibberish, Jessica had a pretty good idea what had gone on. The way she saw it, Bruce wasn't at the mansion when he said he'd be there. It didn't matter why—whatever the reason, Jessica knew Bruce had only been thinking of himself. He had a history of it. And now, because of his selfishness, Jessica's best friend was in the hospital, fighting for her life. If anything happened to Lila, she was going to make sure that Bruce paid for it.

"Does anybody want anything from the vending machine?" Tom asked, reaching in his pocket for change.

"I'll have a diet cola," Elizabeth said.

Tom touched Jessica lightly on the shoulder. "Jess?"

Jessica shook her head. "No, thanks."

Tom stepped out of the waiting room into the hall.

In the corner, Bruce began to stir. His face was all red and swollen, and he brushed away his tears with the back of his hand. *How pitiful,* Jessica thought with revulsion.

A nurse passed by, her white shoes squeaking as

she walked. Elizabeth turned to Jessica. "Did someone call Lila's parents?"

Jessica grimaced. "I knew I forgot something." She felt the pockets of her jeans for a quarter. Elizabeth took one out of her leather change purse and gave it to her twin. "Are you sure you don't want to do this for me?" Jessica grinned pleadingly.

Elizabeth pursed her lips. "She's your friend. You have to do it."

Jessica exhaled loudly and stood up. She walked past the nurses' station over to the pay phone near the rest rooms. She picked up the receiver and dropped the quarter in the slot. Her throat tightened. What would she tell the Fowlers?

The phone was ringing at the other end of the line. *They're probably not even home,* she thought.

"Hello?"

"Uh, hello—Mrs. Fowler? This is Jessica."

"How are you, dear?" Mrs. Fowler asked.

Jessica leaned against the wall. "I'm fine, but Lila's not so good—"

"What happened?" she asked immediately. Jessica heard the panic rising in her voice.

"It was during the quake. There was an accident." In the background Mrs. Fowler repeated everything to her husband. Jessica chewed her lip and patiently waited as they talked. Mrs. Fowler came back on the line, and Jessica continued, "Something fell on her. It hit her on the head . . ."

"How is she?"

The corners of Jessica's mouth drooped. "All I

42

know is that she's in the intensive-care unit. They won't let us see her."

There was a pause and more voices in the background. A moment later Mrs. Fowler came back. "We're on our way right now—please call us on our car phone if you hear any news."

Jessica borrowed a pen from the nurses' station and wrote the number down on her hand. Hanging up the phone, she let out a heavy sigh. There was an ominous hush in the corridor that left Jessica uneasy. Lila was vibrant and full of life—she didn't belong in a place like this.

Everything would turn out all right. It had to.

Back in the waiting room Tom, Elizabeth, and Bruce were speaking to a middle-aged doctor who was holding a clipboard. The doctor wore a white smock, and her gray-streaked hair was cut in a blunt bob. Black-framed reading glasses hung from a silver chain around her neck. Jessica stood beside Elizabeth.

Bruce had just asked the doctor a question.

She slipped on her glasses and referred to Lila's chart. "Clearly the next twenty-four hours are crucial. It will be the best indicator of how well she recovers."

Jessica pushed her way in. "What's going on? How's Lila?"

Elizabeth and Tom looked at each other. The doctor took off her glasses, and Jessica watched the black frames swinging on the chain. Bruce whimpered and sat back down in the corner.

Elizabeth looked at Jessica, her eyes dewy with tears. In an instant she understood. The words turned over in her mind even before her sister spoke them.

"Jess, Lila's in a coma."

Jessica's breath caught in her throat. She leaned against her sister for support.

Elizabeth spoke up. "And what if nothing changes after tomorrow?"

The doctor looked at her gravely. "There's a chance that she may not come out of it at all."

Tom unlocked the door to WSVU and Elizabeth walked into the dark station. It had been a long day for both of them. Thoughts of the earthquake had been pushed to the back of their minds, like memories of a distant time. But all it took was a flick of the light switch to remind them of what had happened.

"Look at this mess," Tom said. His voice was tight, like air hissing out of a balloon. "I'd totally forgotten about it."

The filing cabinet stood several inches from its usual spot, drawers flung open. Elizabeth looked down at the tile floor, which had become a wasteland of videocassettes. Tilted and hanging by only one screw, the wall clock read eleven o'clock. The sweeping second hand continued to move dutifully around the dial, unfazed by its new position on the wall.

Tom scratched his head. "Let's clean up a bit before we start editing the quake footage."

Elizabeth stifled a yawn. "Can't the editing wait until morning? It's getting late." She picked up a few cassettes, scanning the cases for damage.

"I guess you're right." Tom tucked the files carefully into the drawers and inched the cabinet back against the wall. "It has been one tiring day. I can't wait to go back to my room and crash."

Elizabeth stopped and looked at Tom. His eyes darkened as the full weight of reality crashed down on him. She dropped the cassettes and gave Tom a comforting hug.

Tom loosened Elizabeth's ponytail and buried his face in her hair. "It's so late, and I have no place to go. What am I going to do?"

Elizabeth rested her cheek against Tom's and stroked the top of his head. Without giving it a second thought, she said, "You can stay in my room." At the very same moment the words escaped her lips, Elizabeth remembered the list of rules that was still hanging on the door of their room. *Rule 2: No guys in the room after 11 P.M.* She had been so angry at Jessica, it never occurred to Elizabeth how the rules might affect her own life. Elizabeth's heart sank.

Tom gave Elizabeth a tender kiss on the cheek. "It's a sweet offer, but I don't think Jess would go for it. I'll just sleep on the couch here at the station."

Elizabeth glanced at the lumpy couch. It wasn't big enough to even stretch out on. She pictured poor Tom trying to get comfortable, occasionally getting stabbed by the exposed couch springs. There was no way she could let him spend the night like that. *If Jessica doesn't like it, too bad.* When Elizabeth made the list of rules, she didn't account for emergencies.

"You're not sleeping on that horrible couch," Elizabeth said firmly.

Tom shot her a sideways glance. "What about Jess?"

"Never mind my sister," she said, picking lint off Tom's shoulder. "Besides, Jessica is probably going to stay at the hospital all night. You can sleep in her bed."

Bruce sat in a corner of Lila's hospital room, numbly watching everything happen around him. From a distance he saw his girlfriend, lying pale and delicate, her frail body flanked by tubes and monitors. White, gauzy bandages dressed her head wounds. Her expression was serene but unchanging—wherever Lila's mind was at the moment, it seemed like a peaceful place.

"She hasn't moved at all," Mrs. Fowler remarked tearfully.

Bruce's eyes followed Mrs. Fowler as she moved across the room to Lila's bedside. She reached for her daughter's hand with the same elegant gesture that Lila would use. Mr. Fowler sat in a chair on the opposite side of the bed, his gold Rolex gleaming in the yellow hospital light. Jessica's quiet sobs occasionally interrupted the continuing silence.

It was like a play. That was the only way he could

describe it. Movements and characters and events were rapidly unfolding before him, and he had no way to stop it. Life was spinning wildly out of control, taking directions he'd never imagined and suddenly leaving him in the dust. Bruce was helpless, becoming more and more detached from reality. The only thing left for him to do was watch. And wait.

A short, plump nurse stopped in the doorway. "Visiting hours are over," she whispered. "You can stay in the waiting room if you'd like."

Mrs. Fowler began to cry. "My poor baby," she said, clutching Lila's limp hand.

Jessica put her arm around Mrs. Fowler's shoulders. "It's time to go. Let's get some coffee in the cafeteria."

Mr. Fowler stood up reluctantly, wiping tears from his eyes. He leaned over and gave his daughter a kiss on the forehead. His shoulders were slumped.

The three characters moved to the side of the stage, ready to make their exit. "Are you coming, Bruce?" Mr. Fowler asked.

Bruce paused, half waiting for a bright red curtain to come down and sever him completely from the surreal drama. "In a minute," he whispered.

Without another word, they all left.

Bruce stood up and propelled himself toward Lila's bedside. He sat in the same seat her father had taken. It was the closest he had been to her since the accident. Bruce gazed at her with cool observation, as though he were studying a portrait in a museum. Her skin, he noticed, was almost colorless. Under the light it seemed translucent, as though he could look right through it to the bone and muscle underneath.

If only I'd gotten there sooner . . . Bruce swallowed hard. Bits of dried blood still clung to her hair . . . *none of this would have happened*. Lila's arms rested at her sides, her elbows jutting out at awkward angles.

Bruce lifted his hand into the air and held it over her. He lowered it slowly, until it was only a fraction of an inch above her hand. He flinched in anticipation, as if he were about to touch a hot iron. When his fear subsided, he dropped his hand onto hers.

Bruce gasped out loud from the touch of her hand. It was as if he had suddenly plunged into an ice-cold river. Bruce pressed her small hand firmly in his. Being with Lila pulled him back into reality. For the first time since he reached the hospital, Bruce's body shook with emotion.

"Oh, Lila," Bruce called to her, tears streaming down his face. "Don't leave me now. I couldn't stand it." He held her hand against his tear-stained cheek. "I'm sorry I wasn't there for you. Please forgive me."

Lila remained still, the monitors showing the only signs of life.

"Come back to me, Lila," Bruce pleaded. "I can't live without you."

Chapter Five

"What are you doing here?" the nurse asked, arching one eyebrow suspiciously.

Stay calm, the young medical intern thought, *you can talk your way out of this one.* He stared down at the short woman, whose pudgy hands were resting confidently on her hips. He casually ran his fingers through his wavy blond hair and flashed her a bright grin, showing off his perfect white teeth.

"I just finished my rounds and I thought I'd give you guys a hand. I heard you were understaffed tonight." His voice was as smooth as velvet.

The nurse puffed out her cheeks as she sized him up. Her beady eyes scrutinized the ID badge clipped to his smock. "You're one of the interns," she said in a raspy voice. "You have your own wing, so what brings you here?"

It wasn't unusual for an intern to have to pass through the intensive-care wing at least once a week, and today he had made four trips. But it wasn't the ordinary, work-related reasons that had brought him there. It was the young woman who was lying in a coma in ICU room number 4.

Earlier in the day he had been checking on the status of a patient when the medical team rushed by, wheeling the young woman into the unit. His deep blue eyes had caught only a brief glimpse of her, but in those few seconds he knew she was the most beautiful woman he had ever seen.

Her name was Lila Fowler. He'd gotten the name off her chart, which he stole a peek from at the nurses' station. Severe head trauma and loss of blood. And now she was in a coma. The prognosis wasn't good. Even though Lila wasn't on his list of patients to visit, the intern felt compelled to stop and see how she was, hoping her condition had improved.

"Like I said, I heard you were understaffed," the intern lied, knowing full well that there were harsh penalties for visiting patients not on his list. "I'm here to help."

The nurse eyed him. "I bet you're just finishing a double shift, aren't you?"

The intern smirked, showing off the dimples on either side of his cheeks. He did his best to look charmed and amused. "How did you know that?"

"I can see it in your eyes," she answered, crossing her arms in front of her. "You all look the same. By the time the end of your shift rolls around, you all start to get this crazy look in your eyes."

He laughed warmly. "Don't worry, we're just as sane as you."

"That's what I'm afraid of," the nurse answered with a bubbly laugh. She gave him a maternal pat on the arm. "Go on home now and make sure to get some rest."

"I will," he said cheerfully, watching her walk on. As soon as she turned into the next room he glanced around to make sure no one was watching. Then, when it was clear, he opened the door to Lila's room and slipped inside.

Jessica's chin fell to her chest, and her heavy eyelids began to close. It was four fifteen A.M. She'd had three cups of coffee, walked around the hospital wing every fifteen minutes, and read four issues of *Vogue*. Still nothing could keep her awake.

She slowly got up and stood next to Mr. and Mrs. Fowler, who were on the other side of the waiting room.

Mrs. Fowler smiled wearily and put her arm around Jessica. "There's good news," she said, her voice thick with tears. "Lila's out of the coma. The doctor said they're going to run some tests, but they're hopeful that everything will be fine."

Jessica rubbed her red eyes. "That's great," she said with relief. "When can we see her?"

"Not for a while yet," Mr. Fowler answered. "In the meantime, you should go home and get some rest. Come on, we'll drive you."

When Jessica got back to her dorm room, she

heard a loud snoring noise. That was unusual for Elizabeth—normally she didn't snore at all. But tonight she sounded like a buzz saw.

Jessica reached for the light switch but stopped short of turning it on. In the hazy, early morning light she saw the outline of the list of rules on the door. Jessica sighed heavily and changed into her purple silk nightshirt in the dark.

Jessica groggily walked over to her side of the room, her eyes already drooping at the thought of crawling into a nice, warm bed. She'd be out cold in a matter of minutes. Half asleep, she pulled back the comforter and slipped under the covers.

Just as she plopped down onto the bed, someone let out a groan and a loud snore. Jessica froze. The sound wasn't coming from her sister on the other side of the room. It was coming from Jessica's bed. She lifted the covers. Snoring peacefully on the far side of Jessica's bed was Tom Watts.

"I can't believe this," Jessica said out loud, this time not caring who woke up. She gave Tom a forceful nudge. He kept on snoring, his arms clutching her pillow. He looked as innocent as a child. Jessica gripped his shoulder and shook him hard.

"Whuh?" Tom said in his sleep, rolling over toward Jessica. The pillow was still firmly in his grasp.

"You're not getting away with this one, Tommy boy." Jessica moved onto the other side of the bed. Holding the corner of the pillow with both hands, she jerked it away from him. Tom's head landed on the mattress with a thud.

Jessica brushed off her hands with an air of satisfaction. But the job wasn't over yet. She backed up against the wall, then placed one foot squarely on the small of his back. Jessica gritted her teeth, and with an angry kick she rolled Tom's body off the edge of the bed. As Tom fell onto the floor the bedcovers came off with him, softening the fall.

Jessica glared at him as he slept soundly, wrapped in the warmth of *her* blankets. What made Tom think he could come in here and take over her bed? What made Elizabeth think she could let him do it?

Jessica leaned over the bed and with a swift yank pulled the covers out from underneath him. Tom continued to sleep, undisturbed, with his cheek pressed against the cold, hard floor. "I hope you learn from this, Tom Watts," Jessica said menacingly. "Because next time you'll wake up in a garbage dumpster."

"Lila, honey, I'm so glad you're all right," Lila's mom said as she gave her daughter a kiss on the forehead. "You gave us such a scare."

Bruce, who was sitting in a chair beside the hospital bed, reached for her hand. Lila didn't move, but instead she let him pick it up. His touch was cold and clammy. "We were so worried," he said, looking at her intensely.

Lila looked at the faces that were gawking at her around the bed. Aside from her parents and Bruce there was Jessica, Isabella Ricci, Magda Helperin, Denise Waters, and a few other Thetas.

Lila shifted weakly in her bed. "You guys are acting like I did it on purpose."

"Of course not," Lila's dad answered. "But you'll be glad to know the tests came back, and the doctor said you should make a full recovery."

Jessica tapped Lila affectionately on the foot. "Were you scared, Li? What was it like to be in a coma?"

"I was scared at first," Lila said thoughtfully. "I couldn't move my body at all—it was like I was wrapped in heavy, wet rags. All these memories of my childhood swirled around me like in a kaleidoscope—"

"Don't strain yourself," Mr. Fowler interrupted. "If you're tired, you can tell us your story later."

"I'm fine," Lila said, continuing. "Then I remember seeing two doors. I was drawn to the one on the left, and as I got closer to it I felt my body getting lighter."

"What was behind the other door?" Denise asked.

Lila's brow creased in concentration. "Beautiful music and a brilliant, greenish yellow light. I passed through the door, and on the other side was an angel."

Everyone looked stunned. "An *angel*?" Jessica said.

Lila nodded. "There was a golden light around him. His hair was blond and wavy, and he looked at me with the bluest eyes I've ever seen. He told me not to be afraid. He said it wasn't my time to go yet." Her eyes glistened with tears. "I'm here because of that angel."

Lila's dad cleared his throat. "You're here because you had wonderful doctors," he corrected.

Bruce smoothed back the dark hair that was plastered to Lila's forehead. "You were heavily medicated."

Lila flinched. "I didn't hallucinate. It was real. I saw an angel," she said, her tone growing more urgent.

"You've been through a traumatic experience," Lila's mother said. "Don't get yourself worked up over nothing, sweetie."

"It's not nothing," Lila snapped. "Doesn't anyone believe me?"

"Of course we do," Jessica answered, eyeing her strangely.

Isabella looked worried. "You seem a little tired," she said. "Maybe we should leave you alone."

Lila nodded. Denise stepped forward, a cheerful smile plastered on her face. "The Theta fundraising gala is coming up in a few weeks. We still have a lot of planning to do."

"We have a meeting this afternoon," Jessica piped in. "I wish you could be there."

"Me too," Lila answered.

One by one, the Thetas cheerfully said goodbye. Lila knew they were just humoring her, that they all thought she was crazy. They couldn't understand her incredible experience. It was as if a wall had been thrust up between them. On one side was Lila; on the other was everyone else.

"Don't worry, Lila," Bruce said, holding her

hand firmly in his as soon as everyone left. "I'm not going to leave your side."

Lila's body and mind were exhausted. All she wanted to do was drift off to sleep so she could see her angel again. "You don't have to stay," she said. "I'm pretty tired."

Bruce looked at her earnestly. "No—I've made up my mind. I'm going to be with you through everything."

Lila's face flashed annoyance. "How ironic; you're here now that I'm perfectly fine. But let me ask you one question, Bruce." Her blue eyes stared at his eyes, boring deep holes into them. "Where were you when I needed you?"

Chapter Six

"What the heck is this?" Jessica shrieked when she saw the camera tripod set up in front of her closet.

Elizabeth looked up from her book and shot Tom a meaningful glance. "It's Tom's studio equipment," she said lightly. She smoothed the wrinkles of her long floral skirt. "We wanted to get it out of the way."

"You call blocking my closet 'getting it out of the way'?" Jessica picked up one of the tripod legs.

"Easy!" Tom said. He ran up to it before Jessica could do any serious damage. "I'm sorry— I'll put it someplace else."

Jessica kicked a pile of videotapes. "And what about these things?"

Tom scrambled to pick them up. "I'll move these, too. I didn't know where to put them. . . ."

"I know where you can put them," Jessica said furiously as she pointed to a corner of the room. "Right in that trash can over there."

Elizabeth rolled her eyes and slammed her book shut. With all the commotion, studying was out of the question. "Come on, Jessica—it's not like *you* never leave things hanging around. When did you get so neat?"

"About the same time you started breaking your own rules," Jessica said, fiddling with the strap of her red halter top. She tore down the list and handed it to her sister. "Do you need a little reminder?"

Elizabeth glared at Jessica. "Now is not the time to discuss this," she muttered under her breath.

"Why not?" Jessica answered innocently. "I think it's time to get everything out in the open. Don't you agree, Tom?"

Tom moved the equipment onto Elizabeth's bed, ignoring the comment.

"Well, I'll tell you how I feel about this whole situation. I want Tom out of here by tonight."

Elizabeth gritted her teeth. "Jess, don't do this."

Jessica sprawled out on the small couch. "I'm only doing what you did to me a few nights ago. But the difference is that *my* friends were only going to stay for a few hours—not a few days."

"Don't compare this to your little poker party. It's completely different. Tom has nowhere to go."

Jessica leered at Tom, who was smart enough to stay at a safe distance. "I guess that's Tom's problem now, isn't it?"

"Look," Tom began, holding his hands in the air like a referee. "I don't want to cause any problems—"

58

"Tom, you're not going anywhere," Elizabeth said, her eyes still fixed on Jessica. "You're staying right here."

"No, he's not," Jessica scoffed.

Tom grabbed his coat and the video camera. "I'm going out for a while," he said to Elizabeth. He headed out the door.

"Tom, wait—" Elizabeth shouted as the door closed behind him. She turned to Jessica, her face flushed with rage. "Would it kill you to be unselfish for once in your life?"

Lila's eyes fluttered open in the darkness of the hospital room. In the shifting shadows, she heard the sound of someone approaching her bed. Lila's eyes cleared. Her heart leapt as she saw the familiar blue eyes and golden halo of light. He was back. The angel had returned.

Lila pinched her elbow to see if it was all a dream, like everyone had said. But it was real. He bent over her gracefully and touched her forehead. The warmth of his hand filled her with calm. His eyes seemed to speak to her—they were filled with love.

She had to talk to him. Lila opened her mouth, praying she could find the words. At last she said, "Are you an angel?"

The man laughed lightheartedly. He stepped back a bit, and Lila saw that the golden light illuminating his hair was coming from a night-light plugged into the wall behind him.

"No," he answered, his voice soft and gentle

as a lullaby. "I'm just a poor med student."

Lila's hopes fell to disappointment. It was much easier for her to believe that a miracle had taken place instead of a stranger coming to her rescue. She stared, captivated by his eyes. It should have frightened her to have a strange man sneaking into her room in the middle of the night, but she was perfectly relaxed. "Who are you, then?" she asked.

"Porter Davis," he said, formally extending his hand. "I'm an intern here at the hospital."

Lila reached out, firmly grasping his hand. She didn't let go. "Porter, you saved my life last night."

Porter grinned shyly, deep dimples appearing in his cheeks. "You saved yourself."

"No, it was you," Lila persisted. Her initial disappointment was dissolving quickly. There was a yearning inside her, a need to know everything about this intriguing man. She pulled him closer. "Why did you do it?" she asked.

Porter looked down, his thumb stroking the smooth skin of her hand. "After they brought you in yesterday, I came by when no one was around to see how you were doing."

Lila's eyes were shiny with tears. They weren't tears of sadness; she was touched by how humble he was. Porter had an amazing gift, and yet he seemed totally unaware of it. Without giving it a second thought Lila reached up and ran her fingers through his thick blond hair. "Go on," she said.

"I'm not sure why I did it—I just knew I had to," Porter continued, still too shy to look directly into her eyes. "I kept talking to you, hoping you'd come out of the coma."

Lila smiled. "Thank you," she whispered. "Without you, I don't think I would've come out of it." She held his face in her hands and slowly turned him toward her so that they were looking directly at each other. "But you didn't answer my question—why did you do it?"

Porter swallowed hard, his eyes unswerving. "I think I fell in love with you the moment I saw you."

"Did you bring a flashlight?" Tom asked Danny. He zipped his dark coat and turned the collar up so that it covered half of his face. It was almost midnight, and across the quad they could see only a few scattered dorm rooms that still had their lights on.

"I brought two, and extra batteries," Danny answered as he took them out of his coat pocket. He tossed Tom a black knit cap. "You'd better put this on just in case."

Tom pulled the cap on over his ears.

Danny laughed as he handed Tom one of the flashlights. "We sure do look scary dressed up like this. Don't you think we're overdoing it just a bit?"

"No way," Tom said. "The dean said there'd be a stiff penalty for anyone caught doing this. I know it's only for the safety of the students, but I'm not about to take a chance."

"I guess you're right, buddy. Let's go."

They headed off across the lawn toward their dorm. It stood silent and dark—not even the lights on the front step were on. The grounds crew had cut the electricity because of the water damage. The building was completely abandoned, like a run-down building in an old Western. The sight sent a chill through Tom. He half expected the wind to pick up some tumbleweed to blow across the lawn.

Danny walked ahead, leading Tom around to the back of the building. Each window was covered with yellow tape with the words DO NOT CROSS! printed in bold letters.

"It's a good thing we live on the ground floor," Tom said soberly. When they reached their dorm window, he gently peeled off the tape and spooled it around his hand.

Danny opened the window. "Here we are, breaking into our own room. Kind of weird, isn't it?"

Tom nodded. Did the school really expect them to live without any of their things? "Do you want to go first?"

"Sure." Danny stepped onto the support Tom had made by lacing his fingers together and was hoisted up to the windowsill. He crawled inside, then pulled Tom into the room with him.

Tom's feet landed in a few inches of water. The inner soles of his sneakers filled up like sponges. "This is bad news," he said gravely. He debated whether or not to leave, afraid of what they might find.

"Here goes nothing," Danny said, and clicked on his flashlight. Tom turned on his too. They both stood in silence as they waved the light beams around what was left of their room.

Tom's bureau had fallen over, spilling clean clothes into the inches of murky water on the floor. Books floated by, along with a few videotapes and Tom's prized possession, his autographed football. He moved the beam of light toward his desk. Water was dripping from a leaking pipe directly onto his computer.

"This is awful," Danny moaned. He waded through the ankle-deep water and picked up a framed picture of his girlfriend, Isabella. He dried it off with his coat and stuck the frame in his duffel bag.

Tom's stomach tensed. He picked up the football. "Everything's ruined."

Danny frowned as he wiped off a puddle that had accumulated on top of his stereo. "Do you think this stuff still works?"

"Who knows?" Tom answered glumly as he covered his computer with the sheets of plastic that they brought. "Even if it does, we'll probably get electrocuted just plugging it in."

Danny grunted in agreement. "I thought I'd want to take a lot back to Isabella's, but not much seems worth saving."

Tom waded over to his bureau. A few pieces of dry clothing still clung precariously to the drawers. He snatched them up and shoved them into his bag. The rest of the clothes soaked limply in the water, making the floor look like a gigantic washing machine. Tom took a deep breath and tried to be positive. They were only clothes—they could be replaced.

Tom tossed the few dry books sitting on his desk into his bag, along with the football and some clothes. Fuzzy, the teddy bear that Elizabeth had given him for Valentine's Day, was a little damp but could be easily dried out. The edges of his bedspread were swimming in water. Tom pulled back the cover to find his favorite Snoopy sheets still in perfect condition. He smiled faintly as he took them off the mattress.

Danny laughed. "Glad to see that Snoopy made it."

Tom felt his mood beginning to lighten a bit. "Are you making fun of me?"

"Not at all," Danny said with a smirk. He stuffed a few shirts into the bag.

"Good." Tom flashed him a sly grin. "By the way, how is your collection of toy cars?"

Danny grinned. "Perfect. It was the first thing I grabbed when the quake hit."

"Do you hear that?" Elizabeth whispered across the library table to Nina Harper.

"Hear *what*?" Nina asked, taking a notebook and a few pens out of her backpack. "You could hear an ant walking across the floor in here."

Elizabeth threw her blue blazer on the back of her chair. Rays of bright sunlight came through the window, shining on the reference section. "That's exactly my point. It's so great to finally have some peace and quiet."

Nina pulled her beaded braids back into a ponytail.

She was a natural dark beauty who never needed to wear makeup. "Are Tom and Jess still slugging it out?"

"Constantly." Elizabeth rolled her eyes. "They're always arguing. I can't take it anymore."

Nina raised her dark eyebrows. "And you're in the middle."

"I can understand how they both feel, though. I just wish they'd *try* to get along."

"That's a tough one," Nina answered, chewing the tip of her pen thoughtfully.

Elizabeth sighed and rested her head on her book. One of the library's student workers wheeled a book cart past and started replacing the books on the shelves. "Is this situation even too difficult for Nina Harper, Queen of Diplomacy?"

Nina laughed. "Boyfriend versus sister—that's pretty tough. You might just have to take it to a talk show."

"Come on, Nina, what would you do if you were me?"

Nina pursed her lips. "I don't know—but it *is* Jess's room too. I guess it's only fair that she has more say in the matter than Tom."

Elizabeth played with the end of her blond braid. "But what about Tom? I can't throw him out. He doesn't have anywhere to go."

"You've got a point there." Nina waved her pen in the air in agreement. "An earthquake is a pretty unusual situation."

Elizabeth held her head in her hands. "They're driving me absolutely nuts," she said in exasperation. "I don't know how much more of this I can take."

Lila sat upright and propped a few pillows behind her. Her head was itching under the bandages, and her hair hadn't been washed in days. She was tired of the drab hospital gown and the scratchy bedsheets. She wanted to go home.

In the distance was the familiar squeak of the lunch cart's wheels as it rolled down the corridor. She knew that after exactly four stops, the cart would appear in her doorway. Lila listened for each stop. Part of her was happy to have something to do, but an even bigger part of her thought the whole thing was pretty pathetic.

A plump nurse's aid walked in, proudly carrying a lime green tray with a covered dish on it. "How are we feeling today?" she asked, pulling the bed table across Lila's lap. "Do we have a good appetite?"

Lila looked down at the tray in front of her. "Actually, I *am* kind of hungry."

The nurse's aid smiled a plump smile. "Good— that's exactly what we like to hear. *Bon appétit.*" The nurse turned and strolled out of the room.

Lila waited until she was completely out of sight before lifting the metal lid. A strange odor escaped from underneath. "This is awful," Lila groaned, examining the plate of soggy carrots, pickled beets, and dry, overcooked chicken.

Lila poked the chicken with her fork, as if testing to see if it would move. Beet juice pooled in the center of the plate, turning the carrots and the chicken a purple color. She tried not to gag. *I can't wait to get out of here,* she thought miserably.

"How are you, Lila?" Dr. Santiago asked as she walked into the room. Her thick black hair was pulled back and held in place by a metal barrette. "How's everything going?"

"Fine," Lila said weakly. She covered the plate and pushed the lap table as far away as possible.

The doctor's eyes followed the table. "If you want to finish your lunch, I can come back later."

Lila leaned back in her bed and pulled up the covers. "No, really—it's fine. This hospital food sure does wonders for a girl's figure."

Dr. Santiago laughed. "I know it's not the best, but try to eat something. You need your strength."

"I think I was stronger before I came in," Lila joked. She brushed back a limp strand of hair that had fallen in front of her face. "When do you think I can leave?"

The doctor looked at her sympathetically. "Not for a few days. We still have some tests to do," she said. "And there's someone I'd like you to talk to."

Lila glanced at the dull yellow sunlight that bounced off the sterile hospital-room walls. "But I feel fine. My head wounds are healing and I can do everything I could do before the accident. There's no reason to stay."

Dr. Santiago folded her arms across her chest and took a seat in the chair next to Lila's bed. "You're right. Physically, you're healing very well.

But there's another side to this that you're forgetting. You suffered a tremendous psychological ordeal. I'm not willing to let you out of here until I'm convinced you can handle it emotionally."

"What do I have to do to prove it to you?" Lila asked tiredly. "I haven't cried once in the past two days—isn't that proof enough?"

Dr. Santiago placed a reassuring hand on Lila's shoulder. "It's not that cut-and-dried. There are many emotional issues you're going to need to work out. I've arranged for one of the hospital's psychology residents to work with you. He specializes in posttraumatic syndrome. Please talk to him, Lila. I think it will do you a lot of good."

Lila sighed. The last thing she needed was some flaky shrink analyzing her every word. The sessions hadn't even started yet, and she was already dreading them.

"It won't be that bad," the doctor said, as if she could read Lila's mind. She gave her a knowing wink. "In fact, he's quite wonderful." Dr. Santiago waved to someone out in the hallway. "Come on in," she called.

The psychology resident walked in, and Lila's jaw fell open. She recognized the blond wavy hair, the gentle blue eyes. The heavenly face. He looked at her with the same shy, sexy smile she had seen the night before.

Dr. Santiago motioned for him to come closer. "Lila, I'd like you to meet Dr. Porter Davis."

Chapter Seven

Jessica taped a piece of paper to the door, then stepped back to admire her work. It was brilliant. She smiled to herself as she imagined Tom and Elizabeth reading it, their eyes popping out of their sockets. With a self-satisfied smirk Jessica reread it, just for pure pleasure.

THE <u>NEW</u> RULES FOR ROOM 28

1. *Boyfriends cannot stay in the room, <u>ever</u>. There are no exceptions—including natural disasters.*
2. *This is not a storage facility. Items <u>not</u> belonging to the room's inhabitants must be moved out <u>immediately</u>.*
3. *Roommates are <u>not</u> entitled to change the rules to suit their own wishes.*
4. *Have a nice day.*

"Two can play this game, Liz," Jessica said aloud to herself. One benefit of being close to your sister was knowing her weak spot. And Jessica knew exactly where to aim. If there was one thing Elizabeth prided herself on, it was fairness and consistency. Jessica knew Elizabeth would never condemn her for doing the same thing she had done herself. In fact, Elizabeth's steadfast sense of honor would force her to respect Jessica's rules, whether she liked them or not.

Jessica turned around cautiously, trying not to trip on Tom's things that were scattered all over the floor. Mr. Macho had spread his Snoopy sheets over the floor and laid out everything he owned to dry. It was pitiful. His textbook pages had swollen to four times their normal size. There was some sad-looking video equipment and a set of free weights that Jessica was certain never got any use. The sappy little teddy bear that Elizabeth had given him was on her desk. Tom's clothes were laid out across the backs of chairs and on the couch. They were covered with brown splotches. Jessica gave one of the books a happy little kick. By nightfall, Tom and all of his miserable stuff would be gone.

The door flew open and Tom entered, wearing the same plaid shirt and jeans he'd been wearing for the last couple of days. He was carrying another armload of books. Tom shot Jessica a look of warning, then walked into the room.

"Tom," Jessica said cheerily. "I was just thinking about you."

"Don't start with me . . ." he countered. Opening his arms, he let the books fall noisily to the floor.

Jessica pounced on her bed like a playful cat. "My, my. I know someone who is a G-R-O-U-C-H today." She picked up a fashion magazine and flipped through it.

Tom stood in the middle of his junk, his face in a twisted expression. "I'd like to see how you'd feel if all your stuff got trashed. You'd be pretty grouchy too."

Jessica raised one eyebrow. "Stop—you're making me cry," she said dryly. Leaning over the edge of the bed, she looked out into the hallway at the piles of CDs, clothes, and books that were just waiting to take up valuable space on their floor. "Glad to see you brought even *more* things for me to trip on."

"They need to dry out," Tom snapped. He laid the books carefully, taking up every last bit of walking space. "Try not to step over here," he said in a bossy tone as he gestured to the swollen books.

Jessica gave him a patronizing nod and made a mental note to step wherever she pleased.

"I see you have quite a few books. You must like reading," she said in a conversational tone. "That's good, because there's something I want you to read."

Tom wiped his brow with the sleeve of his shirt. "Jessica, I don't have time for games," he answered with irritation.

"This isn't a game," she said soberly. "Close the door and read the sign."

71

Tom looked at her suspiciously for a moment, then closed the door. As he read the list of rules Jessica could see his face turning an angry red.

"You waited until I moved all my stuff in here before showing me this? You're unbelievable."

Jessica gave her hair a haughty flip. "What's unbelievable is that you keep dragging all your crap in here like you own the place. I want you and your stuff out of here. *Now.*"

Tom crossed his arms stubbornly. "And where am I supposed to put my things?"

"That's not my problem."

He glared at her. "You're all heart."

Tossing her magazine aside, Jessica stood up and glared back at him. "I really don't care what you think of me, Tom. The fact of the matter is this is *my* room, and I want *you* and your water-logged junk out of here. You have ten minutes."

Tom stamped each foot firmly in place, as if they were set in cement. Drawing himself up to his full height, he looked down at her and said, "I'm not going anywhere."

"Are you ready?" Porter asked.

Lila smiled and gave him a nod. It was nice to be out of the drab hospital room for once. The bright red carpet and abstract paintings that hung on the walls of the therapy room jumped out at her. She leaned back comfortably in the leather lounging chair. The soft cotton blouse and pleated miniskirt she was wearing felt good against her skin. Lila touched a silky lock of her freshly washed hair and smiled even more brightly. She was finally beginning to feel human again.

"In honor of our first session, I brought you a little something," Porter said with a wink. A deep dimple appeared in his left cheek, and Lila couldn't help but admire his boyishly handsome face. He set a container on the low table between them and took off the lid. *"Voilà."*

Lila's blue eyes widened with surprise. "Mini brioche filled with pâté?" Hungrily she helped herself to two.

"I know the hospital food can be pretty bad," Porter said modestly. "I hope you like them. I made them last night."

Lila's eyes closed in ecstasy as she tasted the sweet roll and the rich filling. "These are wonderful. You're an incredible cook."

Porter bit into a roll. "It's a hobby of mine. It keeps me from getting lonely."

She looked away from him, focusing her eyes on one of the colorful canvasses. Her cheeks were slightly flushed. "I can't imagine you ever being lonely," she said shyly.

Porter ran a strong, square hand through his mane of wavy blond hair. "You'd be surprised," he said in a low voice.

Popping the last bit of brioche into her mouth, Lila voraciously reached for a third. "Do you mind?"

"Help yourself," Porter said, looking pleased.

"My aunt Katherine used to make these for me," she said sadly. Lila's smile faded and her face darkened.

Porter stopped chewing. He leaned toward her. "Lila, what's wrong?"

A single tear coursed down her cheek. "It's my aunt . . . she was killed last week."

He handed her a box of tissues. "In the earthquake?"

"No, before that." Lila sniffled. Her eyes fixed on a white canvas covered with yellow and orange squares. "She was murdered."

"That's horrible," he said. Porter took her hand in his. "I'm so sorry."

"I'm all right, really." Lila smiled faintly. She blew her nose. "It's just that I miss her. Before my accident, I was devastated about it. The thought of death and of her being buried in the ground just terrified me. It was so strange to think that she was gone, that she didn't exist anymore. But when I was lying in a coma, coming so close to death myself, I realized death wasn't the terrifying experience I thought it would be."

Porter's soft blue eyes gazed at hers, as if he were reaching into her soul. "It sounds like you had an enlightening experience."

Lila leaned back, feeling totally calm. "But don't get me wrong—I'm glad I came back. I'm glad you brought me back."

"Remember—you did it all yourself. You came back because you wanted to." His beautifully curved lips suppressed a shy smile.

74

Lila sighed. Once again his humility touched her, and she suddenly had an overwhelming desire to take his face into her hands and to press her mouth against his. Instead she gave his hand a tight squeeze. "Thank you for saving my life, Porter. I will always be grateful."

He looked at the floor, a blond wave cascading down his forehead. Even in the bright afternoon sunlight he still looked like an angel.

Lila reclined fully in the lounging chair, legs stretched out in front of her and head resting against the arm of the couch. "I hope I can get adjusted to everything again."

"What do you mean?" he asked, pulling the wooden chair closer to her.

"Things seem so different now. Especially with my family and friends. I don't think we connect anymore," she answered. "They don't understand what I went through. They'll never understand."

Porter rubbed his forehead thoughtfully. "Believe it or not, that is a common problem among people who've had near-death experiences. When they come back, they often feel isolated from their loved ones."

"I didn't think my parents would understand," Lila began. "But my friends are more open-minded. I expected more from them."

"They didn't believe you?"

Lila shook her head. "When I told them about the near-death experience, they looked at me like I was insane. Even my boyfriend said it was probably just a hallucination from the painkillers." She toyed with a strand of her hair. "If my closest friends don't believe me, then who will? It's so depressing."

Porter rested his hand on her forehead. Lila's muscles relaxed and she felt a bit sleepy. "Lila, you've been given a special, unique gift that very few people receive. The first thing you need to do is to accept it. Things will be different from now on, especially in your relationships. Ordinary people don't have the capacity to understand the things that you do. It's no one's fault. It's just the way things are. Your gift sets you apart from everyone else."

Lila stifled a yawn. "Including you?"

Porter eased back into his chair. His eyes were distant, as if he were staring at something beyond the walls of the room. "When I was twelve, my father took me out on his motorboat. It wasn't anything special—just a light, aluminum rowboat that my father had attached a motor to. We would cruise the lake near my house every weekend. It was a lot of fun."

Lila noticed Porter's dimples disappearing behind a stony expression. She tried to imagine a younger version of him. She suspected that he didn't look much different than he did now.

"One day my dad wasn't feeling well, so he said we couldn't go," Porter continued. "But I decided that I wanted to go anyway. I waited until he was asleep and my mother was busy doing something, and then I went down to the edge of the lake where the boat was docked. I started the motor and cruised the lake at full speed. It was a perfect summer day, and I was having a great time."

Lila smiled wistfully to herself, enjoying the smoothness of his voice. She closed her eyes.

"About an hour later I decided to go back, figuring that at this point my parents must've realized what I did. As I headed toward the dock, I was going way too fast. I lost control of the boat, and it hit a huge rock only a few feet from the edge of the lake. The boat capsized and wedged itself into the sand, with me trapped underneath. There was a small air pocket in the hull, but the rock had torn a hole into the bottom of the boat, so it quickly filled with water."

Lila's body went rigid as she pictured the little boy trapped underneath the boat. Terror trickled down her spine like cool lake water.

"I struggled to push the boat off me, but I didn't have the strength to budge it. Finally I ran out of air." Porter paused. "I remember the cold sting of the water as it filled my lungs."

Lila's eyelashes were moist with teardrops. "What happened after that?"

Porter was silent for a moment before he continued. "I remember seeing a glowing light cut through the darkness of the water. Then there was a voice telling me to move my arms, to push the boat off. It was the sweetest voice I've ever heard. It gave me strength. I reached up and pushed the boat off me."

Lila opened her eyes and looked at Porter. His

expression was serene. "And do you know what, Lila? I wasn't afraid. Not even for a minute," he said. "I'm sure you understand how I felt."

She understood perfectly.

Elizabeth walked into her dorm room to find Tom and Jessica staring each other down. They looked like two wrestlers trying to intimidate each other before a match. She slammed the door loudly behind her, but neither of them flinched. They continued to glare at each other, their gazes unbroken.

"Okay, you two," Elizabeth said, stepping between them like a referee. "Time out."

"You're just in time," Jessica said to Elizabeth, her eyes still fixed on Tom. "I was explaining the new rules to your significant other."

Elizabeth looked at Tom. He was scowling at Jessica with an anger she had never seen before. "What rules?"

"Ask your evil twin," Tom answered. He nodded in Jessica's direction.

"I guess he means me," Jessica gushed, pretending to be flattered. "They're posted on the door."

With a loud sigh, Elizabeth turned her back on the two of them and read the note taped to the door. Her blood began to boil as she read the note a second time. They were both pushing her to the absolute limit. Elizabeth felt like a soda bottle that had been shaken too many times and was about to explode.

"What is this?" she demanded.

"You know exactly what it is," Jessica answered. She pulled her shoulders back and pursed her lips in a perfect imitation of her sister. "Whether you like it or not, there are going to be a few changes around here," she mimicked.

Tom turned to Elizabeth. "Liz, could you please explain to your charming sister that I don't have anywhere else to go?"

Jessica interrupted before Elizabeth could speak. "And will you please tell Snoopy over here that he hasn't exactly *tried* to find another place to stay?"

Tom was fuming. "What's that supposed to—"

Elizabeth covered her ears. "Both of you—just stop it! You're driving me nuts!"

Jessica and Tom stopped talking but continued to stare at each other. From their stubborn expressions, it was clear that neither one was about to give in.

Elizabeth clasped her head tightly in her hands, then turned to Tom. She put her arms around him and drew him close. "I'm sorry, Tom," she said softly. "I think you'd better move out."

Jessica did a little victory dance, stepping on as many of Tom's books as she could. "I can see there's more to you than just a beautiful face, sis. You're smart, too."

Elizabeth shot her a nasty look. "Cut it out," she said harshly. "This doesn't mean I'm taking your side. It's just that you two have to be separated and it's the only way to do it." She looked back at Tom, her eyes softening from guilt. "I'll help you find a place to stay. Maybe we can move some of your things into the station for a little while."

Tom nodded reluctantly. "I can sleep on the couch there— something I should've done a while ago." He scowled at Jessica. "But I'm only doing it for you, Liz." Tom gave Elizabeth a kiss.

Jessica knocked a few videotapes off a chair and sat down. "Thank you for visiting the Wakefield Hotel, Mr. Watts, but I believe it's checkout time."

Lila sat on the edge of her hospital bed and brushed her hair. She hummed contentedly as she drew the brush through the silky ends. At the top of her head she lifted the bandage slightly and used the bristles to scratch the itchy scalp beneath. With any luck, she'd be able to take the bandages off tomorrow.

Tomorrow. Lila smiled at the late afternoon sun coming through her window. Already she was looking forward to it. Tomorrow she'd have another session with Porter. The cotton blouse and pleated skirt she had worn were neatly folded on the chair beside her bed. It was the nicest outfit she had with her. Lila frowned, wishing she had something different to wear.

Porter doesn't care about making fashion statements, Lila reminded herself. Porter was beyond appearances. He understood it was more important to connect spiritually with someone. Lila admired that. They shared a special connection that went beyond the physical world. Of course, the fact that he was gorgeous didn't hurt, either.

The phone rang, and Lila sprang for it. She waited impatiently for it to ring one more time before picking it up. "Hello?" she said in a velvety voice. Lila held the receiver tightly to her ear, expecting the soft, heavenly voice of Porter.

"Lila, it's me."

The corners of her mouth drooped. "Bruce?"

"How is my sweet girlfriend?" he asked.

Lila put the hairbrush in the nightstand drawer. "I'm fine," she said dully.

"Good. I'm just calling to let you know that I'm going to be a little late visiting you tonight."

Lila flinched as he spoke, pulling the phone about an inch away from her ear. She had never really noticed it before, but Bruce's voice was irritating over the phone. He spoke loudly, full of self-assurance and bravado. It was the exact same way he did everything. Bruce flung himself into situations with complete overconfidence. And it never occurred to him for a moment that he could be wrong.

"Lila, are you still there?" his voice boomed an inch away.

Lila put the receiver back against her ear. "I'm right here."

"Is eight o'clock okay? As soon as I'm done with football practice, I'll be right over."

On the top of the nightstand was a small paper plate covered with a napkin. Lila picked up the plate and uncovered one of the mini brioche that Porter had insisted she take with her. She touched it lovingly, then set it back on the nightstand.

"Why bother?" she asked, as if thinking aloud.

"What?"

"I said, *why bother?*" The words came out louder this time. She scratched at the bandages around her head. "You'll get here toward the end of visiting hours, and then you'll just have to turn right around and go back."

"I'll cut out of practice early," he stammered. "But if you're tired . . ."

Lila examined the tips of her long fingernails. The truth was, she was feeling the best she had in days. But it was as good an excuse as any. "Yeah, I'm tired."

"I guess I'll wait until tomorrow, then," he said sullenly. "Take care of yourself."

"I will."

"I love you, Li."

Lila paused a moment, then instead of answering, she hung up the phone.

Chapter
Eight

Elizabeth tossed her backpack tiredly over her shoulder and walked from the library back to the dorm. The moon was almost directly overhead, casting frosty beams of silvery light on the campus. She strolled past WSVU and noticed that the lights were all off. It was hard to believe the television studio was now Tom's bedroom. She hoped he was able to sleep soundly on that lumpy old couch.

Tomorrow she'd get up early and bring Tom some muffins and coffee for breakfast. She had to make it up to him somehow.

Elizabeth continued on to her dorm. As bad as she felt about Tom, there was the guilty pleasure of being able to go home to a peaceful room. Tonight she'd fall asleep to the sound of her sister's snores instead of relentless bickering. Things would be back to normal.

Elizabeth entered Dickenson Hall. She turned

the corner toward the hallway where her room was and stopped dead in her tracks. Sleeping peacefully on the floor right outside her door was Tom. His hair was tousled and he was wrapped tightly in his favorite Snoopy sheets. He snored softly, his sweet cheek pressed against the rough carpeting.

Elizabeth looked at Tom with love, then gingerly stepped over him and opened the door to her room. She closed it carefully behind her. Jessica was on her bed, balls of cotton stuck between her bare toes. She was painting each nail with ruby polish. Elizabeth threw her book bag on the floor and squeezed her hands into tight fists.

"Did you know that Tom is sleeping out in the hallway?" Elizabeth said in a loud whisper. There was more than a hint of accusation in her voice.

Jessica didn't look up from her pedicure, but instead gave her chewing gum a loud snap. "I know," she said matter-of-factly. "Actually, I don't mind at all if he stays there just as long as he isn't taking up space in my room."

Elizabeth took a deep breath. Every nerve in her body was on edge. "How good of you," she said sarcastically.

"Do I detect an attitude?"

"I can't believe you sometimes," Elizabeth said in complete amazement. "How can you let him sleep out in the hallway? Don't you have an ounce of compassion in your heart?"

Jessica plucked the cotton balls from between her toes. "Compassion has nothing to do with it. We had a deal," she answered nonchalantly. "Tom was supposed to move out and find another place to stay. Everything was cool, and then suddenly he showed up in the hallway. I don't know what happened, and I really don't care. He's not supposed to be here. If he can't find another place, that's his problem."

Elizabeth shook her head in disgust. "You're so stubborn. I can't believe you'd humiliate Tom like that just so you could have your way."

Jessica looked at her blankly. "We had a deal."

Elizabeth was seething with burning rage. Without another word to Jessica, she yanked open the door and took one step out into the hallway. Tom's sleeping body was directly at her feet. Elizabeth knelt on the floor and pulled back the sheet that half covered his face. Her hot anger subsided with one look at his innocent, childlike face.

"Wake up, sweetie," she said in a singsong voice. Elizabeth gently brushed the hair from his face. Tom stirred and opened his eyes. He smiled up at her.

"What a nice way to wake up," he said, his voice thick with sleep. "How long have you been watching me?"

Elizabeth chewed her lip, worry lines creasing her forehead. "Long enough," she said. "Why aren't you spending the night at the station?"

Tom pulled his arms out from underneath the sheets and stretched them above his head. "It was too cold at the station. They turn off the heat at night since no one's there."

"This is a nightmare," Elizabeth thought aloud.

"It's not so bad," Tom said, sounding optimistic. "But the floor is a bit hard. Can I borrow one of your pillows?"

Elizabeth stared into the distance, her eyes fixed on the end of the hall. She shook her head. "No," she said in a firm voice.

"No? You won't let me borrow one of your pillows?" Tom said incredulously.

Elizabeth turned to him. "I'm sorry—what I mean is, no, I can't let you stay out here."

Tom rolled onto his side, propping up his head with his hand. "But what else can we do? I don't have any other options."

Elizabeth wrapped her arms protectively around Tom's neck. There was no way she could abandon the man she was madly in love with. "Don't worry," she said resolutely. "As long as you have me, you'll always have a place to stay."

Tom stiffened. "But what about Jess?"

"Forget about her," Elizabeth said with determination. "My sister thinks she can always get her way. I think it's time to teach her a lesson."

"This is going to sound crazy," Lila said, a blush rising to her cheeks. She shyly curled her toes into the red carpet of the therapy room. "But I think you're the only person who really understands me."

Porter took off his lab coat and slightly loosened his blue-and-maroon-striped tie. The sun's rays, which had poured in brightly at the beginning of their therapy session, were now fading quickly.

"That's not so crazy," he answered with a dimpled grin. "I think you and I really connect on many different levels."

"You think so?" Lila asked in a hopeful voice. She watched intently as Porter unbuttoned the cuffs of his shirt and rolled the sleeves toward his elbow. His forearms were knotted with muscles and covered with downy, golden hair. For a brief instant, Lila imagined one of those strong arms easing seductively around her waist.

"Absolutely." Porter's blue eyes stared at her. "One thing you must learn about me, Lila, is that I never say anything unless I truly mean it."

Lila's stomach did a somersault. She looked away, unable to hold his gaze, and concentrated on one of the thickly painted canvasses on the wall. "I wish everyone I knew was like that."

"What do you mean?" he pressed. "Be specific."

Lila swung her legs up onto the lounging chair and leaned back. She modestly smoothed down the hem of her plaid skirt. "I talked to Bruce last night, and he wasn't being honest with me."

Porter leaned forward, resting his elbows on his knees. She could tell that he was really listening to what she had to say. "What happened?"

She paused, wondering if she wanted to delve into her relationship with Bruce. It would be so much easier to pretend she didn't have a boyfriend at all. After everything that had happened, Lila wasn't so sure she even had one anymore.

Porter touched her arm lightly with his finger-tips. "Go ahead," he coaxed. "Tell me everything."

As if she had just woken from a deep sleep, Lila felt her body come alive. Of course she'd tell Porter. She didn't want to keep anything from him. "Bruce called last night to tell me he'd be late—he was supposed to come visit me. He made some lame excuse—"

"And you didn't believe him?"

Lila frowned. "Why should I? He told me he was going to be with me on the day of the quake and he wasn't. Why should I ever believe him about anything?"

Porter rubbed his chin thoughtfully. "What did you say when he told you he was going to be late?"

"I was tired of hearing excuses. I told him not to bother coming at all."

Lila wondered if maybe she had reacted too harshly. Would Porter think less of her because of it? She studied his face for a reaction. A slow smile grew across his lips, and Lila suddenly realized that he was pleased by what she had done.

He held her hand. "Lila, one of the most diffi-cult lessons we must learn in life is that we cannot depend on other people for our own happiness. Humans make mistakes. You'll find most people are only concerned with themselves and that makes them undependable. Everyone will let you down at one time or another, especially when you need them most. They can't help it. Once you begin to understand this, no one will disappoint you ever again."

Lila listened carefully, absorbing every word he spoke. The more she thought about it, the more she realized he was right. Nearly everyone she knew had let her down at some point—her parents, Bruce, even Jessica and the Thetas. When she told them about her near-death experience, the most significant event of her life, they didn't support her—no one believed her. The only person who had been there for her was Porter.

"That's so discouraging," Lila said somberly. "Why get involved with people at all?"

Porter squeezed her hand. "It's human nature to get involved with others. But you and I—we aren't like the others, Lila. We're different. The best thing we can do is rise above it. Be independent. Separate ourselves. If we are self-sufficient, then we won't have to depend on unreliable people."

Lila lifted her hand slowly toward him, her fingers grazing his blond curls. "I can rely on you, can't I?"

Porter took her hand and pressed it against his smooth cheek. "Always," he said.

The sun descended below the horizon, leaving Sweet Valley in the dusky light of early evening. At that very moment thousands of people were heading home from work to their families, to have dinner and attend to their personal lives for a few hours before going to bed. Lila pictured them scurrying around like little ants, with no understanding of what life was really about. She pitied them. And yet in the middle of all the nonsense, she and Porter had discovered the true meaning of life and relationships. They knew better than to put too much faith in those people who hadn't figured it all out.

Porter stood and put on his lab coat. He gave Lila a lighthearted smile, which indicated that the session was over. "Can you believe we were in here all afternoon?" he said.

Lila slipped her feet into her black flats. "It went by so fast. What time are we meeting tomorrow?"

Porter returned his wooden chair back to its original place behind the desk. "We're not going to meet. I think you're doing well and I'm going to request that you be discharged tomorrow."

Lila jumped up with excitement and, without thinking, threw her arms around him. But then her happiness left as quickly as it came. "We'll still be able to meet once I go home, right?" She dropped her hands at her sides.

"Of course we will," Porter said reassuringly. "I think we'll need a few follow-up sessions."

"Good," Lila answered, hugging him again. As much as she wanted to be self-sufficient, Lila knew that much of her happiness would depend on seeing Porter again.

"Are you all ready, Miss Fowler?" the nurse asked as she stripped Lila's hospital bed. Lila's untouched breakfast of cold scrambled eggs and dry toast was pushed aside as Lila loaded her leather overnight bag. She couldn't even think about eating. All she wanted was to get out of the hospital and go back to campus.

"I'm all set," Lila said to the nurse. She finished emptying the locker near her bed. Lila took a quick peek to make sure she had taken everything, then zipped up the bag.

Lila checked her watch. Bruce was supposed to pick her up in half an hour. That would give her just enough time to say good-bye to Porter. "Have you seen Dr. Davis?" she asked.

"He usually doesn't come in until the afternoons," the nurse said distractedly as she rearranged the flowers.

Lila's face fell. Although he hadn't promised her anything, she thought that Porter would have at least come by to see her off. She picked up her overnight bag and walked slowly out of the room.

Lila checked out and stood in the main lobby by the front entrance, waiting for Bruce's Jeep to come into sight. Gusts of wind periodically entered the building as people entered the hospital through the automatic sliding doors. She stood in place, letting the brief bursts of air swirl through her hair. Lila didn't care if her hair was messed up—it just felt good to be finally free of the bandages.

Her eyes wandered across the lobby, with its plush sectional sofa and scattered magazine tables, to the round clock above the entrance. Bruce was supposed to be here in ten minutes, but he'd probably be late. Lila set her bag on the floor. *This was a bad idea,* she thought. Here she was, dying to leave the hospital, ready to go, and Bruce was going to keep her waiting.

People will let you down. Porter's words echoed in Lila's mind. He was right. Where was Porter right now? She was disappointed that he didn't show, but he'd never said he'd be there. Porter knew better than to make promises he couldn't keep. Lila shifted impatiently from one foot to the other. Suddenly she felt a strong arm encircle her waist. Lila whipped around. She looked up into the kind blue eyes of Porter. As his arms drew her toward him Lila felt all the air escaping her lungs.

"Porter," she said breathlessly.

"Surprised? I couldn't let you leave without saying good-bye," he whispered into her hair.

Lila stared at him with wide eyes. She couldn't think of anything to say. Her mind was reeling from his touch.

"Lila, are you all right?" he asked. A shadow of concern darkened his eyes.

Lila smiled up at him. Bruce's Jeep was nowhere in sight. "I'm fine," she said, resting her head against his chest. She wanted the moment to go on forever. "In fact, I've never felt better."

Bruce parked his Jeep by the back entrance to the hospital instead of the main entrance because it was faster. Not by much—only a minute or two—but at this point, every second mattered. For some strange reason, Lila had suddenly become obsessed with punctuality. Time was the most important thing to her. Bruce figured that it was somehow related to her near-death experience. Perhaps Lila had realized how valuable life was—that every second was precious.

He grabbed the bouquet of champagne roses that was lying across the front seat of the Jeep, then unlocked the doors. The pale peach pink roses were carefully arranged in a box tied with a velvet green ribbon. It was exactly like the first bouquet he had ever given her.

It was right after Christmas break, when Bruce and Lila were flying back to SVU. They were in Bruce's brand-new two-seater Cessna. At that time they didn't get along at all, and the only reason that Lila had gone on that trip was because Bruce had goaded her into it. There was a snowstorm, and they'd crashed in the Sierra Nevada.

They were alone together in the mountains for nearly a week, practically ready to kill each other, when they suddenly realized they had fallen in love. They were rescued and had to spend some time in the hospital. On the day they were discharged Bruce signed out early to buy Lila a bouquet of champagne roses. He returned to the hospital to surprise her with them, and then they went home together.

No wonder I feel like I've done all this before, Bruce thought. He walked through the back entrance, bouquet in hand, to the bank of elevators. He pressed the up button and waited. But the situation was a little different this time. For one thing, he was weighted down by a sense of guilt about the accident. If he had been with Lila during the earthquake, he could have protected her. It was his fault that he wasn't there. The plane crash had partially been his fault too, but at least he had shared in her suffering. At least he had been there for her.

"Come on!" Bruce shouted at the elevator. He punched the button on the wall and glanced up at the numbers over the door. The elevator was on the tenth floor and still going up. Bruce grunted in frustration and headed for the stairwell.

He took the steps two at a time, all the way to the seventh floor. At this rate he was going to barely make it on time. Bruce had even cut out of his geology class early so he'd be there for Lila. When he finally reached the seventh floor, he plowed through the door and jogged to Lila's room.

The door was open, and Bruce darted inside. He'd expected to see Lila sitting in a chair, with her bag packed and ready to go. He expected to see her happy and healthy and excited to see him. Instead he saw a bare room with a perfectly made bed and the window shades drawn. Lila's locker and nightstand were emptied. There wasn't a trace of her left.

"Where is she?" he asked out loud.

Bruce raced out of the room, down the white hallway. The tile floor felt slippery under his sneakered feet. He stopped directly in front of the nurses' station and set the box of roses down on the counter. A nurse with a long braid and a yellow sweater was talking on the phone and looking up some information in the computer. She didn't notice Bruce. He tapped his fingers anxiously against the countertop.

The nurse gave an address to the person over the phone, then repeated it again, slowly spelling the tricky words. *Come on, I don't have all day.* Bruce leaned against the counter, his hands only inches from the phone. With one touch he could disconnect the call. He watched stealthily, waiting for the perfect moment when the nurse would look away so he could carry out his scheme. He concentrated, ready to pounce, when the nurse made things even easier for him. She hung up the phone herself.

"May I help you?" she asked in a dry monotone.

"Yes," Bruce answered immediately, not wasting a second. "Do you know where Lila Fowler is? She was staying in that room across the hall." He pointed to it.

The nurse looked down at a blue binder thick with paper. "She signed out twenty minutes ago."

"You wouldn't happen to know where she is?"

The nurse flashed him a you've-got-to-be-kidding look. "Sir, we are far too busy here to keep track of patients once they sign out." She turned away and started typing on the computer keyboard.

Bruce leaned over the counter. "Okay—I don't expect you to know her exact location, but can you at least tell me where patients *usually* go after signing out?"

The nurse sighed loudly as she continued typing away. "Try the front entrance. Go down the stairs and follow the red line."

"Thank you," Bruce said heavily before dashing off to the stairs. Running down the staircase with the box of flowers under his arm made Bruce feel as if he was on the football field, dodging obstacles to score a touchdown. So far, he wasn't doing so great. The echoed voice of a sports announcer reverberated in his head. *Another dumb move by number 44, Bruce Patman.*

Bruce could see clearly across the imaginary field to the goal line. Lila was waiting there for him. But he couldn't tell if she was cheering him on or ready to tackle him once he got there. She had been so withdrawn lately, so indifferent toward him. Maybe she was tired of being in the hospital. Or maybe it would just take a little time for Lila to get back to her old self. Either way, Bruce hoped that he was still a part of her life. He hoped they were still on the same team.

When he reached the bottom of the stairs, Bruce followed the red line on the floor that led to the main entrance. He ran at full speed, shifting his weight from one foot to the other to make it around the curving hallway and to avoid oncoming people. At last he made it to the front lobby, his feet stopping just over the spot where the red line ended.

Bruce walked slowly, working off the cramp in his side. He glanced around the lobby, when suddenly the realization hit him.

Lila was gone.

Lila rolled down the passenger-side window and rested her arm on the edge of the door. It was the perfect day for a drive along the Pacific Coast Highway. Lila enjoyed every moment, breathing in the clean ocean air. The deep, gorgeous blue of the sky reminded Lila of the waters off the coast of the Hawaiian Islands or the smooth beauty of a star sapphire. Or even the color of Porter's eyes.

"Where did you study medicine?" Lila asked. The sun's rays felt warm and comforting against her pale skin.

"Harvard Medical School," Porter said as he steered his white '64 Mustang convertible around a curve. He lowered the overhead visor to cut the sun's glare. "I stayed in Boston for a while and did a residency at Mass General."

"You're kidding!" Lila exclaimed as she ran a hand over the black leather upholstery. "My uncle,

Chester Cage, was a neurosurgeon there for several years. Did you know him?"

Porter scratched his head, as if trying to recall. "Chester . . ."

"Cage," Lila finished. "He was quite famous."

"I don't think I know him," Porter answered. He turned the corner at the entrance to Sweet Valley University. "Mass General is a huge hospital—we were probably working in different departments." He turned and gave her a sympathetic grin. "I'm sorry."

"That's okay," Lila said. It was so cute the way he apologized, even though he really didn't need to. Porter was definitely the most sensitive man she'd ever met. "You can't be expected to know everyone."

They continued up the campus drive, and Lila took in the scenery like she had been gone for five years. Things seemed sharper, crisper, more colorful. Her powers of observation were heightened. Lila saw details that she never noticed before. The pavement in the student parking lot was darker than that of the campus drive; there was a distinct line where the two different asphalts met. The windows of the buildings where classes were held were each topped with a pediment alternating between triangular and half-moon shapes. The clock on the tower at the end of the quad was two minutes fast.

"How does it feel to be back?" Porter asked.

Lila shrugged. "I'm not sure yet. It's going to take some adjustment, I guess."

Porter drove into the parking lot behind her dorm. "It's going to be a bit difficult, Lila. Don't forget the things we talked about." He parked the car near the side entrance. Reaching across Lila's lap, he opened the glove compartment and took out a pen and paper. He scribbled something down. "I'm giving you my beeper number just in case you need to reach me. Call me for anything, at any time." He cracked a smile. "Even if you're craving mini brioche in the middle of the night."

Lila folded the piece of paper and held it firmly in her grasp. Reluctantly she reached for the door handle. "When are we going to have another session?" she asked.

Porter swallowed hard. He squinted at the side of her dorm building, as if the answer were scrawled on the brick wall. "Lila," he said, his voice faltering. "I can't see you as a patient anymore."

Up until this very moment, Lila felt as though she were hanging over an abyss, clinging to a thin rope. Porter was the rope that was saving her life. But as she sat in the car, in the parking lot outside her dorm, Porter's words were like a sharp knife that slashed the rope in two.

"What do you mean?"

Porter ran a hand through his hair. "I've done something highly unethical. Something a doctor should never do to one of his patients."

Lila looked at him, stunned. Everything seemed to be moving in slow motion. "Porter, what is it? Tell me."

He turned toward her. His face was creased with tortured emotions.

Lila touched his cheek. "Whatever it is, I can handle it."

Porter held her hand there and closed his eyes. "Lila, I'm so in love with you."

Relief swept over her. Those were the words she had longed to hear. Lila moved toward him, her face only inches away from his. "I think I'm in love with you too."

Lila stared at his angelic face, filled with an overwhelming desire to kiss him. She knew he felt the same, but that he was waiting patiently until she was ready. Lila wasn't nervous at all. Porter was someone she could trust completely.

Moving closer, she wrapped her arms around his neck and drew him toward her. Lila tilted her head to the side and pressed her lips against his. Porter's skin was soft and warm, his kiss gentle. Lila felt a spark of pure white light between them. They made a perfect connection. In that instant, Lila knew that they would never be apart.

Tom rolled over on the twins' small couch. Sometime in the middle of the night, in an effort to stretch his legs, he had accidentally knocked over the makeshift coffee table of two milk crates and a wooden board. Also at some point last night, all his bedcovers had fallen to the floor. Tom rubbed his eyes and stared numbly at the heap of Snoopy sheets beside the couch.

"Look who's up," Elizabeth said in a cheery voice. Her bed was already made, and a book bag was slung over her shoulder. "How did you sleep?"

Tom groaned and groggily stood up, his muscles stiff and sore. He felt like a man four times his age. "I think sleeping on the floor would probably be more comfortable," he said in a grumpy tone as he tried to stretch out his tired leg muscles.

Jessica was standing in front of her mirror, covering her face with foundation. "You should try spending the night in the student union. I heard they have a lot of floor space," Jessica said. "You could really stretch out there."

Tom was too tired for a comeback.

"Jess, cut it out," Elizabeth said, coming to his rescue. She planted a big kiss on his cheek. "I'm off to class. Do you think you'll be alive by lunch?"

"Sure," Tom droned. "Usual time and place?"

Elizabeth nodded. "I'll see you there," she said, slipping out the door.

Tom's eyes burned as if he'd been awake all night. He pursed his lips bitterly, wondering how he was ever going to make it through the next few weeks.

"Are you all right, Tom?" Jessica said, starting right in. "You look terrible."

I wonder why? he thought sarcastically, not finding the energy to even say the words aloud. Tom grabbed his toothbrush, toothpaste, washcloth, and towel and sleepily walked down the hall to the men's bathroom.

The bathroom was empty and quiet, except for the repetitive drips coming from one of the faucets. Through hazy eyes Tom unscrewed the cap from his toothpaste tube and squeezed some onto his toothbrush. He put a little water on it and turned off the faucet.

He had so much he had to do today, he wondered if he'd be able to stay awake for it all. While Tom brushed his teeth, he went down the list: three classes to go to, a term paper to start researching, lunch with Elizabeth, pick up clothes from the cleaners (hopefully they got the water stains out), and edit earthquake footage. But the very first stop, of course, would be the coffeehouse.

Suddenly Tom stopped brushing. He was instantly awake, looking at his haggard reflection in the mirror. Tom watched his blank facial expression turn sour, nose wrinkling and lips in an awkward pucker. He plucked the toothbrush out of his mouth. He studied it, noting that it lacked the usual white foam. The bristles were a greasy pink.

Tom slowly lifted the toothbrush to his nose and cautiously sniffed it. It smelled flowery. He froze, his mouth still full, trying not to let any bit of the substance slip down his throat. Carefully he opened his mouth and bared his teeth. Tom had a slick pink smile.

"Jessica!" he hissed as he spit the pink hair gel into the sink. Was she totally insane? Only someone who was completely twisted would even think of filling a person's toothpaste tube with hair gel. What was she trying to do? Poison him?

Tom turned on the faucet as far as it would go and grabbed a washcloth. He stuck out his tongue and rubbed it with the cloth. He rubbed the roof of his mouth and his teeth and flushed his mouth out with water. Already the gel was beginning to dry, and Tom's lips were beginning to stick to the surface of his teeth.

In a fury he stormed out of the bathroom, down the hall, and back to the room. He was ready to give Jessica a piece of his mind. He'd tried to hold back in the past, because she was Elizabeth's sister, but nothing was going to stop him now. Nothing could contain his anger.

He pushed open the door. The room was empty. Jessica had obviously hightailed it out of the room as soon as he'd left. He had to hand it to her, though. Jessica was definitely smarter than she let on.

Tom looked around, peeled his top lip back from his teeth, and let out a short gasp. Hanging from the water pipe above the door, in a purple scarf tied like a noose, was his teddy bear, Fuzzy.

"If that's what you want, Jessica, that's fine with me," Tom shouted to the air. "This is war!"

Lila opened the door, but she didn't invite Bruce in. Without a word, she left the door open and continued unpacking. Bruce took it as an invitation and walked into Lila's room. He put the box of roses on her bed, then sat down at her desk.

"You did say nine thirty, right?" Bruce bravely asked after several minutes of silence. "I wasn't supposed to be there at eight thirty, was I?"

Lila ignored the box with the velvet green ribbon, tossing a pile of dirty clothes into the wicker hamper in the corner of the room. "What difference does it make?" she said ruefully.

"I know it makes a difference to you. I was there on time, Lila." Bruce's eyes followed her around the room, trying to detect any hint of emotion. Lila's face was set in a hardened expression, which she wore like an impenetrable mask.

"How did you get back?" he asked.

"You're only asking to make yourself feel better," Lila retorted.

In seconds Bruce was on his feet, his arms opened wide to give her a hug. "How can you say things like that? I was worried about you." He nodded to the box on the bed. "I brought you flowers."

Lila pushed him away. "I don't need flowers. I needed you to be at my aunt's house when you said you'd be there."

"Lila, I already told you that something came up—" There was a strange look in her eyes, making Bruce stop short.

"I almost died because of you," she murmured. Her eyes flared with hatred.

Bruce's lips began to tremble. He felt as if his chest were caving in. "You're right—I should've been there. But I got there as soon as I could. I smashed that glass door and searched the house for you. I called an ambulance. I lifted that armoire off you all by myself. . . ."

"Why do you always have to exaggerate things?" Lila shot back. "You make it sound like a bigger deal than it really was. Have you ever been humble for one moment in your life?"

Lila's words hit like a stinging slap across his face. He searched her eyes for some trace of the old Lila, the woman he had fallen in love with. But her eyes were cold and distant.

Bruce reached out to touch her lightly on the shoulder, but he thought better of it and pulled away. "If you need anything, let me know," he said as he headed toward the door.

"No, thanks—you've done enough already." Lila kept her back to him and continued to stare out the window.

Bruce paused in the doorway. "I don't understand what's going on with you right now," he said, his voice thick with emotion. "But get one thing straight. It's not over between us."

Lila waited to hear the door close before she turned around. Hot tears threatened to fall from her eyes. She pushed aside the box of flowers and flung herself onto her bed.

"It *is* over, Bruce," she said out loud. Lila tasted the salty tears rolling down her cheeks and onto her lips. Bruce was out of her life forever. Even though it was what she wanted, the finality of it pained her, like a jagged edge that turned itself over and over again inside her stomach. It was becoming clear to her that Bruce wasn't the person she thought he was. The whole time they were together, she had been deluding herself. Bruce didn't love her. He couldn't love anyone.

A cool breeze blew, animating the light cotton curtains that hung in the window near her bed. A few books and magazines lay in silence on Lila's desk, waiting for her to move them to another spot. Gray shadows moved and shifted across the wall.

It was lonely. As much as Lila wanted to be independent, she began to realize just how difficult it was not to rely on anyone. You had to have at least one person you could trust. For her, Lila knew exactly who that person was.

Lila dialed the number for Porter's pager. She left a message with the answering service, then hung up, anxiously waiting for him to call her back. *Please call me, Porter,* Lila thought. *I need you.*

Minutes later the phone rang. Lila picked it up on the first ring. "Porter?"

"Lila," he answered. His voice was filled with concern. "Are you all right?"

"No," Lila sobbed. Hearing Porter's comforting voice was like a dam bursting. Lila was flooded with conflicting emotions.

"Stay where you are—I'll be right over." Porter hung up before she had a chance to say anything else.

Lila waited outside, counting the minutes silently to herself until Porter arrived. In the distance she spotted the white Mustang coming up the drive. It was speeding along at a very fast pace, making Lila feel strangely sad. She had only known Porter for a few days and already he was racing to her side whenever she needed him. Bruce, on the other hand, had been dating her for several months, and not once had he really put himself on the line for her. Life was strange sometimes.

Lila ran to the edge of the road and hopped into the car, with its convertible top down, before it even came to a full stop. Porter drove away without saying a word. Lila took comfort in the wind blowing through her hair and the warm feeling of having Porter's hand in hers.

When they reached the beach, Porter pulled over to the side of the road. Lila slipped off her sandals and walked barefoot in the sand. They walked together, along the edge of the water, in silence. Waves lapped softly over Lila's feet, filling her with a sense of calm. It was good to be with Porter like this—far away from everything. She didn't need to explain herself. Porter understood.

Lila felt the muscles in her neck and shoulders slowly release. All the tension she had felt when Bruce was visiting her was beginning to evaporate into the fresh ocean air.

"Thank you for coming to get me," Lila said with a smile. Porter still hadn't said a word to her since he'd picked her up. She knew he was waiting until she was ready to speak. There was no pressure. That was one of the things she loved most about him.

"Are you feeling better?" he asked.

I am now that you're with me, Lila thought. She tilted her head back so that she could feel the heat of the sun. "Bruce came by and we had a fight."

Porter laced his fingers with hers. "What did he say?"

Lila took a deep breath, letting the salty smell fill her lungs. "He came in, expecting us to pick up exactly where we left off. He couldn't understand why I was mad at him."

Porter's hair captured the rays of sunlight, making his blond curls look like they were made of spun gold. "And what did you do?"

"I was cold. I basically let him know that it was over, but I didn't really tell him why." Lila looked down at the wet sand that covered her feet. "I shouldn't have been so mean. We went through a lot together. Bruce deserves more than that."

Leading Lila by the hand, Porter walked away from the edge of the water and climbed a sand dune. The water below sparkled like a majestic jewel in the sunlight. Beyond were the rocky cliffs and snakes of highway that followed the Pacific Coast. Porter and Lila took a seat, admiring the view.

"I think you did the right thing," Porter said a moment later.

"You do?"

He nodded. "In a situation like that, I think it's best to make a clean break. You knew the relationship couldn't possibly go any further, so why delude both yourself and him?"

Lila pushed away a strand of hair that had fallen

in her eyes. "That makes sense. But it's still painful."

"I know. I wish I could take away your pain." Porter cupped Lila's chin and kissed her softly on the forehead. His eyes were shining like warm tidal pools. "But I can promise you it will pass. Look ahead to your bright future. Life is about living, Lila. Never let go of your dreams."

Lila allowed herself to be swept up in his arms. He rocked her gently, and Lila was overcome with a sense of peace and security that she hadn't felt since she was a child. No matter what problems came her way, there was nothing she and Porter couldn't face together.

"Do you know what my dream is?" Lila said coyly, looking up at him. "My dream is to spend every hour of every day with you."

Porter held her close. Lila felt his body shudder slightly, and she knew he was pleased.

"What's your dream?" she asked.

Porter's eyes became glassy, as though he were focusing on something in the distance. He pointed a strong, square finger toward the cliffs. "Do you see that house over there?"

Lila turned, following his line of vision. Porter was pointing to a yellow Spanish-style house with a red-tiled roof that was standing on the top of the cliff. She knew that house well. It was her aunt Katherine's.

Porter brushed back the hair from her eyes and looked down at Lila. His soft, pink mouth drooped at the corners, making his dimples disappear. His eyes seemed far away—lost. Sad.

"My dream is a long shot," he said wearily. Lila felt the muscles in his arms tense, as if this were something he yearned for with his entire being. "But nothing would make me happier than to live in that house with you."

Chapter Ten

Jessica threw back her head, enjoying the hot spray of water falling from the showerhead. It had been a great day, one of the best she'd had in weeks. Her only class of the day had been canceled—the professor had the flu. Then it was off to the coffeehouse to spend a leisurely afternoon with Isabella, sipping cappuccino and sharing Theta gossip. On her way to the dining hall three different guys asked her out, and for once, all of them had been cute. But the sweetest moment of all came early in the day, when Tom brushed his teeth with a great big gob of hair gel.

"Revenge is *so* sweet," Jessica sang, her voice bouncing off the walls of the shower stall. Clouds of thick steam billowed around her. It was such a simple trick; any genius could've done it.

"I can't believe you did that," Isabella had said earlier in the day when Jessica first told her about it. "How did you manage to pull it off?"

"It was easy," Jessica had reassured her. "As soon as Tom was asleep I snipped off the end of the toothpaste tube and squirted the paste into the trash can. When it was completely cleaned out, I opened the tube and filled it with hair gel. Then I crimped the end with a bobby pin, rolled it up like it was before, and *voilà*—a work of art."

The perfect practical joke, Jessica thought as she poured out a handful of shampoo. Actually, she had never believed Tom would fall for something so simple. After all, didn't he notice that his toothpaste was pink? As smart as Elizabeth made her boyfriend out to be, he sure could be dense sometimes.

Jessica massaged her scalp, working her hair into a thick lather. When she bumped into Tom later on that day in the coffeehouse, she expected him to scream at her. Or at least tell her off. But all he did was walk past her, his eyes focused ahead and his mouth drawn back in a tight line. Jessica smiled with satisfaction. Obviously he was still reeling from what she had done. Either that or his lips were still stuck together.

"You just wait, Tommy boy," Jessica said to the shower wall. "There's plenty more where that came from."

Jessica wrapped a plush royal blue towel around her head and covered herself with a matching bath sheet. Tom was already breaking down, she could feel it. The hanging teddy bear probably hit him pretty hard. One more good prank was all she'd need to get him out forever. Jessica blew on her fingernails and rubbed them against the towel. In a way, she was a little disappointed. *Getting rid of Tom is just too easy*, Jessica thought. *It would've been more fun to have a challenge.*

Standing by the wall of sinks in front of the mirror, Jessica leaned over and towel dried her hair. Then she stood up, flipping back her hair. Jessica froze when she saw her reflection.

"Wait a minute . . ." Stunned, she looked up, thinking something was wrong with the light. But the light was the same as it had always been.

Jessica stared at her reflection in fright. "It can't be." She grabbed a lock of hair and touched it with her fingers. In a panic she grabbed another, then another, until she realized that every piece of hair was the same sickening color.

Jessica's hair was bright green!

"I'm going to get you for this, Tom Watts!" she screamed with all her strength. "You're dead meat!"

Lila slowly unlocked the door. "This is ours now," she said.

Porter followed her inside, his eyes wide with excitement. He looked at her and smiled. "It's all I ever wanted. Thank you." Porter wrapped his arms around her and kissed her passionately.

Lila giggled and pulled away. "Wait until you get inside and see what I've done with it."

They ran up the stairs like two excited children. When they reached the top, Lila beamed proudly as she gestured to the new decorations. Every inch of wall was covered with narrow shelves, evenly spaced apart. They continued all the way up the ceiling, which was several hundred feet above them. The shelves were lined with pretty pieces of crystal arranged in perfect rows. There were delicate crystal animals, cups and saucers, wine goblets, bud vases, and miniature sculptures. They sparkled like prisms.

"It's beautiful," Porter said breathlessly.

At that very moment the room began to shake. Lila looked out the enormous window and saw Bruce, who was as big as a giant. He gripped the house in his gigantic hands and rocked it back and forth on its foundation. His eyes burned like red-hot coals.

A few pieces of crystal smashed to the floor. "Bruce, stop it!" Lila screamed. The house continued shaking and the shelves collapsed, one by one, crystal pieces falling down around them.

Lila cried and reached out for Porter. Just as she was about to touch him he eluded her, scrambling around the floor and picking up the pieces. "Porter, come here. Help me," Lila begged. "I can't," he said in a calm, unnatural voice. He filled his pockets with the broken crystal. "I have to put it all back together again."

Lila bolted upright in bed, her heavy breathing the only sound in the darkness. She clicked on the light. The room was perfectly still, everything in place. She lay back uneasily, waiting for the pounding in her chest to subside.

114

"It was just a dream," she told herself, "the crystal, Bruce as a giant . . ." It seemed silly now that she thought about it. But the shaking was very real to her.

She sat up again, suddenly seized with anxiety. Eyes darting around the room, she noticed that so many things hung perilously above, ready to crash on her head. Lila bolted out of bed, snatching pictures off the walls, clearing shelves. She removed the glass cover of the ceiling lamp. Her bureau was pushed against the corner and braced with a solid chair. Everything that could possibly move was secured. In the morning she'd buy some brackets to nail everything down.

Lila shook uncontrollably. Even though all her things were out of harm's way, she still felt helpless. When the next quake hit, she'd probably be alone in her room with no one to help her. It would take search parties days to find her, buried under all the rubble. Lila rocked back and forth, hugging herself, while anxious tears streamed down her face. She couldn't stand the thought of being alone ever again.

With shaky fingers, she dialed Porter's number.

"Hello?"

"Porter—" Lila broke down in tears.

"What's wrong?" She knew she had woken him up in the middle of the night, but his voice was as kind and sweet as if she had called him in the middle of the afternoon.

"Porter, I'm scared . . ."

"Is it about the quake?"

Lila nodded furiously, but then remembered that he couldn't see her. "Yes. I keep thinking it's going to happen again."

"I want you to close your eyes and relax," he said in a hushed voice. "Are you doing it?"

"Yes," Lila said, straining. A prickly sensation was crawling up her spine, making the hair stand on the back of her neck. "I can't relax, Porter . . ."

"Shhhh. Take a deep breath. I'm here for you."

Lila tried to breathe, but she broke down in tears again. How could she relax when at any moment the earth could start moving again? "It's not working," she said weakly. "Can't you come get me?"

Porter was silent for a moment. "I would, Lila, but I live in a one-room studio. There's no place for you to stay."

"Porter, I can't stand this anymore. I need you."

"I know," he answered quietly. "I wish I could do something." He was silent, as if he were lost in thought. "I'd even buy a bigger apartment if I could afford it."

Lila's head was spinning. "If you had a bigger place, you'd let me live with you?"

"You know I would. Don't you remember my dream?"

How could I forget? Lila pictured the stately house rising through the trees on the top of the cliff. More than anything he wanted to live there with her. Little did he know that she owned it. She dreaded living in that house, the same place where Aunt Katherine died so horribly and where she too had almost died. But if Porter moved in with her, she'd never be alone again.

"Lila, are you still there? Are you all right?"

"I'm here. I was just thinking." *Don't tell him; just forget about that terrible place.*

"Hang in there, Lila. I almost lost you once. Don't make me go through it again."

Lila looked around her room. Everything had been tossed to the floor. Every piece of furniture was moved aside. It was the best temporary solution she had, but it was no way to live. She needed real security.

Lila breathed in and took the plunge. "Porter, I have the most wonderful secret."

Tom cued up the videotape player. He ran a ten-second clip, showing footage of the crowd of students outside the library after the earthquake. "I'm going to trim this a bit," he said to Elizabeth. "But what do you think we should say over it?"

Elizabeth put the microphone down on the editing table and leaned back in her chair. "You're not going to include that dumb creamed-spinach story, are you?"

Tom laced his fingers behind his head. "Well, it *is* a news item. And at the moment, we really don't have much to work with."

"We have to draw the line somewhere." Elizabeth twirled the end of her ponytail pensively. "Why don't we just show a shot of the crowd and I'll say something about everyone's day being disrupted."

Tom moved the tape forward to the exact frame where they needed to start. "Do you want a dry run or do you just want to go for it?"

Elizabeth picked up the microphone and cleared her throat. "I think I'm just going to wing it," she said.

"What a pro," Tom marveled. "On the count of three. One . . . two . . ."

Elizabeth did the voice-over in her most journalistic voice, careful to make the words match the footage. *"The earthquake was a disruption to academic life at SVU. Many students were forced to abandon papers and research projects for the day, due to the closing of the library. This left the more studious members of SVU to find other ways to put their time to good use . . ."*

The tape cut to the guy in ripped jeans as he said, "I cranked up my stereo. It was cool."

Tom laughed out loud and drummed his fingertips against the table. "That was absolutely brilliant, my dear."

Elizabeth took a bow. "I didn't know that was going to happen. Do you think we should leave it? It's harsh."

"Nah." Tom shook his head. "It's just a joke. Besides, the guy won't even know the difference. He'll be thrilled that he made the news."

"You're probably the wrong person I should be asking about what's harsh and what isn't," she said with a teasing smile. "After all, this is coming from a man who dyed my sister's hair green last night."

"Jessica dyed her own hair," Tom corrected. His serious expression melted into a sly grin. "I just gave her the supplies."

Elizabeth giggled. "I shouldn't laugh, but it *was* pretty funny. If you want to get to Jess, toying with her appearance is the best way." She moved from her chair and sat on Tom's lap. "Of course, she got you pretty good too."

Tom's eyebrows furrowed. "There's nothing funny about that. My teeth still feel like an oil slick."

"Poor baby," Elizabeth cooed. She held his head close to her and planted a great big kiss on the top. "At least I haven't had to listen to you two screaming at each other for the past few days. Still, I hope this will be the end of it. These things can really get out of hand."

"Don't you worry," Tom said, touching her lightly on the nose. "There's no way Jessica can top that one."

"What are you going to have, dear?" Grace Fowler lowered her menu and smiled at her daughter. "Order whatever you like. This is your night."

Lila hid behind her menu and rolled her eyes. If it was really her night, why did her parents drag her to a restaurant when she didn't want to go? If she had any say in the matter at all, she would've told them both to stay home so she could have a quiet dinner alone with Porter.

"I'm sorry Bruce couldn't make it tonight," Lila's dad said. A waiter in a white tuxedo shirt and black bow tie set a basket of bread in the center of the white tablecloth. Next to the basket he placed a tiny silver bowl filled with butter rosebuds.

"Bruce had something else to do," Lila answered pointedly, even though she had neglected to invite him.

"Are you ready to order?" the waiter asked.

"Yes," Lila's mother said, flashing a plastic smile that made Lila shiver. "I'm going to have the stuffed pheasant *en cro te.*"

"And for you, sir?" the waiter asked, turning to Lila's dad. "I'm in the mood for beef Wellington. Madeira sauce on the side, please."

The waiter nodded appreciatively. "And you, miss?"

Lila looked up, and everyone was staring at her. She'd spent so much time thinking about Porter, she hadn't even had a chance to look at the menu. "I'll have . . . whatever," she said, giving him a dismissive wave.

"Lila," Grace Fowler whispered indignantly.

The waiter stood patiently with a servile grin on his face. "May I suggest the capellini with capers and prosciutto in a tomato cream sauce? It's superb."

"Fine." Lila handed him her menu. Lila's mother forced a weak smile.

"And one more thing," Lila's father called to the waiter. "We'd like a bottle of your most expensive champagne."

"Certainly." The waiter scurried off to get the bottle.

Lila grabbed a sourdough roll from the bread basket and broke it with her hands. Out of nowhere another waiter appeared, taking a linen napkin out of its silver holder and draping it elegantly across Lila's lap. His white-gloved hands reached for a set of miniature tongs and carefully placed a butter rose on her bread plate.

"Thanks," Lila murmured tiredly. The waiter nodded and retreated to his post, directly behind Lila's chair.

Grace looked lovingly at her daughter, her gray eyes squinting as she smiled. Lila stared at her mother's long, slender fingers and flashy gold rings. "Please pass the bread basket, dear." No sooner did Lila's mother take a roll than the waiter stepped forward and did his routine all over again.

Lila's father took a sip from his crystal water goblet. "We wanted to take you out tonight for a celebration of sorts. We're so happy you've made a full recovery."

As if on cue, Grace's eyes sparkled with tears. "When I think of it—my poor baby in the hospital. I couldn't bear the thought of losing you. You have no idea how scared we were."

Lila chewed furiously on the roll. *You have no idea how scared* I *was,* she thought bitterly. It had been so easy for everyone to watch it all from the sidelines when *she* was the one who almost died. She was reaching her flash point, like a dry piece of paper smoldering under the magnified rays of the sun.

The original waiter returned, carrying an un-corked bottle of champagne. He took the cham-pagne flute in front of Mr. Fowler and filled it with an inch of the golden, sparkling liquid. The waiter poured skillfully, pressing his thumb against the base of the bottle and balancing it with his re-maining four fingers.

Mr. Fowler held the flute by its delicate stem and took a sip. He smiled. "Marvelous," he said, then took another drink.

The waiter refilled his glass, then proceeded to fill Lila's and her mother's.

"I propose a toast," Lila's father said. He raised his glass high in the air. "To our daughter, Lila. May she have a long, healthy, and happy life."

"Hear, hear," her mother chimed in. They clinked glasses and sipped the champagne.

Lila brushed away a few bread crumbs that had fallen onto her Hermes scarf. *When is this night going to end?* While her body sat primly in the cream-colored brocade chair, her mind had already escaped. Past the army of tuxedoed waiters and through the green marble lobby, Lila's thoughts were already hours ahead, anticipating the next time she'd see Porter. She hadn't told him about the house yet—only that she had a wonderful surprise. She couldn't wait to see the look on his face when she told him the truth. The more she thought about it, the more she realized that moving in with Porter was the best thing she could possibly do.

"Lila? Are you listening?"

Lila felt as if she'd fallen off a cloud and crashed rudely back to earth. "What, Mom?"

"I was *saying* that your father and I were planning to extend his business trip so we could spend some time in Europe." She gracefully dabbed the corners of her mouth with a napkin. "But after what's happened, I think we should stay home. What if you should need us?"

Why should you stay home now? Lila thought bitterly. *You never did when I was growing up.* She was a fraction of a second from blurting it out, when suddenly she thought the better of it. Getting them upset would only cause them to worry more—they'd definitely stay home and paw all over her. If she was going to start being independent, she had to make them believe she was perfectly capable of taking care of herself.

Lila flashed them her best dutiful daughter smile. "I won't hear of it," she said in a syrupy voice. "You two go and enjoy Europe. You deserve it."

Both her parents exchanged curious glances. "Are you certain you won't need us for anything?" her mother asked.

"I've never felt healthier or happier." Lila gave her mother's hand a reassuring pat. "I'll be fine. I promise."

"Don't peek," Lila said, eyeing Porter playfully. She cut the steering wheel left and drove Porter's white Mustang up the steep mansion drive. Her spine tingled in anticipation. In a few minutes Porter would know her secret.

Porter tugged at the edges of the silk scarf that covered his eyes. "I know I sound like a kid, but are we there yet?"

"Almost." Lila inched the car so that it was parked a few feet in front of the garage doors. "Believe me, this is going to be worth the wait."

Excitedly Lila jumped out of the car, ran around to the passenger side, and helped Porter out. She held his hand, leading him to the front of the house. The tree that had fallen during the quake was still leaning precariously against the smashed porch. It wasn't a pretty sight, but it didn't matter. Lila knew Porter would still be excited.

"Any last-minute guesses?" she asked. Lila's heart pounded eagerly in her throat. She gave his hand a tight squeeze.

"All my guesses have been wrong so far," Porter said with a wry smile. "But I still think it's a picnic in the woods."

Lila let out a nervous giggle. "You're still wrong. This is a thousand times better than a picnic." She reached behind him to untie the knot. "Are you ready?"

"You've kept me in suspense for twenty-four hours. I'm definitely ready."

With a flourish, Lila removed the blindfold. Her lips twitched with pleasure as she watched Porter's expression change from confusion to surprise, and back to confusion again. Porter was speechless.

"Well, do you recognize the house?" she said.

Porter's blue eyes were clouded. "Of course, but why did you bring me here?" he asked slowly. "Did you want to show me the wrecked porch?"

Lila shook her head. "Porter, I own this house."

Porter stared at her. His jaw went slack, and his eyebrows arched in amazement.

Lila looked deeply into his eyes. "I'm not kidding. This house belongs to me."

Porter's face brightened as Lila's words seeped in. His eyes sparkled with excitement as they looked up at the red-tiled roof and traveled all the way down to the lush green lawn. "I can't believe it."

"It belonged to my aunt Katherine—the one I told you about. But I didn't mention that she left it to me in her will. When we were on the beach and you told me your dream to live here with me, well . . ." Lila wrapped an arm around his waist.

"Nothing would make me happier," Porter said huskily. He looped the scarf behind her neck and tugged on the ends, pulling her closer. Porter pressed her against him and kissed her amorously. Lila felt herself weaken under his touch. He pulled away slightly, his gaze sending shivers through Lila all the way down to her toes. "Can we go inside?" he asked.

Lila stood still, afraid that the slightest movement would make the moment disappear forever. "Of course," she whispered. "We can get in through the back door."

Porter turned and looked at the porch. "Did that happen in the quake?"

Lila nodded. "I was in the house at the time. That's how I got hurt." She pressed her cheek against his chest, remembering the crash she had heard just before the armoire fell. There had also been chimes and voices calling her to the attic. Lila started to shake, pressing herself harder against him. What if the voices were still there? What if they still wanted her? She closed her eyes and concentrated on the sound of Porter's heartbeat, its steady rhythm comforting her like a lullaby.

He gently touched her soft brown hair. "Don't be frightened. I'm here. Nothing will happen."

He knows me so well, Lila thought. She didn't have to say a word, and he understood how she felt. It had never been that way with Bruce. Even when she told him exactly what she was feeling, he still didn't understand. "Let's go inside," she said.

It was late afternoon, and the sun was low in the sky. Its rays darted through the trees, covering the house in golden, dappled light. Porter followed Lila behind the house to the terrace and the glass doors that led to the kitchen. Broken glass was everywhere, and a few shards hung perilously over the doorway.

"Wait a minute," Porter said, holding Lila back. He threw small rocks at the remaining pieces of glass, which crashed noisily and scattered in hundreds of fragments. He looked down at Lila's open-toed sandals, showing off her perfectly painted red toenails.

Lila wiggled her toes. "I guess I wasn't being very practical."

126

Porter brushed a blond curl out of his eyes. "It's not a problem." In one quick motion he tipped her backward and lifted her into his arms. Lila let out a squeal of delight and clung to his neck. Porter smiled. "I guess I'm supposed to do this anyway," he said, carrying her over the threshold.

He let her down in the middle of the kitchen. Lila looked around at the black-and-white-tiled floor and the shelves of cookbooks. Lila took a deep breath and smiled to herself. She wasn't frightened anymore.

Porter was already walking ahead, wandering out into the hallway. Lila ran to catch up with him. "Where are you going?" she asked teasingly.

"To the parlor." He took an immediate right, walking as though he had done´it a thousand times before.

Lila's eyes narrowed. "How do you know where the parlor is?"

Porter flashed her a boyish grin. "I don't. But it's usually not too far from the kitchen," he answered.

"Right," Lila said with a laugh. She walked under a curved archway into the parlor. A thin layer of dust had accumulated on the beautiful furniture. Lila swiped a finger across the top of one of the end tables, leaving a snaking trail in the dust.

"It's incredible. Even better than I'd dreamed." Porter walked around the room, inspecting every inch of the parlor. He opened drawers, looked inside vases, lifted paintings to look at the wall space underneath. "Exquisite.

Absolutely exquisite," he said, running his strong hand over the top of a lacquered Chinese box.

Lila blushed. She was so happy that he was pleased. "My aunt must've bought it when she was on one of her culinary tours. She was a world-class chef." Lila pointed to a picture frame on the mantel. It was a photograph of Aunt Katherine, wearing one of her eccentric aprons that she loved to collect. This one in particular was covered with sequins and gaudy plastic jewels. Uncle Chester had given it to her on her birthday. The words *Queen of the Kitchen* were spelled out in silver piping.

"This is my aunt," Lila said, showing Porter the photo.

Porter grimaced. "What is that *thing* she's wearing? It's horrible."

"She collected unusual aprons," Lila said in her aunt's defense. "It was one of her hobbies. I think it's charming."

Porter opened the lacquered box and looked inside. "Doesn't it bother you to have all of your aunt's things around you?"

"What do you mean?"

Porter paused. "Considering everything that happened . . . doesn't it bring back painful memories?"

As the words escaped Porter's lips, Lila felt the chill returning. The cold covered her skin with goose bumps, threatening to sink deeper until it became a permanent part of her. She wanted Porter to fulfill his dream, but living among Aunt Katherine's things would be a constant reminder of her horrible death. Lila touched one of the piano keys. A clear note resounded, cutting through the silence of the room. Even though she felt safe with Porter, what would happen when he wasn't around?

Porter sat down on the red velvet covered piano stool. "If it's going to bother you, why don't we move all her things up to the attic? We could leave the furniture, of course, but then we could decorate it with our own things. We'll make it ours."

Lila glanced at his beautiful, dimpled face. Porter's nose had a pinkish sunburn from their afternoon at the beach. *Would Aunt Katherine be upset if I moved her things?* Lila wondered. She thought about it for a moment, then realized that Aunt Katherine would want her to be happy. And being with Porter was what made her happy. If moving her things to the attic was what Lila needed to do to start her wonderful life with Porter, then that was what she'd have to do.

"I'll have it all done before we even move in. I'll board up the attic door and you'll never have to see those things ever again, never be reminded of what happened." His face was full of hope. "I'll have the porch and the glass doors fixed, too."

"That sounds great," Lila said enthusiastically.

Porter's mind was already at work, making plans for their new home. "Is there a phone around here? Do I need to have one put in?"

Lila sat on his lap and wrapped her arms

around his shoulders. "There's one upstairs. It's the only one in the house."

"That's all we'll need. I'll make that room my study," he said decidedly. "If it's okay with you."

"Of course it's okay with me. I want you to be happy." Lila sighed to herself, thinking how perfectly happy she was at that very moment. Finally they were going to start their lives together.

Chapter
Eleven

When Bruce heard a knock at the front door of Sigma house, he flew down the stairs with a cardboard box in his arms. Without missing a beat he quickly opened the front door, so he wouldn't give her a chance to change her mind.

Lila stood on the front step, tapping her foot impatiently. Bruce tried not to notice the beautiful shape of her calves. "Thanks for coming by," he said with a tinge of nervousness. "Come inside."

Lila flipped her hair over her shoulder. Her blue eyes reflected the annoyance that was brewing underneath. "Why don't you just give me my things so I can go? I still have a lot of packing to do," she snapped.

Don't leave yet, Bruce pleaded silently. "Just come in for a second. I'm not quite done yet."

Lila looked at him skeptically. Bruce stepped aside and pointed to the brown-and-green-plaid couch in the living room. Lila curled her upper lip in disdain and walked inside.

Bruce breathed a sigh of relief. He had made it through the first hurdle. Lila sat stiffly on the couch, primly smoothing her skirt. Tony Calavieri lounged at the opposite end with his feet propped up on the coffee table, munching on a slice of pizza.

Bruce cleared his throat loudly. "Tony—do you mind?" he said, nodding in Lila's direction.

"Sorry. I wasn't thinking," Tony said. He nudged the pizza box toward Lila. "Do you want a slice?"

Lila glared at the pools of orange grease floating on top of the pizza. "No, thanks."

"Tony." Bruce flashed him an intimidating look.

Tony was instantly on his feet, gnawing on a piece of crust. "I can take a hint." He bounded out of the room with his pizza.

Bruce took a deep breath, setting the cardboard box on the table in front of Lila. "This is most of your stuff, but I think I'm forgetting something." He scanned the room, hoping to buy some time.

Lila looked into the box. There were a couple of her CDs, a T-shirt, the spare key to her room, some books, and a few odd things she had left in Bruce's room. Lila took out a small plastic dinosaur she had won at a carnival. She held it up for him to see. "I gave this to you. You can keep it."

Bruce took the dinosaur from her. His fingers brushed hers. Bruce let the touch linger for a moment. "Do you remember that night at the carnival?

132

There was something wrong with the Ferris wheel and we were stuck at the top for almost an hour," he said wistfully. "But we were so busy talking that it was fifteen minutes before we even noticed."

Lila looked away. "Bruce . . . I know what you're trying to do."

Bruce pushed the box aside and sat down on the table. "I'm trying to save our relationship. Can you blame me?"

She moved uncomfortably in her seat. "Bruce, it's over."

"According to who?" Bruce leaned forward, elbows resting on his torn blue jeans. "I thought things were fine with us, and suddenly you tell me it's over. Would you please explain what's going on?"

"I told you, things are different now," she said, touching the string of pearls around her neck. "The accident has changed me in ways you'll never understand."

A sickening feeling hit Bruce in the pit of his stomach. "I think there's more to it than that," he said thickly.

Lila's eyes dropped. She picked invisible lint off her navy skirt as though she didn't hear him.

Bruce touched her lightly on her arm. "If you've met someone else, just tell me. I want to work this out. I'm not ready to let you go."

Lila didn't answer. Her lips were drawn tightly and her eyes were cold. He could tell that she was working hard not to betray any emotion. Just when he thought he'd started communicating with her, she pulled away.

Bruce gripped his head with his hands. His temples were throbbing. "At least answer one question for me," he said in a shaky voice. "Do you still love me?"

Lila bit her lip. Her eyes glistened. "That has nothing to do with—"

"Tell me, Lila," Bruce interrupted. "I need to know. Do you still love me?"

"I'm in love with someone else," she blurted through clenched teeth. Her face was red. "We're moving into the mansion together."

Bruce felt as though his heart had just been crushed by a gigantic fist. He stared at her numbly. "Who is he?"

She stood up and grabbed the box. Walking past him, she headed for the door. "Someone who understands me better than you ever did."

"What are you in the mood for—espresso or cappuccino?" Isabella leaned against the counter of her kitchenette. The heavy aroma of freshly brewed coffee wafted across the room toward Jessica, who was seated at the kitchen table.

"Cappuccino. And don't forget to sprinkle a little cinnamon on top." She touched her blue baseball cap self-consciously, tucking in any stray hairs. Jessica made a mental note to get to a hat store as soon as possible. She had a feeling she might have to spend the rest of the semester with her head covered.

Isabella poured some skim milk into a small metal pitcher. She turned a knob on the cappuccino machine and put the steam spout in the pitcher of milk. "So, have you heard from Lila? Has she moved in yet?"

"Tomorrow," Jessica said, checking her reflection in the round mirror hanging on the wall. "She's all packed and ready to go."

A strange gurgling sound erupted from the cappuccino machine. "I can't believe she's moving in with this guy," Isabella's silver bracelets clinked as she frothed the milk. "But from what she said about him, he sounds fabulous."

Jessica snickered. "He could be a toad and still be a better catch than Bruce Patman."

"Ouch! That one hurt."

"It's true," Jessica said flatly. "I could never understand why she was interested in him in the first place."

Isabella poured the milk into two cappuccino cups and carried them over to the table.

"Don't forget the cinnamon—" Jessica reminded her.

Isabella set a shaker of cinnamon on the table next to Jessica. "Bruce isn't that bad," she said, licking a bit of milk foam off her fingertip. "He was pretty good to her."

"Please," Jessica said dramatically. "Patman is totally stubborn and selfish. He doesn't care about anyone but himself. I guess Lila finally figured that out."

"I don't know—I feel sort of bad for him. Don't you think this has all happened pretty suddenly?"

Jessica sipped the sweet, milky coffee. "Who knows? Maybe the breakup was coming on for a long time, and this Porter guy finally tipped the scales for her."

Isabella brushed back her long dark hair. "I can't wait to meet him. She says he's gorgeous."

"And he's a doctor." Jessica arched one eyebrow impressively.

"Sounds like a dreamboat," a male voice said.

Jessica and Isabella looked up to see Danny Wyatt stroll out of the bathroom and into the living room.

"Hey, Danny," Jessica said.

Danny pulled on a sweatshirt and picked up his duffel bag. "How's it going, Jess?" he said with a smirk. "Nice hat."

Jessica's eyes narrowed threateningly, but she didn't answer.

Isabella gave Danny a quick kiss on the cheek. "Heading out?" she asked him.

"I'm going to the gym," he said, tying the laces of his sneakers. "I'll come by to pick you up for dinner."

"Bye," she called sweetly as he closed the door. She pointed to Jessica's hat. "What was that all about?"

Jessica frowned. "Evidently Tom's got a big mouth."

Isabella's gray eyes were filled with confusion. "Jess, I don't follow."

136

Jessica grabbed the visor of her hat and took it off. Silky green hair tumbled to her shoulders.

Isabella covered her red mouth. Her eyes were wide. "What happened?" she said, stifling laughter.

"Remember that little trick I played on Tom?" Jessica said ruefully. "This is the payback."

Isabella reached for a bright green lock of hair. "Don't worry—I know a hairdresser who can get this out."

"Oh, *I'm* not worried," Jessica said with a touch of sarcasm. "The only person who should be worried is Tom. I've already thought of several ways I could torture him."

"That might not be the best way to go," Isabella said, taking another sip of coffee. "You just might make things worse. Being mean to him probably isn't the best approach."

Jessica puckered her lips in thought. If being mean wouldn't drive him away, what could possibly work? Suddenly she had a great idea. A sly smile crossed her lips. "You know what, Izzy? You're absolutely right. You just helped me think of the perfect way to get even."

"Oh, no," Isabella said. "Am I going to regret this?"

"No, but Tom will," Jessica answered with an evil grin. "He's going to regret the day he was born."

Porter dropped the last box in the middle of Lila's new bedroom. He brushed his hands to-

137

gether and smiled at her warmly. "I guess that's it. How do you like it?"

"It's beautiful," Lila said, glancing around the room. Porter had done a wonderful job of setting up the house. All Aunt Katherine's things were safely tucked away in the attic, the door boarded up so Lila would never have to see them again. Porter bought a white lace bedspread for her with matching curtains. There were silver makeup and hairbrushes on the vanity. He'd even filled a crystal vase with delicate white flowers.

"Thanks for everything," she said, glancing out her bedroom window to the front lawn and the driveway.

Porter caressed her cheek. "I'm glad you like it," he said. "My room is right next door, so I'll be close by if you need anything." He turned her face so that she was looking directly into his eyes. "I set up my study in the room across the hall. Please don't go in there. I have some confidential medical records, and I want to be able to work freely without worrying that you'll see something you're not supposed to. Do you understand?"

"Of course I do."

"Good," Porter said with a smile.

Lila suddenly became aware of the musty smell of the room. It was a damp mixture of old linen and lavender soap. "I'm going to air out the room a little," she said, trying to open the window. It wouldn't budge.

"I'll fix that later," Porter said, pulling Lila

away from the window. He sat her down on the bed. "We have a lot to do today. I want to go shopping for some things we still need. But first, I wanted to give you this." He took a small box out of his pocket.

"Porter—" Lila's graceful hand reached for her throat. Her pulse quickened as she imagined all the incredible things that could be in such a tiny box.

He handed it to her. "Consider it a 'moving in' present."

Lila touched the box gingerly. She looked at Porter with expectation, then quickly took the top off the box. Inside was a gold, heart-shaped locket. An intricate design was engraved on its tiny surface. Lila was certain that she had never seen anything so glorious in her entire life.

"It's an antique," Porter said. "It's been in my family for generations."

Lila felt tears of happiness coming to her eyes. "I'm going to put our pictures in it," she said, trying to open the locket.

Porter took it out of her hands. "Don't force it. The hinge is broken. I thought we'd drop it off at the jeweler's while we're out shopping."

Lila thought her heart would burst. "Porter—I don't know what to say . . . I'll treasure it forever."

"I hope you will. It's a family heirloom." He reached for her brown leather purse and slipped it into one of the side pockets. "Leave it in here for safe-keeping until we get to the jeweler's. We wouldn't want you to lose it, the way you lose everything else."

Lila was about to ask him what he meant when the passionate heat of his kiss came down upon her.

Lila and Porter cruised the aisles of the housewares department, looking for things to furnish their new home. Not everything that belonged to Aunt Katherine was whisked away to the attic; Porter decided to keep the pots and pans and cooking tools, because they would be too expensive to replace. But they still needed glasses and dishes. When Aunt Katherine's body had been found, the cupboards had been emptied and the glassware was smashed to pieces.

"Ooo, I love those," Lila cooed, pointing to a set of dark blue water glasses. "They'd look great in the kitchen cabinets. That's definitely one of the advantages of having cabinets with glass doors. You can see all the pretty things inside."

Porter inspected the glasses, holding them up to the light. "They're flawless. Good choice, Lila." He put them into the shopping cart.

Lila smiled proudly, gazing up at the terracotta vases stacked on a high shelf. This was more fun than she had ever imagined. Lila wove her way through the fragile aisles, her walk light and graceful. She felt ready to conquer the world.

"Do you see anything else?" Porter called from the other end of the aisle. The cart he was pushing was packed with glasses, towels, kitchen utensils, and an automatic pasta maker.

"I guess that's it," Lila answered happily.

"I'll go pay," he said, turning toward the row of cash registers.

Lila wandered through the china patterns over to the baking section. As her eyes scanned the rows of mixing bowls and wooden spoons, it suddenly occurred to her that the earthquake was probably the best thing that had ever happened to her. If it hadn't been for the accident, she would have never met this perfect man. She wouldn't have had this wonderful day of moving into the mansion and shopping for household items with Porter. And he would've never given her that beautiful little locket. The accident was definitely a blessing in disguise.

Lila was about to head for the cash registers when she noticed a box sitting on the lower shelf. It was a cookie press—almost identical to the one Aunt Katherine used to bring out whenever they'd made cookies together. Lila picked up the box, smiling with sentiment. Aunt Katherine used to fill the tube with cookie dough and slide a metal plate with a pattern cut out of it over the end of the tube. Lila, wearing one of her aunt's tacky aprons, would press down on the top, and a pretty patterned cookie came out onto the cookie sheet. Occasionally Aunt Katherine would color the dough and they'd make different-colored flowers. It was one of Lila's happiest memories of Aunt Katherine.

Lila suddenly had the urge to make those flowers again. The old cookie press was probably somewhere in the house, although Porter might have taken it upstairs to the attic. She would have

141

asked him to go get it, but she didn't want him to go through the trouble of taking the boards off the attic door. Plus, he might not understand her reasons for doing it. The only thing left to do was to buy a new one.

Lila dashed to the cash registers, hoping to catch Porter before he'd paid for everything. When she reached the counter, the cashier was handing him the change and his receipt.

Porter grabbed the two white shopping bags. "Did you find something else?" he asked.

Lila nodded, putting the press on the counter. "That's okay," she said. "I'll pay for this one."

The cashier rang up the purchase, and Lila reached into the side pocket of her purse, where she always kept her money.

"Ten forty-six," the cashier said as he slipped the press into a shopping bag.

Lila's fingers felt for her money, and she pulled out a crisp ten-dollar bill. She reached in again for the forty-six cents. Her hand searched the pocket, but she didn't have any change. She was about to reach for another bill, when it suddenly dawned on her that something was missing. She froze.

The locket was gone.

"Just a second," she said to the cashier with a panicked smile. She searched the other pockets once, then over again. *It can't be,* Lila thought frantically. How could she lose something so valuable? She remembered feeling it when she paid for something at the last store they went to.

Maybe it's in one of the aisles, she reasoned. *It can't be far.*

"Lila, is something wrong?" Porter asked.

Lila laughed weakly. "I think I'm out of change. Do you have any?"

Porter set down the bags and searched his pockets. While he was looking for the change, Lila slipped away to search for the locket. Her heart pounded as she retraced her steps through the baking section, to the china patterns, and back to the glassware. She moved quickly through, her eyes glued to the floor. As she reached the far wall Lila's lower lip began to tremble. The beautiful antique locket was gone.

Lila retraced her steps again, her heart heavy. *What am I going to do?* she thought miserably. Porter wanted to take the locket to the jeweler. She had to do everything in her power to make sure they didn't go to the jeweler's.

"Lila," Porter called, his arms loaded down with bags. "I was looking everywhere for you."

Lila forced a smile. She brushed away a stray tear. "I was just looking around," she said casually.

Porter nudged her quickly out of the store. When they reached the sidewalk, he stopped and turned to her. His expression was grave. "Don't ever do that again!" he said harshly.

Lila did a double take. *Does he know about the locket?* "What . . . what's wrong?" she stammered.

Porter's angelic face took on a hard edge. "You can't just take off whenever you feel like it, Lila.

You're still recovering from a serious head injury, and you need to be more careful."

"I was only looking around," she said defensively.

Porter softened. "Look, I don't want to frighten you—but it's too soon for you to be running around. You have to tell me what you're doing." His eyes pleaded with her. "I'm worried about you, Lila. I just don't want anything to happen. Understand?"

Lila nodded. A tingling fear gnawed at the base of her spine. She thought she had recovered completely, and now he was saying that she still wasn't out of danger. What could possibly go wrong?

"Promise me you'll tell me everything. It's the only way you'll get better."

The last thing she wanted to do was disappoint him. "I promise."

They continued down the busy street. Cars whipped past them, and Lila felt the heat of the pavement through the soles of her sandals. Her legs were starting to ache. Up ahead, she spotted the green-and-white awning of the jewelry store on the corner. She turned to Porter. He was looking at the window of the card shop, which was decorated with shelves of stuffed animals. He apparently hadn't noticed the jewelry store yet.

Think of something, Lila told herself. She had to distract him in some way. She had to buy time until she could find the locket.

"Ow!" Lila shouted, grabbing her foot. She hopped up and down in place.

"Are you all right?" Porter asked.

Lila grimaced. "I stepped on something," she said with drama. "I'm really tired, Porter. Can we head home?"

Porter's brow furrowed. "I thought you were having a good time."

"I am . . . I mean I was. I'm tired now," Lila said. "Let's just go back."

Porter supported her as she massaged her foot. "We're almost done. One more stop and we're finished." He smiled brightly at her. "Don't you want to get the locket fixed?"

Lila dropped her foot. Losing and forgetting things, maybe that's what Porter was talking about when he said she hadn't fully recovered yet. She felt fine physically—it didn't make sense that she'd lost the locket. Whether it made sense or not, she *had* done it. And now she had to own up to it. As much as it pained her to tell Porter, she'd made a promise to him. She had to tell him everything.

"Lila, something's wrong. I can see it in your eyes," he said worriedly. "Are you really not feeling that well? Maybe we should go back."

"It's not that." Lila walked on, with Porter at her side. The jewelry store loomed closer and closer. With each step, she did her best to summon the courage to tell him what she had done. When they reached the store, she stopped in her tracks.

"Aren't you coming inside?" he asked.

"I can't." Lila glanced at the sparkling necklaces and earrings in the window. Her heart caught

145

in her throat. "Porter, I have something to tell you. Promise you won't be angry."

"What is it?"

Lila looked down as she nervously wrung her hands. "I lost the locket."

Porter stared at her without saying a word.

"I know how much it meant to you—it meant a lot to me, too." Lila swallowed hard. "One minute it was there, and the next minute it was gone."

Porter looked at her strangely. "Lila, things just don't disappear. Think—what did you do with it?"

"I don't know," Lila said, on the verge of tears. "I've been racking my brain, but I can't remember."

Porter sighed, shaking his head. Lila knew that she had disappointed him.

"I blame myself," he said. His eyes locked on the store window filled with jewels. "I should've known it was too soon to take you out. I hope I haven't made things worse."

Lila covered her face with her hands. "I'm sorry," she cried. "I don't know what's wrong with me."

Chapter Twelve

"What can I do for you?" the policeman at the front desk asked. He wasn't much older than Bruce, but he had an eager look and a neatly pressed uniform. His new badge flashed proudly under the precinct's fluorescent lights.

Bruce gave him an appreciative nod. "I'd like to speak to the chief homicide detective."

The young officer took a pen out of his uniform pocket. "And what is this regarding?"

"I'd like to discuss a case with him."

"Are you a witness?"

"No," Bruce answered.

"Then I'm afraid you'll have to fill out this form—" He reached for a yellow sheet of paper. "Leave your name, number, and the case you're referring to, and Detective Desmond will be in touch at his earliest convenience."

Bruce gripped the edge of the counter. It wasn't

soon enough. He needed to talk to him *now*. Ever since Lila broke the news to him that she was moving into the mansion with a stranger, he'd had a gut feeling that something was terribly wrong. In a few short weeks Lila had changed into a completely different person, and Bruce was determined to find out why. The best place to start, he decided, was right at the beginning—with her aunt's murder.

Bruce pushed the form away. "This is extremely important. I need to speak with him immediately."

"I'm sorry, it's just not possible," the officer said in a firm voice. "Detective Desmond is extremely busy."

"Rourke!" someone shouted from across the bustling office. The young officer bolted upright. "Get over here!"

"Fill this out and leave it here," he said quickly. He straightened his tie. "I'll make sure he gets it."

"Thanks." Bruce waved as the officer hurried away.

He scanned the area. No one was watching the front desk. Secretaries and officers scurried about, absorbed in their own work. This was exactly the break Bruce was looking for. For once, something was going his way.

Bruce casually walked around the counter. He marched through the office with a purposeful walk, even though he had no idea where he was going. He continued past a secretary's desk and down the hallway to the windowed offices in the back of the building.

His eyes shifted from side to side until he found the black-and-silver nameplate with the name Detective Gerald Desmond engraved on it. Through the blinds Bruce caught a glimpse of the detective, who was rocking in his desk chair and talking on the phone. He was muscular, with dark, thinning hair and a mustache. Bruce opened the door and walked inside.

Detective Desmond abruptly hung up the phone. "Who are you?" he demanded.

"Bruce Patman. I want to talk to you about the Katherine Cage murder."

A spark of interest flashed in his eyes. "Do you know anything?"

"I wish I did."

The detective rolled up the sleeves of his blue-and-white-striped shirt. "Then why are you here?"

Bruce sank into a chair, his black motorcycle jacket creaking as he sat down. "I want some information. My girlfriend is Katherine's niece."

The detective unwrapped a minted toothpick and stuck it in his mouth. "What do you want to know?"

"Do you have any suspects?"

"None," he answered bluntly. "Any other questions?"

Bruce clenched his jaw. "Look, my girlfriend has been acting very strangely. She broke up with me and is living with some guy I've never seen before in the house where Katherine was murdered."

Detective Desmond's mustache twitched in amusement. "I'm really sorry about your messed-up

149

love life," he said with a touch of sarcasm. "But my job is to solve crimes, not patch up relationships."

"Somehow I think there might be a connection to the murder," Bruce argued.

"Then you're two steps ahead of us," the detective snapped. "Our team went through that mansion with a fine-toothed comb. All they found was some broken glass around the body and a few missing items, including Katherine's diamond. It was a robbery that turned bad—plain and simple."

Bruce threw his hands into the air. "Aren't you interested in trying to find out who did it?"

"We have no leads. If you want to try and solve it by yourself, then be my guest," the detective challenged. He leaned back in his chair and propped his feet on top of his metal desk. "As far as this department is concerned, the case is closed."

"Lila, please come down here!" Porter called from the bottom of the stairs.

Lila threw back the lace bedcover and stopped in front of the mirror. The rims of her eyes were tinged with red, and her face was still puffy from crying. She combed her hair with a silver-handled brush and forced a feeble smile. *Just relax*, she told herself. *Everything will be fine*.

Lila descended the stairs, using all her strength to look cheerful. Porter was smiling patiently up at her. "I have a surprise for you," he said. His eyes were shining.

Lila's face was lit with hope. "Did you find the locket?"

"No," he said seriously. "But it's still a good surprise." He stepped into the parlor entrance for a moment. When he returned, there was a young woman standing next to him. "Lila, I want you to meet Nancy."

Lila's face fell. "Hi, Nancy," she said, trying to sound friendly. Nancy had short, ash blond hair and big green eyes. She was tall, with legs that seemed to go on forever, and she took advantage of it by wearing the shortest skirt possible. She also wore a white cotton T-shirt that was three sizes too small and silver hoop earrings. Nancy gave Lila a red, glossy smile.

"Nancy's our new housekeeper and cook," Porter said proudly.

Lila cringed as he gave Nancy's shoulder a squeeze. Nancy giggled.

"That's great," Lila said dryly. Her eyes locked with Porter's. "Porter, can I talk to you for a minute?"

"Sure." Porter turned to Nancy. "Is it all right if we have a moment alone?"

"Certainly," Nancy said with a little curtsy before retreating to the parlor.

Porter grabbed Lila by the waist and tickled her. Lila stifled a shrill of laughter. "Isn't she great?" he said with a dimpled grin.

Lila straightened up, her smile fading. "She seems a little—strange," she whispered. "Are you sure we really need a housekeeper?"

Porter touched her chin. "Lila, I did this for you. I was hoping you'd be happy. You won't have to think about taking care of this place. And I won't have to worry about you being here all alone when I'm at the hospital." He looked deeply into her eyes. "I'm doing this so you can get better. I'm doing it for us."

Lila tilted her head back, feeling the soft warmth of his lips on hers. She opened her eyes to see Nancy's reflection in the hall mirror. She was staring at them.

"Nancy, you can come back now," Porter called.

Nancy swayed into the front hall, moving very close to Porter. "When can I start?" she asked excitedly.

"Right away," he answered. "Lila will show you to your quarters."

Lila smiled meekly. They walked down the long hallway all the way to the back of the house, where the old servant's quarters were. Lila wasn't prepared to have someone staying there, and she had no idea what kind of state the room was in. She sighed heavily and opened the door.

"This is your room," Lila said, clicking on the light. The last time she had seen it, the room was a storage space for extra pieces of furniture. But now it was decorated like a real room, with a bed, writing desk, and vanity mirror. Lila couldn't help noticing that the lace bedspread, silver brushes, and crystal vase filled with flowers looked exactly like hers. "It's small, but cozy."

"Small isn't the word," Nancy said. Her lips twisted into a sneer. "But I suppose if I'm feeling claustrophobic I can always visit another room."

Lila swallowed nervously. "I hope you like it."

Nancy lit a cigarette. "Thanks, Lolita."

"Lila," she corrected.

Nancy gave her a once-over. "Whatever."

Elizabeth dropped her book bag onto the library table and slumped into a seat in the middle of the reference section. She had spent so much time in the library over the past week, she had managed to get her work done several days ahead of schedule. If there was a good result of the fighting between Tom and Jessica, that was the only one.

Elizabeth took a paperback novel out of her bag and opened up to the spot where she left the bookmark. Ever since Jessica's dye job, the fights between them had been fewer. It was almost eerie how quiet the room had been. Tom was convinced that it was because Jessica was backing down, but Elizabeth knew better. Jessica would never let Tom get away with it. Whenever she was in the room, Elizabeth felt an unbearable tension, as if something terrible was about to happen. It was like a time bomb ticking down each second. And she didn't want to be there when the whole situation exploded.

Elizabeth looked around the library. The study carrels were filled with the usual faces, the same students who could be found at almost any time, day or night, in the reference stacks. Their desks were crammed with piles of books, candy wrappers, balled-up pieces of paper. In between studying, a few of them would take hour-long naps. Elizabeth was convinced that these people didn't have dorm rooms of their own—they actually lived in the library. Then again, she was here so often herself, they probably thought the same thing about her.

Elizabeth sighed and leaned back in her chair. She looked at the computer work station and saw a face that she almost never saw in the library. It belonged to Bruce Patman. He looked washed out and there was stubble on his chin, as if he hadn't shaved in days. *Poor guy,* Elizabeth thought sympathetically. *It must be rough to have your girlfriend almost die from a terrible accident, then have her leave you as soon as she gets better.* Even though Elizabeth had never had an occasion to feel badly for Bruce in the past, her heart went out to him.

Bruce was typing furiously on the keyboard. He stopped, then looked at the screen. Something on the computer must have irritated him because he muttered to himself, then started typing again.

Elizabeth dropped her book, then went over to see what was going on. "Hi, Bruce," she said. "What's up?"

Bruce leaned back heavily in his chair. He looked as if he were about to snap at any moment. "Hey, Liz. This stupid computer won't work." He ran his fingers through his dark hair, making it stick up even more. "I guess doing computer searches just isn't one of my talents."

154

Elizabeth pulled up a chair. "Well, you're in luck. It just happens to be one of mine," she said. "What exactly are you looking for?"

Bruce looked at her wearily. "It's a long story. Do you have all day?"

"You'd be surprised at how much free time I have," she said jokingly. "Try me."

Bruce tipped his chair back a bit and crossed his arms in front of his Sigma sweatshirt. "You must've heard about Lila moving in with that guy, Porter Davis."

Elizabeth nodded. Everyone on campus knew about it. "Who is he?" she asked.

"I don't know," he said with a shrug. "The only thing I can think of is that she must've met him while she was in the hospital. He's a doctor." Bruce looked away as he spoke, as though he was telling the story to the computer screen. "Ever since she told me, I've had this strange feeling that something's not quite right."

Elizabeth slipped her hands into the pockets of her linen trousers. "I don't know Lila that well, but it does seem odd that she'd move in with some guy she's only known for a week."

"I *know* Lila, and it's definitely strange," Bruce added. He balled his hands into tight fists. "The weirdest part is that she's acting like she doesn't care about me anymore. It doesn't matter what she says—you just can't turn your emotions on and off like a light switch."

Elizabeth was touched. She sensed that Bruce

loved Lila very much. "What are you going to do now?"

"I'm not giving up, if that's what you mean." Bruce blinked back a tear. "I'm trying to find out exactly what it was that caused this change in Lila. I think the best place to start is with her aunt's murder."

Elizabeth's face fell. "Did they ever find out who did it?"

Bruce shook his head. "They don't have any suspects. All the detective would tell me is that there was broken glass scattered around the body, and some of Katherine's things were missing. That's all they know." He looked directly at her. "They've closed the case, but I'm not about to give up on it yet. They must be missing something."

Students walked in and out of the aisles, gathering books for their research projects. Elizabeth watched the flurry of activity around them. She understood what Bruce was going through—what it was to rely on your instincts. Working for WSVU, she had uncovered major stories many times just by following her intuition. Even if Bruce's research didn't amount to anything, it would be worth it, just for some peace of mind. But Elizabeth had her own sense of the situation, and her instincts told her that Bruce had a reason to worry.

"Why don't we do a computer search of all the articles that were written about the murder?" Elizabeth suggested. "The first step is to gather all the information about the case."

156

Bruce moved his chair over to make more room for Elizabeth. His face lightened a bit, as though he were slowly waking from a deep sleep. "Thanks for doing this," he said softly. "It's nice that someone is finally taking me seriously."

Elizabeth typed at the keyboard, then waited for the information to come up on the screen. "I think you're absolutely right, Bruce. The whole thing does sound kind of fishy."

Several newspaper articles popped up, and they scanned them one by one. All of them had the same information, trying to reconstruct the murder scene and speculating on a possible motive. None of the articles had any new information, and the information they did have was sketchy.

"I guess we've hit a brick wall," Bruce said tiredly as he finished the last article.

"Wait a minute," Elizabeth said, pointing to the screen. "What about this one? *Boston Doc Gives Wife 30-Carat Diamond.*"

Bruce shook his head. "I've read that one already. Katherine had a pink diamond that was supposed to be one of the largest in the world. The detectives never recovered it."

"It must be priceless," Elizabeth said thoughtfully. "And with press like this, it's not surprising that someone would steal it."

"Or kill for it," Bruce added.

"Valentino! You must help me!" Jessica said with a sigh. She sat in the hairdresser's chair. Her green hair clashed perfectly with bright red vinyl upholstery.

"You don't like it?" Valentino said with a vague European accent. His skin was a dark bronze, and his curly black hair stayed exactly in place, no matter how many times he turned his head. "I think the look is very sexy," he said with a pout.

"I want my blond hair back!" Jessica whined. She stared at his billowy, multicolored shirt. "I'm tired of wearing hats in ninety-degree weather."

Valentino waved his arms in the air above her head as though he were conjuring a spirit. "Valentino will fix it for you," he said with a flourish.

Isabella, who was sitting at the manicure table only a few feet away, gave Jessica a thumbs-up sign with her free hand. "Go for it, girl!"

Seconds later Valentino was slathering Jessica's hair with a thick orange paste. Jessica stared at her reflection in horror.

"Don't worry," he said, reading her expression. "You will be gorgeous."

Isabella watched as a middle-aged manicurist named Irene pushed back her cuticles. "If it doesn't come out, Jess, we could always find a green gown for you to wear to the Theta gala."

Valentino shook his head in disgust. "A green gown! Never! You should complement the hair, not match it." He scratched his head with a black comb. "Plum would be a better color. No?"

Jessica covered her face in distress. "I forgot about the gala. What am I going to do?"

"Plum," Isabella said thoughtfully. "You know, Valentino, you're absolutely right. Plum is definitely the right color. You are a genius."

"Thank you, Miss Isabella. You are too kind."

"Would you two stop it?" Jessica shouted, placing her hands firmly on her hips. "Can't you see I'm having a crisis here?"

Valentino massaged the orange paste into the roots of Jessica's hair. "What I don't understand is, if you don't like green hair, why did you dye it in the first place?"

"She didn't," Isabella cut in. "Someone did it for her."

Jessica seethed. "And that someone is going to pay dearly."

Irene finished shaping Isabella's nails. "What color polish would you like today?" she asked.

"Definitely plum," Isabella answered, surveying her nails. She smiled. "Jess, you still haven't told me what you plan to do to Tom," she said.

The corners of Jessica's mouth turned from a frown to a sly grin. "You'll just have to wait to find out."

"Come on, Jess. You can tell me."

"No way," Jessica answered, shaking her head. Orange paste splattered all over Valentino's multicolored shirt. "Sorry," she said sheepishly.

"It's not a problem," Valentino said, ignoring the orange splotches. "It blends in. I *love* it. It's a whole new look."

"Why won't you tell me?" Isabella asked as Irene applied the base coat.

"You're closely associated with the enemy," Jessica reasoned. "If I told you, I'd have to kill you."

"I swear, I won't tell Danny," Isabella begged. "You can trust me."

Jessica leaned back in the chair, resting her neck against the edge of the sink. Valentino turned on the water and started rinsing out the orange goo. "All I can say is that Tom is in for the shock of his life."

"It's such a beautiful day," Lila said, peeking through the heavy red drapes in the parlor. "Why do we always have to keep the drapes closed?"

Porter looked up from his medical journal. "We don't have to keep them closed. Open them if you want."

Lila smiled at him from across the dark parlor. "Good," she said. "I will." She pulled one of the heavy drapes to the side, letting in a beam of sunlight. Already she was starting to feel better.

"Don't do it yourself," Porter said firmly as he watched her tie back the drape with a gold silk cord. "Call Nancy."

Lila shook her head. The less she saw of Nancy, the better. "It's no trouble, really. It'll only take a second."

Porter looked at her with exasperation. "Must you fight me on this? I hired Nancy to do these things so you wouldn't have to. That's what she's here for."

Lila twisted the ends of her hair nervously.

"She's washing the kitchen floor . . . I don't want to bother her."

"Lila, how do you expect to get better when you're constantly fighting me? Don't you think I know what's best for you?" He waited for her to answer. "Don't you?"

"Of course," Lila said. She pressed the intercom button on the wall to call for Nancy. Lila knelt beside Porter and spoke to him in hushed tones. "It's just that I think she hates me."

Porter chuckled. He touched her cheek with the back of his fingers. "Nancy doesn't hate you."

"She does, I swear," Lila whispered, eyeing the door. "I think it's because she's attracted to you."

"Don't be silly, Lila," Porter answered. "She's not here to like or dislike anyone. She's just here to clean the house."

Nancy appeared in the doorway. "You called, sir?" She was wearing a white apron, which covered more of her than the clothes she was wearing.

"*I* didn't call," Porter said with a gracious smile. "Lila did."

Lila did a double take. "Could you please draw back the drapes?" she asked nervously.

"Yes, ma'am," Nancy said in an obedient tone. Porter went back to reading his journal. As soon as his head was buried in the magazine, Nancy turned to Lila and shot her a dirty look. Lila recoiled.

"I've been thinking," Lila said, turning back to Porter. The dark room was instantly filled with bright sunlight. "Now that we're all settled in, why don't we entertain—"

"Anything else, sir?" Nancy interrupted.

Porter gave her a wink. "No, that's all." Nancy scuffled out of the room. He looked down at Lila. "What were you saying, dear?"

Lila forgot for a moment what she had started to say, but then it quickly returned. "Why don't we invite the Thetas over to show them the house?"

"I thought you wanted to stay away from the Thetas," Porter said calmly. "You told me they didn't take your near-death experience seriously."

Lila turned away from Porter, her face in the sunlight. "It's true, but it's not their fault they can't understand. I haven't seen them in a while and I'm starting to miss them. After all, they *are* my friends."

Porter gripped her shoulder. His eyes darkened. "Lila, what about everything we talked about? I thought you agreed that it was better to be independent, not to rely on outsiders."

"I can still be independent," Lila reasoned. "I just want them to meet you and to see our new house. Why don't we invite them over for dinner tomorrow night?"

Porter stood up angrily, the magazine falling loudly to the floor. "I don't want to share you with anyone!" His voice thundered across the parlor.

Lila backed away a fraction of an inch at a time. Porter's icy gaze held her like a tightrope suspended over a canyon. Lila knew that one wrong move would cause everything to come crashing

162

down. She held her breath, watching and waiting, as he towered above.

"Porter—what's gotten into you?" Lila asked in a frightened voice.

Porter swallowed hard. His icy look instantly melted, and he sank to the floor beside her. "I'm so sorry, Lila." His voice broke. Tears started to stream down his cheeks. He put his arms around her and buried his face in her neck.

"Shhh—it's all right." Lila stroked his head. The sound of Porter's sobs touched her so deeply that tears were starting to flow from her eyes. Suddenly it occurred to her that one of the biggest differences between Porter and Bruce was that Porter was much more passionate. He had a depth of feeling and an understanding of life that Bruce just wasn't capable of. Even though his outburst had frightened her a bit, Lila knew it would make them stronger as a couple. She knew they could get through anything together.

"I'm sorry. I didn't mean to get so angry," he whispered in her hair. He pulled back and wiped the tears from his face. "I'm overtired from working at the hospital. But I guess I was a little disappointed when you wanted to make other plans for tomorrow night. You've obviously forgotten again."

Lila froze. *What were we supposed to do tomorrow night?* Anxiety climbed up her neck as she struggled to remember. She tried to recall even the slightest fragment of conversation about their plans, but she only drew a blank.

He must have recognized the confused look in Lila's eyes, for Porter's expression changed from sadness to pity. "You don't remember, do you?"

Lila fidgeted and smiled uneasily. "I'm sure it will come back to me if you give me a hint."

"The ballet—we'd planned to go to the ballet tomorrow."

Lila's face lit up. "We're going to the ballet?" she exclaimed.

Porter stared at her bleakly. "Don't tell me this is a surprise to you. We talked about this many times."

"Are you sure?" she said incredulously. "I would've definitely remembered something like this."

Worry lines creased his forehead. "Don't be so certain," he said gravely. "Sometimes a coma can have lasting effects."

Chapter Thirteen

Tom reached for the doorknob, then stopped. *Please don't let Jessica be here,* he pleaded silently. Elizabeth was still in the library and wouldn't be back for another hour or so. Tom's stomach tightened. He hadn't been alone with Jessica since the day he'd poured the green dye into her shampoo bottle. She hadn't said much to him since then, but Tom had a feeling she was probably waiting for Elizabeth to leave before letting him have it. He dreaded the battle that awaited him.

Tom sighed and opened the door. The room was dim—only Jessica's desk light was on. Soft jazz music floated from the stereo speakers. He put down his video equipment bag and cautiously walked into the room. Jessica was nowhere in sight.

"Are you looking for me?"

Tom whipped around. Jessica was standing behind the open door. Her hair was back to its normal golden blond, and she was holding a white silk scarf in her hands.

Tom eyed the scarf and backed away. He nervously cleared his throat. "Glad to see you got the dye out," he said with a strained laugh.

Jessica inched closer. The corners of her pink mouth quivered. "You thought that was pretty funny, didn't you?"

"No . . . uh, not that funny," Tom stammered. He continued to back up, not tearing his eyes away from Jessica for even a fraction of a second. "Actually, it was pretty mean."

"Mean but funny," Jessica said pointedly. She looped the scarf around both hands and pulled it taut. A saxophone shrilled in the background.

Tom started to sweat. He tripped and fell backward onto the couch. "It was wrong . . . I shouldn't have done it."

Jessica sidled up to the couch. She peered at him through hooded eyelids. "Do you want to know what I thought of your little trick?"

Tom's throat tightened as he watched her pull the scarf tighter.

Jessica leaned heavily against him. She smiled. "I thought it was brilliant."

Tom's heart nearly stopped.

"I've got to hand it to you, Tom. It was the best prank I've ever seen," she said.

"Really?" he asked suspiciously.

"Absolutely," Jessica said with a nod. She loosened her grip and waved the scarf at him like a flag. "There's no way I can top that one. So I guess the only thing left to do is surrender." She held out her hand for him to shake. "Friends?"

Tom's brow furrowed. "Jessica, are you serious or is this another trick?"

She leaned back against the couch. "Come on, Tom. Don't you think we've fought long enough? To tell you the truth, I'm kind of tired of it."

Tom nodded. "Me too."

"Well, then, that settles it." Jessica held out her hand again. "Truce?"

Tom shook her hand. "Truce," he said, with a sidelong glance.

"Now that *that's* over, there's something I want to give you." Jessica walked over to her closet and reached for something on the top shelf.

This is it, Tom thought, breaking into a sweat again. *She's going to get the last laugh.* He knew she wouldn't let him off the hook so easily. *What's she going to do?* Terrible thoughts raced through his mind. He imagined Jessica reaching for one of his expensive video cameras, then smashing it on the floor. Or maybe she'd stolen all his computer disks and had erased them. Or even worse—maybe she had some sort of weapon. Something to get rid of him. Permanently.

Jessica turned around, the object hidden safely behind her back. "I hope you like it," she said mysteriously. "Consider it a peace offering."

Tom drew in his breath and recoiled. Jessica shoved the object in front of him.

"A box of doughnuts?" Tom gasped.

Jessica pouted. "You don't like doughnuts?"

"No, no—I *love* them." He scratched his head in confusion. Was it possible that Jessica really wanted to make up after all?

"Good," Jessica said sweetly. She set the box down on the coffee table in front of him, then went over to the stereo to pop in a new disk.

Tom looked inside the box, his mouth watering. She had bought all his favorite kinds: cream filled, jelly, double-chocolate glazed. He didn't know which one to choose.

Jessica hummed a tune as she flipped through her collection of CDs. "Take whichever one you want," she called from the other side of the room.

Tom's hand was about to reach for a lemon-filled doughnut when suddenly he snapped it back. *Now I get it,* he thought in sudden realization. *I'm onto your trick, Jessica.* When he'd seen her reaching into the closet, he thought she was probably reaching for a gun or knife or lead pipe. But he was wrong. He should've known that Jessica would try to get rid of him with the least amount of fuss. She was trying to poison him.

Tom's eyes bulged as he stared down at the sweet, poisoned spheres. It was so easy. All she had to do was inject some poison into one of the cream doughnuts. No one would know the difference just by looking at them. "Aren't you going to have one?" he said to her.

Jessica shook her head. "Don't worry about

me. You just go ahead and enjoy yourself."

Tom's hands began to shake. *Which one could it be?* he wondered as his hand hovered over the box. His hand stopped above one of the jelly doughnuts. *No, the filled ones are the easiest to poison.* He moved over to a chocolate-powdered one. *Then again, she could dust it with poison, too.* He touched a glazed doughnut. Sweat beaded his brow.

"Can't decide?" Jessica said. She put a disk in the CD player. A heavy beat pounded from the stereo.

Tom smiled weakly.

"What's wrong?" Jessica's eyes narrowed. "Don't you trust me?"

Tom wiped the sugar glaze off his fingers and pushed the box away.

Jessica shook her head in disbelief. "I tried to do something nice—"

"You *did* put hair gel in my toothpaste," Tom reminded her. "Forgive me if it's hard to forget."

"If it makes you feel any better, I'll eat one." Jessica sat down on the couch. "You can pick."

She's even smarter than I thought. Tom's hand moved from doughnut to doughnut, watching Jessica's expression for clues. Finally he picked a puffy, cream-filled doughnut covered in powdered sugar. "This one," he said confidently, holding it in front of her face.

"Good choice," Jessica whispered. She held Tom's wrist and pulled it closer to her. Closing her eyes, she bit into the doughnut. "Mmmmmm," she said, licking the sugar off her lips.

Tom put the doughnut on the table. He waited for her to grimace, clutch her throat, and fall over, but nothing happened.

"Your turn." Jessica picked up the doughnut and took another bite.

Tom picked out a plain one. No coating and a big hole in the middle—it was the safest bet.

"How is it?" she asked.

Tom took a bite. It tasted like a normal doughnut. "Pretty good," he said.

Jessica picked out a chocolate cream. She took a bite, then shoved the doughnut in Tom's mouth before he had a chance to protest.

"We're friends now, Tom," she said with a provocative smile. "You can trust me."

Lila finished off the last bit of her morning tea and gazed out through the brand-new glass doors in the kitchen, leading to the patio. The world continued on, as it always did, beyond the silence of the glass. At times Lila wondered if it was all an illusion. Tiny sparrows hopped in the green grass, searching for food. Cars traveled down the steep slope of the mountain road. Beyond the cliff, the surface of the ocean glimmered in the sunlight. There was only a single pane of glass between Lila and the outside world, yet she felt completely removed from it. Life was played out before her like a movie on a screen.

"Why don't we take a walk this afternoon?" she suggested, pressing her palms flat against the glass.

The warmth of the sunlight felt good against her skin. "We could go down by the dunes."

Porter spread some raspberry jam on his toast. "Why don't we just stay inside today? There's no sense in pushing our luck."

"But I stayed inside all day yesterday—" Lila raised her voice. She tightened the sash of her red satin bathrobe.

"Lila." Porter spoke softly. "You need your rest." He opened the newspaper. "Come, sit down and have some more tea."

Lila put her mug down on the counter with a bit more force than she had intended. "I've had four cups already. I don't want tea, Porter. I want to go outside."

Porter scanned the newspaper headlines. "You can do whatever you want," he said evenly. "But I don't recommend going out twice in one day, and we're already planning to go out tonight." He looked at her with concern. "You do remember, don't you?"

Lila sat down in the chair beside him. Her lips formed a proud smile. "We're going to the ballet tonight."

"Good girl—you remembered." Porter's eyes glowed. He traced the line of her jaw with his thumb. "That's a good sign."

Lila fingered one of his blond curls. She smelled the musky scent of his aftershave. "I'm trying so hard, Porter. I really want to get better. I want us to have a normal life."

"We will." He left a trail of kisses across her

cheek all the way to her ear. "Please promise me you won't overdo it. You need to take care of yourself."

Lila closed her eyes, feeling shivers of delight running down her back. She tilted her head to feel his hot breath against her neck.

Porter is right, Lila thought, *I shouldn't push myself.* She needed to take things slowly so she could have a full recovery. As soon as she was better, they could start their lives together.

"I guess I didn't realize how much fun it can be to stay inside," Lila said with a giggle.

Porter massaged her shoulders, digging his thumbs into her knotted muscles. "So, my love, what are your plans for today?"

"Good question." Lila sighed with pleasure as he kneaded away the tension. Across the room she noticed a white box sitting on one of the cupboard shelves. It was the cookie press she had bought on their shopping trip. "I know! I'll make some cookies—just like my aunt Katherine used to make." Porter's strong thumbs suddenly dug too deep, and Lila yelped in pain.

"Sorry, love," Porter said, dropping his hands at his sides. "Cookies sound wonderful."

Lila happily bounded to the other side of the kitchen. She went to open the glass door of the cupboard but suddenly stopped short. "Porter . . ."

"What is it?" Porter asked, returning to his newspaper.

Lila opened the cabinet door slowly, then poked her hand through the wooden frame. "The glass is missing," she said as she examined it. All the other cupboard doors were still intact. "Where is it?"

Porter drank some tea. "It's broken," he said, not looking up from the paper.

"Broken? When did that happen?"

Porter looked up. His eyes darted around the room. "I don't know when exactly," he said abruptly. "But it's the obvious explanation. Maybe it fell when Nancy was cleaning. You could ask her."

Not on your life, Lila thought. She took the cookie press down from the shelf. Nancy already hated her enough without Lila accusing her of breaking something.

She threw on an apron over her bathrobe. The apron was bright white, with fresh creases in it. It even smelled brand new. Lila secretly wished she could use one from Aunt Katherine's old apron collection, like the one with the sequins and plastic gems all over it, but they were all tucked safely away in the attic.

Fortunately Porter had left Aunt Katherine's recipe books downstairs. Lila insisted that they remained on the shelves in the kitchen, exactly where they belonged.

"I hope I can find her cookie recipe," she thought aloud as she picked up an old cookbook with a yellowed cover. Flour residue coated the pages, and colored splotches covered a few of the recipes. Lila made a mental note to try the recipes with the most splotches. They were obviously the ones Aunt Katherine liked the best.

173

"Do you want to help me make them?" Lila asked.

Porter's head was buried in the stock market figures. "You go right ahead. I'll watch."

Lila scanned the index. *Cookies . . . page 134*. As she flipped through the pages a piece of paper fell out of the book and onto the floor.

What's this? Lila wondered as she unfolded the sheet. It was a letter. Lila strolled over to the table, reading the letter to herself. "You won't believe what I just found," she said, smiling as she read. "This is one of my aunt's old letters."

Porter looked up from the financial section.

"I haven't seen you in a while. When can we get together?" Lila read aloud. *"I know you have other obligations, but I really must see you. Please call me and let me know. I'll be waiting. All my love— David Carrier."* Lila smiled. "Sounds like Mr. Carrier was one of my aunt's admirers."

Porter swiped the letter out of Lila's hand and slid it into his bathrobe pocket.

"What are you doing?" Lila's face fell.

Porter folded up the newspaper and tucked it under his arm. His mouth was drawn into a thin line. "I can't sit here and watch you torture yourself with memories of your aunt," he said gravely.

"I'm not torturing myself," Lila answered lightly. "I like reading her old letters."

"This morbid fascination you have is very disturbing."

Lila frowned. "It is?"

174

Porter rubbed his temples. "Of course it is—but I couldn't expect you to understand it, considering the state you're in."

Lila fell to her knees and clutched Porter's arm. She was numb with fright. "What state? What's wrong with me, Porter? Please tell me."

Porter touched her cheek. "I've said too much. I didn't mean to frighten you." He smiled at her. "Go and bake your cookies. Forget any of this ever happened."

"She did *what*?" Danny shrieked. His voice echoed off the walls of their trashed dorm room. He slipped on a pair of rubber gloves. "Did I hear you right?"

Tom leaned against the handle of a broom. "I'm telling you, it was really weird. I came home, and Jessica was being all nice to me. She had jazz music playing and the lights were low."

"And she brought you *doughnuts*?" he asked incredulously. He picked up a soapy sponge and started cleaning the dirty water marks off all the furniture.

Tom nodded. "I thought she'd poisoned them or something."

"Did you eat one?"

"I let her take the first bite," Tom said, sweeping the damp floor.

Danny laughed out loud. "I can't believe this."

Jason Armstrong, carrying a box of muddy clothes, popped his head in the doorway of their room. His eyes narrowed as he studied the nearly empty room. "Where's all your stuff?"

Tom and Danny exchanged knowing glances. "We moved it all out," Tom answered.

Jason wrinkled his freckled nose. "But they only let us back in the dorm half an hour ago. What's your secret?"

Danny shrugged, a smirk across his lips. "We're fast workers."

"Well, you guys can come help me in my room as soon as you're done here," Jason said with a grin. "Unless you want me to tell the resident assistant just *how* fast you work."

Tom picked up a dirty sock from under the bed and threw it at Jason. Jason tried to dodge it, but it hit him squarely in the face.

"Forget it," Tom said.

Jason relented. "Okay, you don't have to clean—just send over a large pepperoni pizza."

Danny shook his head. "No dice. And you can tell the RA if you want to," he said. "We'll just let him know the next time you're planning a keg party in your room."

Jason made a face. "You really know how to hurt a guy," he said, heaving the box into the air to gain some leverage. "See ya later."

"Bye," Tom said. He swept a pile of debris onto a piece of cardboard and threw it into the trash can. It was already overflowing with wet, disintegrated paper, ruined videotapes, and dirty clothes that were beyond repair.

As they waded through the muck Tom became more and more aware of the extent of the damage and of just how many things he owned. Even items that had seemed meaningless to him before suddenly took on new significance. An undeveloped roll of film that had been sitting in his desk for almost the entire school year was destroyed by the water, but Tom felt a pang of nostalgia as he threw it away.

In the bottom drawer of his desk Tom found a file folder that was brimming with old test booklets. He turned page after page to find the essay questions he'd answered had dissolved into a wet, inky mess. Even though the words in the booklets were completely illegible, Tom still didn't want to part with them.

"Are you going to tell her about it?" Danny asked as he continued scrubbing his desk.

"Tell *who* about *what?*"

Danny squeezed out a sponge in the bucket of murky water. "Are you going to tell Elizabeth about what Jessica did?"

Tom's finger grazed the blurry lines of a test booklet. The damp ink smeared onto his skin. "What's there to tell? Jessica was just being nice."

"I can't believe you don't see what's going on here," Danny said, laughing. "Here's a question for you. When is Jessica Wakefield ever *nice?*"

"I don't know." Tom sighed and threw the folder into the trash heap.

Danny scratched his head. "Answer—she's nice when she wants something. And I think *you're* that something."

Tom's eyes bulged. "Come on, man."

"I'm not joking around," he said seriously. "It's a vibe I have."

"I'm the last person Jessica would be interested in. She's my girlfriend's sister, for God's sake."

"That doesn't mean anything." Danny wiped down the desk with a rag. "If I were you, I'd sleep with my eyes open."

"Thanks for helping me out again," Bruce said as he typed away on the library's computer. "But I think it's a waste of time. I haven't found anything."

Elizabeth, who was sitting at the computer station directly behind Bruce, pressed a key that set the printer in motion. "Well, you won't believe what I just found," she said, tearing off the piece of paper.

"What?" Bruce whirled around. He leaned over so far that Elizabeth thought he was going to fall out of his chair.

"I decided to do a different kind of search," she said. Her blond ponytail bobbed excitedly. "Instead of searching for articles on the murder, I did a general search on Katherine and her husband." She handed him the sheet. "This is what I found."

FAMOUS SURGEON AND PROTÉGÉ PART WAYS

BOSTON—*Dr. Chester M. Cage made an announcement Friday, in front of the Massachusetts General board of directors, that he would be parting ways with longtime friend and protégé Dr. David Carrier. While he would give no specific details, Dr. Cage cited "fundamental differences of opinion" as the cause of the breakup. David Carrier could not be reached for comment.*

Dr. Cage earned the reputation of being one of the country's leading neurosurgeons after discovering a safer, more successful method for the removal of brain tumors. Dr. Carrier aided Cage in developing the technique and is considered to be one of the rising stars among Mass General's interns.

An inside source claims that the two were inseparable and the breakup comes as a complete shock. "It's a shame," said a Mass General spokesperson. "They were an incredible team."

Cage and Carrier spent much time together outside the hospital. In addition to being a doctor, Carrier is also a gourmet and a fan of Katherine Cage, the world-renowned chef and wife of Dr. Chester Cage.

"Where did this come from?" Bruce asked.

"*The Boston Herald*. The article is about three years old." Elizabeth shot him a sideways glance. "What do you make of it?"

Bruce rubbed his chin thoughtfully. "The whole situation seems vague—they don't even mention why they split up." He handed the sheet back to her. "It's interesting, but I don't think it's anything out of the ordinary."

179

Elizabeth pointed to the text. "Rule number one in investigative reporting—always read between the lines," she said emphatically. "The article hints at a lot of possible reasons as to why they broke up. Think about it, Bruce. What could cause a sudden falling out between two men?"

"Money," Bruce said, scanning the article a second time. "Or a woman."

"Bingo!" Elizabeth chimed. "It says here that David Carrier was a fan of Katherine's."

Bruce's brown eyes widened. "Are you saying that Katherine was having an affair with Carrier?"

"Not necessarily," she said, folding her arms in front of her. "But Carrier might've been getting a little too close, and Dr. Cage didn't like it."

Bruce folded up the article and put it in the pocket of his blue Sigma jacket. "Interesting theory, but what exactly does it have to do with the robbery?"

"I don't know," Elizabeth admitted. "But my instincts tell me that this whole thing might be more complicated than we originally thought."

Lila hummed softly to herself as she slipped into a pair of black stockings. *We're going to the ballet tonight,* she thought with a smile. This was going to be their first real date. Lila marveled at the strangeness of it. Here she was, living with Porter in this enormous house, feeling like they had known each other all their lives, and yet they had never been out on a real date. It definitely wasn't a conventional romance. But Porter and Lila connected on a level much deeper than conventional couples. There was no use in even making the comparison.

Still, Lila wanted tonight to be special.

She flipped through the hangers in her closet, trying to find an outfit that would knock Porter off his feet. Lately she had been so concerned with relaxing and taking it easy that she hadn't really given much thought to fashion. Cotton loungers and loose housedresses had become her everyday clothes. It was no wonder she occasionally caught Porter glancing in Nancy's direction, with her miniskirts and cropped tops. *It's time to start trying a little harder,* Lila decided.

She chose a long, sleek, body-skimming skirt and matching black high heels with ankle straps. For a top she wore a cream-colored fluttery rayon blouse. Lila tied a black ribbon choker around her throat and surveyed her form in the full-length mirror. She moved her body in several model-like poses and leered at the mirror seductively. "Very chic," she said to her reflection. She tossed her shiny chestnut hair over one shoulder. "Even if I do say so myself."

"Lila!" Porter called from outside her door.

Lila quickly ran a brush through her hair. She had spent so much time getting ready that she hadn't realized they were late for the ballet. Her pulse quickened and her palms were damp. *Just like a sixteen-year-old out on her first date.*

She couldn't wait to see Porter's face when she

opened the door. His soft blue eyes would melt at the sight of her. He'd sweep her up in his arms and they'd walk right past Nancy, out the door and into the crisp evening air.

"Lila, are you in there?" Porter called again.

Lila took one last look in the mirror, breathed in deeply, and opened the door.

Porter looked straight at her. But instead of the soft, romantic look on his face that she'd imagined, his jaw had a hard edge and his eyes were cold.

"Sorry to keep you waiting," she said cautiously as she grabbed her beaded evening bag. She closed the door behind her and walked into the hall. "I'm ready now."

Lila noticed that Porter was still wearing the same khaki pants and cotton shirt he'd been wearing all day. He grabbed her firmly by the wrists and pulled her toward the top of the stairs.

"Some pills are missing from my medicine cabinet," he said, looking at her with a penetrating stare. "Where are they?"

Lila tried to pull away, but Porter's grip remained firm. "I—I don't know where they are," she stammered. "What kind of pills? What do they look like?"

Porter leaned so close to her that Lila felt his hot breath on her face. "Don't play games, Lila. This is serious." His voice was full of accusation. "Now *think*. Did you go into my room without my permission?"

Lila's lower lip began to tremble. Her vision of

the perfect evening was slowly dissolving. "I never go into your room without asking, Porter. Maybe Nancy moved them or something."

Still holding firmly to Lila's wrist, Porter leaned over the top of the staircase. "Nancy! Get up here. *Now!*" he barked.

Lila exhaled, allowing herself to finally breathe. Porter was angry, but not necessarily at her. He wasn't singling her out. Nancy would know where the pills were, and everything would be fine.

"Yes, sir?" Nancy ran up the stairs in her five-inch heels, scarcely out of breath.

The hard edges of Porter's face took on softer lines. "Lila said you took some pills out of my medicine cabinet."

Lila squirmed. "I didn't say—" Porter tightened his grip, and she fell silent.

Nancy continued to stare at Porter as if Lila wasn't even in the room. "She must be mistaken," Nancy said evenly. "In fact, I saw them in her room when I was making the beds this morning."

"That can't be," Lila erupted. She felt hot blood rushing to her face. "I would've seen them."

Porter nodded. "Thank you, Nancy. Would you be so kind as to show me where you saw them?"

Lila strained against his grip. "Porter, I don't have them. I swear I didn't touch them."

Nancy opened the door to Lila's room and walked inside. Porter followed behind, pulling Lila along with him.

"This is crazy! I don't have your pills!" Lila's

voice reached a fever pitch. She watched in horror as Nancy opened the top drawer of Lila's nightstand and pulled out a prescription bottle filled with red capsules. She handed them to Porter.

Porter clenched his jaw. "Thank you, Nancy," he said in a low voice. "That will be all."

Nancy did a small curtsy and shot Lila a look of disgust before leaving the room.

Lila avoided Porter's stony gaze. She felt her stomach heave as she burst into tears.

"What are these?" Porter shook the bottle of capsules right in front of her nose.

Lila sobbed. "I've never seen them before. I don't know where they came from."

Porter dropped the bottle into his shirt pocket. "I thought you were going to try harder," he said in a tense voice.

"I *am* trying," she said through her tears. "I honestly don't remember how they got here. I'm sorry."

"I won't tolerate this behavior in our home." He released her. "I hope you realize that our evening plans are off now."

Lila threw herself onto the bed, exploding in tears. "Please, Porter—I need to get out. It will be good for me. I don't know what I did, but I promise to be more careful. I promise not to do it again."

Porter brushed back a tear that ran down his cheek. His eyes were filled with pain. "Please don't make any more promises. It's going to take some time for me to trust you again." He looked

184

out the window as the last bit of sunlight dipped below the horizon. "I don't understand why you're getting worse—I blame myself," he said in a husky tone. "Maybe I shouldn't have brought you here."

There was a deep aching in Lila's chest; she could feel the heaviness of his disappointment. If only they could start all over again. Lila rubbed her wrist—the sensation of Porter's grip lingered. "Don't blame yourself," she cried. "It's my fault."

Porter turned to her, his eyes tinged with red. "It's just that I'm so scared, Lila," he said, his voice wavering. "You may never be the same again."

Chapter Fourteen

Lila buried her head in the pillow and cried, racked with shame. The pillow muffled her mournful sobs and gasps for air. It was as if she were ten years old again, shaking with humiliation after being caught doing something she wasn't supposed to. The only difference was that when she was ten, she had disobeyed intentionally. Now she didn't even realize she had done it.

Night began to fall, and Lila's room was getting dark. Colors were indistinguishable—everything had turned to different shades of gray.

The ballet probably started an hour ago, Lila thought with a heavy heart. One or two cars whirred past the house, down the mountain toward town. Lila wished desperately that she was in one of those cars on her way to some glorious party or concert. Even to a movie. *Anything but here in this lonely, silent room.*

The door creaked open, and Lila lifted her head. Black streaks of mascara stained the white lace pillow cover. Porter stood in the doorway, his face nothing but a shadow. The outline of his body was illuminated by the lights in the hall. His hair glowed, reminding Lila of the first time she'd seen his heavenly face as he'd stood over her bed.

"I'm going out," Porter said. He was holding a key ring.

Lila pushed back her tangled hair and straightened her skirt. "Where?" she asked.

"To the hospital," he said smoothly. "I'm going to do some paperwork I've been neglecting."

Lila's face was puffy. Her eyes burned from crying. "Can't you bring the paperwork back here?"

"I think it would be best for both of us if I went out for a while."

Fresh tears sprang to her sore eyes. "I need you, Porter. Please don't go."

"I have to go." Porter turned away and headed down the stairs.

"Don't!" Lila called. She ran after him, nearly tripping on her heels. When she reached the top of the stairs, Porter was already in the foyer, talking to Nancy. Lila stood by the banister, watching in silence.

"I'm going out for a while—you'll be here to look after Lila, won't you?" Porter said as he put on his trench coat.

"Of course I'll be here." Nancy nodded. "I don't have any plans."

"That surprises me," Porter said as he reached

for his briefcase. "It's Saturday night—shouldn't a pretty girl like you have a date?"

Lila roughly wiped away a bit of lipstick that had smeared across her cheek. She gritted her teeth as she listened to the conversation.

Nancy giggled. "I'm afraid not, sir."

"Well, in any case, just keep an eye on Lila to make sure she doesn't go anywhere," he said in a hushed voice. Lila strained to hear. "And if anyone should come by to see her, do not, under any circumstances, let them inside. Lila's health is fragile and I don't want anything to jeopardize it," he said firmly. "And one more thing—take some tea up to her. She must be hungry by now."

"Certainly," Nancy answered.

Porter gave her a wink and a smile. "Thank you, Nancy. I don't know when I'll be back tonight."

"That's all right, sir," Nancy said coyly. "Everything will still be here when you return."

Lila turned on her heels and stalked angrily back to her room, slamming the door behind her. She stood by the window and watched as the white Mustang pulled out of the driveway onto the mountain road. She pressed her fingertips against the window, feeling the cold smoothness beneath her fingertips.

Why didn't you take me with you, Porter? The air inside the room was hot and thick, smelling of tears and sleep. Lila's lungs craved the cold, fresh ocean air just beyond her window, like a glass of icy water in the hot desert. She undid the latch and tried to lift the sash. The window didn't move.

"Stupid window!" Lila pounded her fist against the frame. Suddenly the lights came on, and Nancy stood in the doorway. In her arms was a tray of tea and cookies. A smoldering cigarette dangled from her lips.

"Boy, you look like hell," Nancy said.

Lila brushed her swollen face with the back of her hand. She gnawed on the inside of her cheek. "Thank you for the tea."

"Porter told me to bring it." She stood with her arms crossed and her feet apart. Her critical eyes traveled from Lila's toes to the top of her head. "Let me give you a little advice, honey." Puffs of blue smoke curled out of her mouth as she spoke. "If you want to keep that man of yours, you've got to stop crying like a baby and start acting like a woman."

Lila poured herself a cup of steaming tea without looking up. "That will be all, Nancy," she said dryly, even though her insides felt like molten lava. She angrily pinched a lemon wedge into the amber-colored tea as Nancy walked out the door.

Lila took a sip of tea and relaxed as the soothing liquid trickled down her throat. While she hated to admit it, there was a kernel of truth to Nancy's advice. Getting hysterical every time something went wrong with Porter probably wasn't the way to go.

Lila bit into a shortbread cookie. When they'd first met, Porter had been attracted to her sense of independence. Yet somewhere along the way, she had lost it. What had happened? How did things get so messed up?

Lila slipped off her shoes and dug her toes into the plush carpet. From this moment on, she was determined to be stronger. She'd prove to Porter that things could be different. Their lives could be better. She'd stop being so forgetful. She'd stop acting like a child and start being an adult.

And the first step was to get through the evening alone.

Lila took a deep breath and poured herself another cup. In the back of her mind the anxiety lingered, crackling like hot lightning, trying to work its way to the surface. Lila kept her fears at bay by concentrating only on the cup in front of her and the plate of cookies on the tray. Any images of the earthquake that threatened to emerge were tucked back safely into the recesses of her mind.

I don't need Porter, she repeated silently. *I can do this alone.*

Suddenly a loud noise came from directly above Lila's room. It sounded like something had fallen over in the attic. Startled, Lila sprang up, knocking over her cup and the pot of tea. The hot liquid soaked into the carpet. Lila looked around to make sure nothing in the room was moving. She dashed out into the hallway. "Nancy! Nancy! Come here," Lila yelled.

Nancy strolled over to the bottom of the stairs, looking up at Lila with annoyance. "What?"

Lila swallowed hard. "Did you hear that?" she asked, panic rising in her throat. "Did you hear the noise in the attic?"

Nancy's red lips twisted into an amused smirk. "It's probably just your imagination, dear," she said in a patronizing voice. "Eat some cookies and go to bed."

"Thanks for being so nice to Tom lately." Elizabeth bit into a crusty piece of garlic bread and looked across the cafeteria table at Jessica.

"No problem," Jessica answered casually as she ate a spoonful of frozen yogurt. "Tom's a great guy."

Elizabeth brushed a few bread crumbs off the front of her green blouse. "That's not something you would've said a few weeks ago."

Jessica licked the back of her spoon. "I was under a lot of stress with Lila in the hospital and all."

Elizabeth's brow furrowed. "How is Lila doing?"

"Great, I guess." Jessica shrugged. "With a gorgeous doctor by her side, she must be."

Elizabeth stared at the back wall of the cafeteria, where the plastic cereal containers were lined up. "But haven't you talked to her recently?"

"Not since she moved in with him. I figure she'll call when she's settled in."

"Don't you think that's strange?"

Jessica pulled up the sleeves of her white bodysuit. "I hadn't really thought about it." She squinted in Elizabeth's direction. "Why are *you* so interested, anyway?"

Elizabeth twirled a few strands of spaghetti around her fork. "Bruce's really worried about

191

her. Katherine's murder was never solved, and he's afraid that Lila could be in danger."

Jessica sneered. "I think Bruce I-love-myself-more-than-anything Patman should keep his nose out of it. He's just trying to ruin her happiness," she said. "Besides, who's going to hurt Lila with Porter there to protect her?"

"I don't know, but I think Bruce might be on to something." Elizabeth wiped her mouth with a paper napkin. "I've seen some of the evidence, and something's not quite right."

"That's ridiculous—Lila's fine," Jessica scoffed. "She can take care of herself."

Elizabeth pushed her tray aside. "Maybe you're right. But I suppose it wouldn't hurt to make sure she's okay."

An hour later Jessica and Elizabeth pulled up the steep driveway to the mansion. The house was magnificent—it wasn't difficult to understand why Lila decided to move in after all, Elizabeth thought.

Only a few lights were on downstairs, and one light shone on the second floor. Elizabeth cut the engine and listened to the peaceful chirping of crickets in the grass.

"This *was* a good idea," Jessica said as they walked toward the front porch. She smoothed down her short knit skirt. "I'm dying to see what this Porter guy looks like."

Elizabeth rang the doorbell. "This is your best friend's boyfriend. At least have the common courtesy *not* to flirt with him."

Jessica's lips curved into a pouty frown. "Me? Flirt? I'd never do such a thing."

"I don't think anyone's home." Elizabeth rang the bell again.

A moment later the door opened. A young woman with heavy makeup and a cigarette stood in the doorway. She was wearing a maid's apron. "Yeah?" she said gruffly.

Jessica and Elizabeth exchanged curious glances. "Is this Lila Fowler's house?" Jessica asked.

"What do you want?" the maid demanded.

"We'd like to see her," Elizabeth cut in.

The maid shook her head. "Sorry—she can't have visitors. She's not feeling too well."

Elizabeth craned her neck, struggling to see inside. "That's all right. We'll only stay a minute."

Lila clasped the pillows until her knuckles turned white. The footsteps continued above her head, pacing back and forth with deliberate steps. She pushed the pillows harder against her ears to block out the sound. Still the thumping continued, as if it wasn't coming from an attic, but from inside her own head.

Lila dropped the pillows, overcome with exhaustion. Her body was limp, and every movement was an effort. Her stinging eyelids drooped, begging for sleep to take her away from the terror. And yet she couldn't sleep. The crackling anxiety continued to resurface again and again, keeping her nerves on edge.

Please stop it, her mind cried out, *just go away*. The footsteps halted. *It's all in your mind. You can control this*. Lila's palms were soaked with sweat and her jaw ached from being clenched. She lay back gently in her bed, not wanting anything to disrupt the perfect silence.

That was when she heard the wind chimes.

They started softly at first. So softly, in fact, that Lila wasn't sure she'd heard them at all. Then they grew louder, clanging tonelessly in her head. Lila pressed her damp palms against her ears, praying to get from one moment to the next without losing her sanity. Each frightening, poisonous tone filled her, and then another and another, until Lila thought she'd split apart at the seams.

Is that you, Aunt Katherine? It was just like the day of the earthquake when Lila had traveled from room to room, feeling her aunt's spirit everywhere. She had heard the wind chimes just before the armoire had fallen on her. Lila cowered in fear as the realization came to her. That day, Aunt Katherine was trying to warn her. She didn't want Lila to be there. But Lila didn't understand her message. And now here she was, living in the house against her aunt's wishes. Lila braced herself as the chimes continued, waiting for the house to come crashing down upon her.

Where are you, Porter? None of these things happened when he was around. Lila rocked back and forth nervously, remembering how he'd winked at Nancy as he walked out of the house. He left her all alone when she was feeling terrible. No, she didn't need him. But she did need someone.

Lila ran out of her room to the study across the hall. She paused, her hand on the brass knob. The door was unlocked. Porter had told her never to go into that room, and normally she wouldn't, but it was the room with the only phone in the house. Lila's forehead was cold and moist. She had to get in there and call someone. She was desperate.

Lila quickly closed the door behind her and looked around the room. Porter's antique rolltop desk was in the corner, the top of it locked. There were a few wooden file drawers and a simple bookshelf. On a small table near the door was an old-fashioned telephone. She picked up the heavy black receiver and dialed Jessica's number.

Please pick up, Lila pleaded silently as she bit her knuckles. The phone rang several times, but there was no answer. She tasted salty blood on her lips. *Please be there, Jessica.*

There was a *click* at the other end of the line. "Hi, this is Jessica and Elizabeth's room. We can't come to the phone—"

Lila bit down harder, hoping the pain in her fingers would take her mind off the pain in her heart.

Tom clicked on the light and collapsed tiredly in a chair. He breathed a sigh of relief with the realization that both Jessica and Elizabeth were gone. As far as Jessica was concerned, Tom wasn't quite sure what to make of that whole doughnut incident, and being around her still made him a bit uneasy. On the other hand, he'd really wanted to see Elizabeth, but he was too tired to give her the attention she deserved. His muscles ached from working with Danny all day, cleaning their room. What he needed was to take a long, hot shower and then to go to bed early.

Tom peeled off his dirty rugby shirt and jeans. Both were covered in brown mud and smelled like they had been in a damp basement for ten years. It was amazing to him that he and Danny had spent the entire day cleaning the room and it still wasn't enough. At the rate they were going, it looked as if they wouldn't be able to move back into the room until sometime next week. The whole situation was completely discouraging.

Tom opened the bottom drawer of Elizabeth's bureau. That was the drawer she had cleared out to give Tom some space for his things. It was a tight squeeze, but he found that he could fit almost all his clothes in there. He pulled the drawer as far as it would go and stuck his hand all the way in the back. It was empty.

Tom's shoulders slumped forward. "Don't tell me I'm out of clothes," he whined. Suddenly he remembered that everything he owned was in a smelly heap in a corner of the room, waiting to be washed.

Tom chewed the inside of his cheek and his eyes started to water. He was too tired to take a shower, let alone do a couple loads of laundry. He threw one of Elizabeth's towels over his shoulder and decided to look through the pile of dirty clothes. Maybe there was something he could wear for just one more day.

But when he spun around to look at the pile, it was gone. Every bit of clothing he owned that hadn't been destroyed had been in that pile. Now it was gone.

And he knew who was responsible.

"I'm going to get you for this, Jessica!" he shouted violently at her side of the room. "I should've known better." This time she had gone way too far.

Tom opened the window, then ran over to Jessica's bookshelf. The veins in his arms and neck were throbbing. He picked up Jessica's stereo. Just as he was about to hurl it out the window, something caught his eye.

On the coffee table was a stack of clothes. Tom eased the stereo down and went to take a closer look.

Tom's anger quickly subsided. All his clothes were freshly washed and folded perfectly, sitting in a neat pile. *You're incredible, Elizabeth,* he thought with love. She always knew the right thing to do.

On top there was a note. *Since you're so busy cleaning out your room, thought you might need a little help. See you around— Jessica.*

Tom's jaw went slack. This was, by far, the nicest thing Jessica had ever done for him. Tom clutched the note in his hands as Danny's words turned over again and again in his mind. *Jessica's only nice when she wants something . . . and that something is you.*

Lila hung up the phone. *Where are you, Jessica?* she wondered. Her hands were shaking. Her heart pounded in her ears. Who could she call now? She thought of calling her parents, but then remembered they'd left for Europe two days ago. *Why isn't anyone ever around when I need them the most?*

"You can't come in now. Go away!"

Lila spun around. It was Nancy's voice coming from the front entrance. Maybe someone had come to visit. Lila ran out of the study and stood at the top of the stairs.

"And don't come back!" Nancy slammed the door shut before Lila even had a chance to see who was there. She turned around and glanced up at Lila.

"Who was that?" Lila asked.

"No one important," Nancy said dismissively. "Just some pesky salesman."

Lila gave her a long, hard stare. "Who was it really, Nancy? I need to know."

Nancy tugged at the back of her skirt. "I already *told* you," she snarled, then stalked off to the kitchen.

Lila stared wearily at the door. "Whoever you were, thanks for dropping by." Then Lila leaned her head against the banister and cried.

Chapter Fifteen

"Magda, I need to talk to you," Bruce said, taking a seat beside her.

Magda Helperin sat in the middle of the Theta house kitchen, with piles of mint green invitations stacked around her. They were RSVP responses to the Theta's annual gala. Magda and a few other Thetas were sorting through the responses. There were two huge boxes in the middle of the table, one marked yes and the other no. So far, the yes box was half filled while the no box was nearly empty.

"Fire away, Bruce," Magda said, handing him a stack of green cards. "But we're going to put you to work while you talk."

"That's okay," Bruce said, taking off his Sigma jacket and hanging it on the back of the chair. "It's about Lila."

Isabella tossed one of her cards into a box.

"What about Lila?" she chimed in.

Bruce tossed a card into the yes box. "I really need to see her. I don't want you to think I'm being a jealous ex-boyfriend. It's not like that. I'm really worried about her."

Magda reached for another stack of cards. "Actually, we're worried too."

Bruce's throat tightened. "You are? I can't tell you what a relief it is to hear you say that. I thought I was going out of my mind."

"She hasn't talked to any of us since she left," Denise Waters added.

Magda nodded. "And no one's seen her in any of her classes. It's strange that Lila would isolate herself like that."

"Unless someone's making her do it." Bruce tossed another card into the yes box.

Isabella pulled her dark hair back into a silver barrette. "Jessica told me that she and Elizabeth went to the mansion to see her, but some creepy maid wouldn't let them in the door."

Bruce shook his head sadly. "I blame myself. I never should've let her move in with that Porter guy."

Magda touched his shoulder reassuringly. "To be honest, Bruce, there was very little you or any of us could do. You know Lila—once her mind is made up, nothing can stop her."

Bruce dropped the cards on the table and covered his face with his hands. "Well, *I'm* going to stop her. I can't sit by and watch her put herself in a dangerous situation. I have to do something, even if it means that she'll never speak to me again." The phone rang, and Denise went into the living room to answer it.

Bruce rubbed his temples. "That's why I need your help."

"What do you want us to do?" Isabella asked.

"I want you to seat me next to her at the gala," Bruce said earnestly. "All I need is five minutes alone with Lila and I think I can convince her to come back to SVU."

"Sounds good to me," Magda said. "Consider it done."

Bruce smiled gratefully. "Thank you, Magda. You don't know how much this means to me."

Magda tossed a card into the box. "Lila means a lot to us—we want her back."

Denise came into the kitchen and sat down. Her face was somber.

"Who was on the phone?" Isabella asked.

Denise looked down. "It was Porter."

Everyone stopped what they were doing and looked at her.

"What did he say?" Bruce asked.

"He called to thank us for the invitation to the gala," Denise said slowly. "But he said that he and Lila would *not* be able to attend."

Lila slid a rhinestone-studded comb into her hair, then stood back to look at her reflection in the mirror. Her lips were painted scarlet red, making her delicate complexion look even paler than it already was. She touched her face with her fingertips. It had been days since she'd felt sunlight on her skin. Lila ran a finger over her pallid cheeks, which were starting to hollow out. She dabbed a bit more concealer on the dark circles under her eyes, then smoothed the makeup until it was blended in.

Maybe a white gown wasn't the best choice after all, she thought gloomily as she stared at her reflection.

The Theta gala was the biggest event of the year, and Lila had shopped for her gown months ago. Finding the perfect dress was no easy task; it often took weeks of rigorous searching. But this time, things had been different. The moment she had stepped out of her car, in Sweet Valley's most exclusive shopping district, she looked up into the store window of a tiny French boutique and saw the dress. It was love at first sight.

The gown was creamy-white raw silk. It had a sweetheart neckline and off-the-shoulder gathered sleeves. The bodice was fitted close to her body, emphasizing her tiny waist, while the skirt was draped, following the contours of her hips. It was simple, but elegant.

All that had been before the accident, when Lila had envisioned herself with a golden tan to contrast with the whiteness of the dress. She had imagined Bruce on her arm, in his black tux, and the two of them swirling around the dance floor like a royal couple, totally in love.

It was amazing how quickly things could change in a matter of weeks.

Lila smoothed the bodice of her dress. "Smile," she told herself. "And try to look beautiful." She felt anything but beautiful tonight. Lila's ashen complexion against the silk made her feel more like the bride of Frankenstein than a princess. The relationship she had with Bruce had fallen apart, and she hadn't heard from any of her friends in weeks. As far as they were concerned, she might as well be dead.

"Then why am I going?" Lila questioned her reflection. She had told herself that she didn't want anything to do with her friends—that they didn't have anything in common anymore. It was true, she thought, that her life was taking a much different course than theirs. But even though she had this beautiful home now, and had Porter to take care of her, Lila still felt empty. She missed her old life, and she missed her friends. Most of all, she wanted them to miss her too.

Lila applied one more coat of mascara, then grabbed her beaded handbag and headed down the stairs, holding the hem of her dress with one hand. *Even if the evening is a complete disaster, I'll at least get out of the house for once,* she thought.

Lila stood in the arched doorway of the dim parlor. Porter sat on the couch, thumbing through a thick medical book and jotting down notes. He was dressed in jeans and a sweatshirt.

"Lila, you look absolutely breathtaking," he

said, looking up from his work. His eyes traveled the length of her body. "What's the occasion?"

"I'm going to the Theta gala," she said, looking at him curiously. "Why aren't you dressed?"

Porter got up and took her by the hand. He looked distressed. "I don't know how to tell you this—" he started.

"Tell me what?"

Porter's fingers caressed the back of her hand. "I thought you were too sick to go, so I declined the invitation."

Lila pulled her hand away. "You *what?*"

"It was that day we were supposed to go to the ballet—you were so upset. I didn't think you'd be up for the gala."

"Why didn't you ask me first?" she demanded, her voice cracking. "It's *my* party."

Porter touched her hair lightly. "I'm sorry."

Lila stood with her shoulders back and her head held high. She desperately wanted to go to the gala, and a little thing like an invitation couldn't stop her. "I guess it doesn't matter. I'm going anyway."

"I had no idea it meant so much to you," Porter answered. He quickly picked up his books. "Give me a few minutes to get ready, and I'll go with you."

"Hey there, stranger," Jessica said as Tom walked through the door. She threw back her head and sprayed a little perfume on her neck, pretending not to notice his sappy stare.

"Hi, Jess," he mumbled, walking into the room like a zombie.

Men are so weak, Jessica thought. Of course, who could blame him for staring when she looked so devastating. Jessica had picked out a sexy black sheath dress with spaghetti straps and a daring slit up the side. To top it off, she wore long black gloves and had pulled her hair up into a chic French twist.

"How was your day?" she asked sweetly as she preened in the mirror.

"Uh, fine," Tom answered. His face was red. "Is Elizabeth around?"

Jessica spritzed her twist with a bit of hair spray. "Probably in the library. Knowing Liz, she won't be back for quite a while."

Tom sat down on the couch and opened a textbook. Although he pretended to be reading, Jessica could feel his eyes wandering over to her every few seconds.

"Did you get the note?" Jessica put on her rhinestone earrings.

Tom looked up, but wouldn't make eye contact. "What note?"

"You know, silly. The note I left with the laundry."

"Ah, yes, the laundry," he said. Jessica detected the slightest note of nervousness in his voice. "Thanks for doing that, Jess. It was really kind of you."

"My pleasure," she said huskily. "Anything for my sister's boyfriend."

Tom shifted uncomfortably in his seat and buried his face in the book.

Jessica's glossy lips twisted into a sly smile. She reached into her jewelry box and took out the rhinestone necklace that matched her earrings. "Tom, can I ask you a favor?"

He looked at her warily. "What is it?"

"Can you put on this necklace for me? The clasp is hard to do. I'd ask Liz to do it, but she's not here."

Tom swallowed loudly. "Sure."

Jessica turned around and handed him the necklace. Tom lifted it over her head. She leaned back slightly, so that her shoulders rubbed up against him. Tom's fingers felt cold and thick against her neck as he struggled to get the clasp to lock.

"It's not working," he said in a shaky voice.

Jessica smiled wryly to herself. "Keep trying."

Tom sighed. Finally the clasp slipped into place.

"Thanks." Jessica spun around and flashed Tom a bright smile. "So—how do I look?"

Tom looked at her for a moment, then quickly looked away. "You look incredible."

"Would you like some champagne?"

Bruce nodded gratefully at the tuxedoed waiter and took one of the bubbling champagne glasses off the silver tray. He took a sip and stood with his back against the wall, watching the decked-out couples as they entered Xavier Hall. The room had been decorated with white and silver balloons, and vases of fresh flowers adorned the round linen-covered dinner tables.

There was a small hors d'oeuvres table filled with a variety of cheeses and bite-size quiches to nibble on before dinner was served. On the other side of the hall was a twenty-piece orchestra for after-dinner dancing. Magda and the Thetas had really outdone themselves. The whole room gleamed with elegance and polish.

The only thing missing was Lila's beautiful face.

Bruce took another sip of champagne and slipped his hand into the pocket of his black tuxedo jacket. *If only Lila could be here tonight.*

Ever since he had fallen in love with her, Bruce had carried that love inside him like a glowing fire. It burned steadily in his heart, and no matter where he went or what he did, he always felt her warmth within him. Even after the accident, when Lila said she didn't want to see him anymore, it continued to burn, if not more brightly than before. And now, fearing that he'd never see her again, Bruce felt the fire burning out of control. It was ready to consume him. As hard as he tried, nothing could extinguish the flame.

"Are you all right?"

Bruce looked up from his glass to see Magda in a shiny blue strapless dress, staring at him with a look of concern on her face.

"I'm fine," he answered.

"You looked a little flushed. Maybe you ought to loosen that bow tie," she said with a sympathetic smile. "I'm sorry that she isn't going to be here. It was good of you to come anyway."

Bruce smiled politely. "Thanks."

Magda gave his shoulder a squeeze. "Hang in there. If you need anything, just give me a holler."

Bruce nodded and watched as Magda greeted the next couple that entered the door. He didn't know who they were, but they looked happy, holding hands and gazing at each other. He sighed heavily, thinking how ridiculous he must look to everyone, still pining for a woman who'd moved in with a doctor. He imagined their pitied glances and whispers. *Poor, pathetic soul—he can't take no for an answer.*

But Bruce was the last person who'd stick around to be made a fool of. If he truly believed that Lila was happy with Porter, he'd let her go. All Lila had to do was admit that she was no longer in love with him, and Bruce would wish her well and move on with his life.

But he needed a moment alone with her to find out the truth.

"I'm so glad you're here!" Isabella shouted.

Bruce turned his head toward the entrance. The Thetas were crowding around the door. His heart stopped. At the top of the stairs was Lila, with Porter on her arm.

Bruce's knees began to tremble. Lila looked thin and tired, as if she'd been through a tremendous strain. Her skin was pale, just the way it had been in the hospital, fighting for her life. The inner radiance that Bruce had been so attracted to was gone, like a candle that had been extinguished.

What on earth have you done to her? Bruce seethed as he looked at Porter in his white tuxedo and English ascot. Porter smirked arrogantly, surveying the room as if he were a king and the room was his court. Bruce squeezed his fist in a tight ball, fighting every instinct to walk up the steps and deliver a crushing blow to the side of Porter's smug face.

"Bruce, did you see who's here?" Magda called to him as she scurried among the tables, rearranging place cards. She gave him an encouraging wink.

Bruce smiled and made his way through the crowd to where Lila was standing. A few of the Thetas spotted him and moved aside. A hush fell over the crowd.

Bruce walked up a few steps and held out his hand toward her. "It's good to see you, Lila," he said.

Lila looked at Porter, then down at Bruce. "Hi, Bruce," she said with a faint smile. She placed her hand delicately in his.

Bruce curled his fingers around her cold hand. The fire inside him raged, spreading from his heart all the way out through his limbs. The flames traveled from his arms to his fingertips. He prayed that Lila could feel the heat of his touch.

"Bruce, this is Porter Davis," she said, pulling away from him with the slightest hesitation. "Porter, this is Bruce Patman."

Porter extended his hand with confidence and flashed Bruce an aloof smile. "How do you do?"

"Very well, thanks," Bruce said through gritted teeth. He forced his lips to twist into a smile, but it turned into more of a sneer. "I think dinner will be served shortly. Why don't I show you to your table?"

"That would be nice," Lila said as she followed him down the steps.

At least she's talking to me, Bruce thought as he led them both through the maze of tables. His heart soared when he thought of how she'd looked at him. There was still a glimmer of interest in her eyes. Maybe he had a chance after all. The only thing to stop him was that snotty boyfriend of hers, who was hanging on to her at every second. If only he could be alone with her— Bruce was certain he could win Lila back.

"Right here," Bruce said, motioning to their seats. Porter moved over to the farthest chair while Lila took the seat between the two of them. At the very same moment both Porter and Bruce reached for Lila's chair to pull it out for her. Porter tugged the back of the seat, inching it closer to him, while Bruce pulled it in the opposite direction. They struggled for a few seconds as the chair was yanked from left to right. Finally Bruce grabbed the chair with both hands and released it from Porter's grip. Porter's hand fell away, and his cuff link dropped to the floor.

Lila eyed both of them and sat down.

Porter faced forward, seemingly unaware that he had lost his cuff link. "You're very good at that, Bruce. Have you worked as a waiter before?"

Bruce reached down and swiped the shiny cuff link from under Lila's chair. He slipped it stealthily into his pocket. "No, but I know how to treat a woman with respect."

Lila held up her hands. "Please, stop it—both of you," she said with agitation. "I came here to enjoy myself. I won't be in the middle of any arguments."

Porter glared at Bruce. "I think it would be best if you sat at another table."

Bruce ignored him and turned to Lila. "Is that what you want me to do?"

"Please don't put me in the middle," Lila said.

Bruce felt as if he was balancing on a very fine line between winning her back and losing her forever. One wrong move could mean disaster. "Okay, I'll leave," he relented. "But if you need me, you know where I'll be."

Porter flashed a look of haughty triumph as Bruce got to his feet.

Just as he was about to leave, Bruce bent down and whispered to Lila, his lips brushing against her ear as he spoke. "I miss you," he said.

Lila felt a burning color rise to her cheeks. She took a drink of water to cool herself down.

"Are you all right?" Porter asked, covering her hand with his.

"Yes—I'm fine," Lila answered distractedly. Her eyes didn't follow Bruce as he crossed to the other side of the room, but she felt the reassuring comfort of his presence nearby. Her ear still tingled with the words he had spoken, his hot breath against her skin. He *had* missed her after all.

And so had the Thetas. Lila looked around the table at all her friends, who seemed so happy to see her. It was like coming home.

Lila picked up a butter knife and tapped it gently against her water glass. "May I have your attention—" she said to everyone at the table. "I'd like you to meet Dr. Porter Davis."

Porter grinned charmingly, his dimple showing. Lila gave his hand a proud squeeze. "Porter, I want you to meet my friends," Lila said. One by one she went around the table, introducing everyone. "Jessica Wakefield, Magda Helperin, Denise Waters and her boyfriend, Winston Egbert, and Isabella Ricci and her boyfriend, Danny Wyatt."

Porter smiled. "I'm not going to be quizzed on this, am I?"

The table broke into polite laughter. "Just make sure you remember *my* name," Jessica said teasingly. "It's the one that'll be famous someday."

"You mean *in*famous," Winston cut in.

"Whichever," Jessica answered, nibbling on a roll. "As long as it's a household word, I don't care."

Danny held up his water glass. "How about *Jess the Ripper*?"

"No—I like *The Loch Jess Monster*," Denise offered.

"I've got it!" Winston said excitedly. "*Jess-zilla* versus King Kong."

Everyone groaned.

"Okay, okay—I take it all back!" Jessica shouted. "Porter, you don't have to remember my name."

Porter laughed graciously. "It's such a lovely name, I couldn't forget it even if I wanted to."

A waiter came around and placed a spinach-and-mushroom salad in front of each of them. Jessica leaned over and whispered in Lila's ear, "He's a real charmer, and definitely cute."

"I'm glad you've all finally had a chance to meet him," Lila whispered back. A lump formed in her throat as she looked around the table. She had almost forgotten how good it was to be with her friends. Lila sighed contentedly, feeling better than she had in weeks.

When everyone was finished eating their salads, the waiters cleared the empty plates and brought in the main course. It was baked stuffed chicken with a white wine sauce, rice pilaf, and a mix of fresh garden vegetables. Lila ate hungrily.

"So when can we come see your house?" Jessica asked, spearing a piece of chicken with her fork.

Lila looked at Porter with apprehension.

"We still have a little more work to do," Porter said. "But as soon as it's finished, we'd love to have all of you over."

Lila smiled at him lovingly. For the first time since the night of the ballet, she felt that things were going to work out. If she could get better and stronger, their lives would be back to normal in no time.

Jessica patted the back of her French twist. "Actually, Liz and I stopped by your place the other night to surprise you, but the maid wouldn't let us in."

Porter dropped his fork.

Lila stopped chewing. "I didn't know you came by. . . ."

Jessica wiped her mouth with her linen napkin. "It was just to say hi and to see how you were doing. The maid said you were sick and told us to leave." Jessica turned to Porter. "If you don't mind me saying so, that maid of yours is pretty weird. If I were you, I'd let her go."

There was a sudden chill in Porter's eyes. "I assure you that Nancy does a fine job."

"I'm sure she does," Jessica answered quickly. "But she'll probably scare away anyone who comes to your door."

A tense silence fell over the table. Lila looked away, her gaze wandering across the room. Bruce was sitting at a table near the orchestra.

Lila felt an odd tingle in her stomach as their eyes met.

Chapter Sixteen

As soon as the dinner tables were cleared the orchestra began to play. The lights were dimmed as couples moved off to the dance floor. Lila sat back contentedly as she watched the commotion around her.

Denise jumped up and grabbed Winston's hand. "Come on, Winnie! Let's show them how to dance!"

Winston made a reluctant face. "Can't we wait until there're a few more people on the dance floor?"

Denise rolled her eyes. "There must be at least fifty people out there now," she said, dragging him along behind her.

"How about you, Iz? Are you up for it?" Danny asked.

Isabella smiled, tossing a red chiffon scarf glamorously over her shoulders. "I thought you'd never ask."

Magda excused herself and Jessica stood up, surveying the crowd. "Looks like I'd better find a partner before they're all taken." Jessica gave Lila's hand a squeeze. "Don't you go anywhere—I want to talk to you before you leave."

Lila smiled. "I'll be here."

Jessica headed off into the thick of the crowd. A waiter came by and placed a silver tray filled with chocolate-covered fruit in the center of the table.

"Looks like there's more for us," Lila said cheerfully. She picked up a chocolate-dipped strawberry and bit into the succulent fruit. Lila found her eyes wandering over to the other side of the room, looking for Bruce. At the moment he had disappeared from view behind the dancing couples, yet she still felt his gaze on her. Would he have the nerve to ask her to dance? Part of her wanted it to happen. But at the same time, a greater part of her wanted to avoid any sort of confrontation between Porter and Bruce.

"Thank you for coming," Lila said, reaching for a dried apricot. "I'm having a great time."

Porter didn't respond. Lila turned her head to look at him. The sparkle was gone from his eyes, and his mouth was drawn into a thin, stern line. She had seen that face before.

"What's wrong?" she asked. His expression made her blood run cold.

Without a word, Porter pulled back his shirt-sleeve. Reluctantly Lila's eyes dropped to his wrist. Porter's watch was missing.

"Oh, no . . ." Lila clamped a shaky hand over her mouth. "I didn't do it. . . ."

"Not *again*—" he said under his breath.

Panic pricked her spine like a thousand jabbing needles. "Porter, I don't have it. You were right here—how could I have taken your watch?" Her voice was rising. "You could've dropped it anywhere."

Porter reached angrily for Lila's evening bag.

It can't be in there. Lila's breathing became faster as she watched Porter sift through the contents of the bag . . . *it can't be in* . . . A sour, sickening ball rolled around in the pit of her stomach, rising higher and higher to her throat . . . *it can't be* . . . Blood pounded in her head, shifting from side to side, making her feel light and off balance . . . *it can't* . . .

Porter pulled his fist out of the bag and slammed the watch down on the table.

"Nooo!" Lila screamed.

The orchestra stopped mid-song, and the dancers looked around to see where the commotion was coming from. Lila tilted her head back and screamed with all her strength, until she squeezed the last bit of air out of her lungs.

"Lila!" Bruce shouted across the dance floor.

"I'm sorry, everyone," Porter said calmly to the crowd as he pulled a hysterical Lila up the stairs and out the door. "She's not feeling very well."

Bruce was about to run after the two of them when he felt an arm holding him back.

"Don't," Magda said. "Just let her go."

Bruce's body shook with rage. "What is he doing to her?"

"Maybe Lila's trauma over the accident is worse than we thought," Magda said gently.

"That's bull!" Bruce shouted harshly. "Lila was fine when she left the hospital. She's only been with that guy for a few weeks and he's turned her into a basket case."

"Bruce . . ."

"I'm not going to just sit and watch while Porter Davis plays with her mind," Bruce said in a threatening tone. "I'm going to get to the bottom of this."

Before Magda could respond, Bruce was running out the back entrance into the cold night air. Adrenaline flowed through his veins, making Bruce's head reel. *Porter's not in love with Lila.* Bruce could feel it in his gut. *But why is he with her?*

Bruce ran at full speed toward the library, the cold air stinging his lungs. The answer to the puzzle loomed ahead of him like the light over the library's main entrance—it was directly in front of him, but he couldn't quite reach it. Bruce didn't think he'd ever discover the answer alone.

But he knew someone who could help.

"Elizabeth—" he wheezed as he jogged over to the reference section.

Elizabeth looked up from her notebook. Her eyes widened with surprise as she surveyed Bruce, red-faced and breathless, in his tuxedo.

218

"Is there a new dress code in the library that I don't know about?"

Bruce leaned against the back of a chair, trying to catch his breath. "I was at the gala," he said seriously. "I need your help."

Elizabeth's eyebrows narrowed. "What's wrong?"

"Lila was there tonight." Bruce told Elizabeth the entire story. He told her how sickly Lila seemed; how arrogant and cold Porter was. And that the strangest moment of all was when Lila screamed at the top of her lungs and Porter dragged her out of the party.

Elizabeth listened quietly, seemingly collecting her thoughts. "This whole thing sounds incredibly strange," she said, tapping the tabletop with her pen. "But what can you do about it?"

"I don't know," Bruce said helplessly. "All I wanted was a few minutes alone with Lila to talk some sense into her." A trickle of sweat ran down the side of his face. He was reaching into his jacket pocket for a handkerchief when his fingers touched a small round object. It was Porter's cuff link.

Elizabeth leaned back in her chair. "But Lila's so headstrong. Even if you did talk to her, there was really very little you could do to change her mind. She'd think you were just jealous," she said slowly. "The only way to sway Lila is to *prove* to her that he's bad news. You need hard evidence."

"Frankly, I'm a little short on that right now," Bruce said ruefully. He took the cuff link out of his pocket and held it up to the light. The silver cuff link was engraved with initials—but they weren't Porter's initials. Bruce felt the air catch in his throat. "Then again, maybe I'm wrong. This is Porter's cuff link—but look at the initials."

Elizabeth studied the silver cuff link, tracing the swirling letters with the tip of her fingernail. "D.C. I don't get it—why would Porter Davis wear cuff links with the wrong initials?"

"There's only one reason I can think of," Bruce said, his voice thick with emotion. "And that's because he's not really Porter Davis."

"How could you humiliate me like that?" Porter shouted as he tossed Lila roughly onto her bed. "It's bad enough that you took *my* watch— who knows what you've stolen from your friends."

"I can't take it anymore!" Lila screamed hysterically. Her fingers clawed wildly at the lace bedspread. She poked a hole through it, then tore it to pieces with her hands and teeth.

Porter stood in the doorway and watched as she pulled apart the pillow seams, sending a cloud of goose feathers into the air.

"Stop it!" he barked, lunging at her. Porter grabbed her by the wrists with his strong hands. "Stop it right now!"

Lila squirmed, trying to break his steely grip. Bits of feather clung to her hair and gown like snowflakes. She pulled and twisted, barely able to move his hands a fraction of an inch. Suddenly she stopped. Her red-rimmed eyes darted crazily around the room. Porter dropped her hands into her lap and Lila pulled away, whimpering like an injured animal.

Porter shook the feathers out of his curly hair. "How can you treat me like this after all I've done for you?"

Lila numbly wiped her mouth with the back of her hand, smearing red lipstick across her cheek. "Sorry, Porter," she said in a childlike whisper. "I'll try . . . harder."

"I don't even know what to do with you anymore," he said, brushing off his jacket. He stood up and headed for the door.

Lila shrieked. "Where are you going?"

"To the hospital. I have late-night rounds," he answered flatly. "Have Nancy draw you a bath, and then you should get some sleep."

"Don't leave me!" Lila crawled across the floor on her knees and wrapped her arms around Porter's legs. "Don't leave me here alone!" she sobbed.

"Nancy will be here."

Lila squeezed tighter, her breath coming in short spasms. "It's the sounds . . . footsteps . . . wind chimes."

Porter shook his leg at her. "What on earth are you talking about?"

Lila's chest heaved. "The sounds in my head. I only hear them when you're gone," she cried. Her lips twisted in horror. "I can't take it anymore. You have to help me. I'm losing my mind."

Porter yanked himself away from her. "I'm

221

afraid I've done all I can," he said icily. "You're beyond help."

"Can you slow it down a bit?" Elizabeth said nervously. Off to the right the city lights glimmered in the distance, growing more hazy as they climbed the mountain. Despite the beautiful view Elizabeth kept her eyes forward, looking only at the section of road illuminated by the Jeep's headlights.

"Don't worry," Bruce said reassuringly. He let the speedometer drop a few notches. "I know this road so well I could drive with my eyes closed."

Elizabeth gripped the armrest. "Don't feel like you have to prove anything—I'll take your word for it."

The green light from the dashboard illuminated Bruce's features, giving him an eerie glow. His face was creased with lines of worry and determination. Elizabeth felt the tiny hairs on the back of her neck stand up. What was going to happen when they reached the mansion? This was a personal matter between Bruce and Lila, and Elizabeth felt as if she shouldn't really be there. As much as she wanted to help Bruce, Elizabeth started to wonder if maybe she was getting in too deep.

An empty, heavy silence fell between them, drowned out only by the roar of the engine. "Do you really think Porter is actually David Carrier?" Elizabeth asked.

"Absolutely," Bruce answered through clenched teeth.

222

She wanted to diffuse his anger somehow, to cool him down before he got to the mansion and did something he was going to regret. But Bruce's determination was like the fuse on a bomb. Once it was lit, he could never go back. "But Carrier was a fan of Katherine's. What would he want with Lila?"

Bruce swerved to the side of the road and stopped the Jeep. "That's what I want to find out."

Elizabeth looked out the driver's-side window. They were across the street from the mansion. Through the trees they could see that only a few of the rooms had lights on, but the drapes were drawn, making it impossible to see inside.

"What are you going to do?" Elizabeth asked nervously.

Bruce pursed his lips in thought. "I'm not sure." He turned to Elizabeth. "If only I could get to see her without that bozo hanging all over her."

Elizabeth saw the figure of a man run out of the house and jump into the white Mustang parked in the drive. "Looks like you got your wish."

Bruce clicked off his headlights and stared intently as the rear lights of the Mustang came on. Seconds later the white sports car was backing out of the driveway.

"Where do you suppose he's headed?" Bruce thought aloud.

"Who knows—maybe the hospital?"

"Wherever it is, it ought to give me enough time to talk to Lila."

The Mustang backed out into the road, but instead of cutting right to head down the mountain, it turned left to continue up to the very top.

"That's crazy . . ." Bruce said in wonder. "He can't keep going up—there's a dead end at the top."

Elizabeth chewed her bottom lip warily. "Are you sure?"

"Positive," Bruce answered. "Eventually he'll have to turn around and head back down the mountain."

They sat in the darkness for several minutes, waiting to see the Mustang's headlights reappear.

But the car never came back.

Porter turned down the road that ran behind the mansion and clicked off the car's headlights. The last few yards he could manage without light, guiding the car by the feel of the gravel underneath the tires. When he got close enough, Porter cut the engine and let the car roll quietly in neutral until he felt the familiar give of soft earth and grass. He pulled on the emergency break and got out.

Porter threw off his trench coat and doctor's smock and zipped up a pair of dirty coveralls that were stashed under the driver's seat. Work clothes. When Porter had bought them, he thought he'd only have to wear them once, but there had been a slight delay, a change in his original plan. Things were quickly becoming more complicated by the day.

He grabbed his hat and a backpack and closed the car door. It was a dark night. The moon was under a cover of clouds, not even offering a sliver of light to guide his way. Porter walked in a zigzag pattern through the family plot, careful not to stub his toe on any of the gravestones. Moving quickly through the darkness he made his way to the back of the mansion, stopping when his hands touched the rough stucco wall.

Why didn't you just give me the diamond when I asked for it, Katherine? You could've saved us both a lot of trouble.

Porter leaned with his back against the wall and his arms spread out. He felt his way as he moved along, his fingers memorizing every bump and ridge of the textured plaster. Smooth, then rough. Then another ridge. Porter smiled. Only a few more inches. There. He'd found it.

Porter scaled the fire escape ladder easily and without fear. When he reached the top of the building, he slid open the attic window and climbed inside, brushing against the wind chimes that hung in the window frame.

Porter clicked on the flashlight that was strapped to the visor of his hat and aimed the beam of light directly in front of him. How he hated the musty, dirty attic, with its piles of useless junk. Cookie jars shaped like animals, tacky cut-glass vases, that horrid apron collection. Spending night after night sifting through the heaps, Porter came to the conclusion that someone with an obvious lack of taste did not deserve to own such a stunning jewel as that priceless pink diamond.

That's why Katherine had to die.

He remembered that night well. It had just rained and the air smelled of promise. He'd showed up on Katherine's doorstep unexpectedly, but she'd let him in. There was no reason not to.

"David, it's so good to see you," Katherine had said. Her hair was particularly beautiful that night, pulled back in a bun. Soft curls fell loosely around her face. "I got your letter."

Porter pushed aside a few straight-backed chairs and walked across to the other side of the attic. His footsteps were heavy, and the floorboards creaked under his weight.

She'd made him dinner that night, just like old times.

"I wonder what Chester would say if he could see us now," he'd said with a laugh.

"Please don't talk about my husband that way," she'd said. "He was a good man."

"Of course he was," he'd said. "His only fault was taking credit for other people's work."

The other night, Porter had gone through the drawers of the small wooden bureau, the old trunk filled with clothes, and a stack of hatboxes. Those were the last few places he had to check, and still he couldn't find the diamond. The only thing left to do was start at the beginning and look through everything again. It had to be there—somewhere.

"You helped him a great deal," Katherine had insisted. "But it was his discovery."

Porter kicked a box of cookbooks over. The

books tumbled noisily on the floor. From below, he could hear Lila's muffled shrieks. Every time he made some sort of noise, she flipped out. She was really starting to lose it. Porter smiled to himself. This was going to work out even better than he'd planned—as long as he could find that diamond.

"It was my discovery, too," he'd said to Katherine.

Porter snapped back and crossed to the other side of the room, stomping his feet forcefully with each step.

Bruce rapped on the door with the brass knocker for a second time, but still there was no answer.

Elizabeth glanced over her shoulder anxiously, looking at the dark driveway. "What if he comes back? What'll we do?"

Bruce dropped the knocker and rapped on the door with a solid fist. "Don't worry about a thing. I'll deal with it."

That's what I'm afraid of, Elizabeth thought. Two men interested in the same woman didn't make for a pleasant confrontation. The veins in Bruce's neck were already starting to pop out, and Elizabeth imagined that his blood pressure was rising. She twisted her fingers nervously, praying that Bruce would be able to keep his temper in check.

Bruce banged on the door. "Open up!" he shouted.

As if by his command, the door creaked open. In the doorway stood the same maid that Elizabeth had seen that time when she'd come by with Jessica.

The maid looked at them testily. "What do you want?"

Bruce folded his arms across his chest, making his muscles ripple under his long-sleeved shirt. "I want to see Lila."

The maid took a long drag on her cigarette, then blew the smoke in his face. "You can't."

Elizabeth fanned away the blue smoke with her hand. "We just want to talk to her for a minute. We don't even have to come inside—she can come to us."

"I told you before—she's not well."

Bruce's face turned a dark red. "Did it ever occur to you that she's not well because you never let her outside?"

"Bruce, don't—" Elizabeth said.

The maid cocked an eyebrow at him, unruffled by his anger. "Hey, I'm just following orders."

"It wouldn't hurt you once in a while to use your head instead of acting like a puppet," Bruce barked at her.

The maid sneered at the two of them, then moved to slam the door shut. Bruce stuck his foot in the door.

Elizabeth jumped to the side.

Bruce pushed against the doorframe, his arms shaking. "I'm getting in here whether you like it or not."

"Stop it!" Lila shrilled at the ceiling. She clutched her feather-covered hands over her ears,

228

but the footsteps continued to pound. Each step was louder than the one before it, throbbing in her brain.

"Stop it!" she screamed louder, but the pounding went on incessantly. In desperation Lila lunged for the vase on her bureau. The flowers Porter had put in it when she'd first moved in were dead—brown and crisp and smelling of rot. She turned the vase upside down, the dead flowers and slimy water spilling onto her gown. With one hand she took the glass vase and hurled it up toward the ceiling. The vase hit the ceiling with a loud *crack!* and was crushed on impact. Jagged pieces rained down around her.

I'm losing my mind . . .

Lila stepped out of the way of the glass splinters. Her chest rose and fell in shaky sobs. First she was forgetting things. Then she was taking things without even realizing it. Now she was destroying everything in sight. Yet she couldn't help herself. Lila felt a large vacuous hole opening inside her. It was growing, taking over the person she once was and turning her into an empty shell. How long would it be before it completely took her over and there was nothing left?

Lila pushed back a stringy strand of hair and sobbed quietly. Downstairs the front door creaked on its hinges, opening and closing repeatedly. Nancy was talking to someone, her voice so low that Lila couldn't make out the words. Porter must have returned.

Lila stumbled out into the hall, bleary eyed,

letting the hem of her stained gown drag along the floor. She leaned against the banister, waiting for Porter to come up the stairs.

"Get out of here before I call the police!" Nancy hissed, struggling to close the door. Her voice was severe—not the kind of tone she'd ever use with Porter.

Lila rubbed her eyes. Her hands still smelled of moldy flowers. She blinked twice, and her vision cleared just in time to see Bruce's face as Nancy closed the door on him.

"No . . . wait! Bruce, don't go . . ." Lila yelled, but no one seemed to hear her.

Nancy bolted the door firmly and turned around, stopping suddenly when she caught a glimpse of Lila at the top of the stairs. Their eyes locked.

Lila gripped the banister. *What was Bruce doing here?* She wanted desperately to run down the stairs, throw open the door, and call to him. But something cold and ominous in Nancy's stare stopped her.

Nancy backed up slowly, her eyes still fixed on Lila. She leaned against the door. Her meaning was clear: *You're not going anywhere.*

Lila turned around in a flurry and burst through the door of her room. Pulling back the drapes, she peered through the window. She saw the headlights of Bruce's red Jeep come on as he started the engine.

I miss you . . .

That's what he'd said to her at the gala. There

had been something in his voice—a tenderness—that made Lila believe he'd meant it. And now he showed up on her doorstep, even after the scene she'd made at the gala. Bruce's gesture touched something inside her. It was the feeling of passion and intrigue that had made her fall in love with him in the first place.

She had to stop him before he left.

Lila unlocked the window latch and pulled up on the window frame. It didn't move. Porter still hadn't done anything to fix it.

"Come on! Open!" Lila shouted. She tugged again, struggling with all her strength. The Jeep's brake lights turned off and it started to roll down the driveway. Lila panicked. She pulled harder. Her muscles ached as she strained to open the window. Her fingernails dug deep into the wood of the frame.

"Wait!" She knocked on the glass with her knuckle.

The Jeep rolled slowly, moving closer to the end of the drive.

"Bruce! Wait!" she screamed. Tears of frustration coursed down her cheeks. She clenched her hands into tight fists and banged on the window.

The Jeep came to the very end of the driveway, then stopped for a second.

He sees me. . . .

Lila caught her breath, waiting for the taillights to turn white as the Jeep retraced its path. Instead the wheels turned to the right and the Jeep rolled onto the mountain road.

"Nooo!" Lila wailed.

In a fit of hopelessness she slammed her fists through the pane, shattering the window. Hot pain seared her wrists as the broken glass pierced her skin.

"Help me!" Lila screamed in agony, watching crimson rivers gushing down her arms, covering her in blood.

Chapter
Seventeen

_____

"You poor thing! You've been working so hard, you fell asleep on your books."

Tom smiled sleepily. He loved being woken by the sound of Elizabeth's sweet voice. He lifted his head off the desktop, looking at her with blurry, half-closed eyes. "I was waiting up for you," he said.

"I was hoping you would," she said. Her arms encircled his neck.

He rubbed his eyes. "You know, we haven't spent much time alone lately."

She didn't say a word. Tom felt her blowing softly in his ear. It sent shivers through him. Obviously she felt the same way.

Tom's smile widened as his hand reached up to touch her arm. But instead of feeling the warmth of her skin as he'd expected, his fingers skimmed cool satin.

Tom gripped her arm. He opened his eyes. "What the—"

Jessica looked at him, a sly smirk playing on her ruby lips.

"Why did you do that?" he snapped. Tom's cheeks burned in anger.

Jessica touched him playfully on the nose. "Come on, Tom," she said in a husky voice. "You knew it was me. Would Liz wear satin gloves or a dress like this?" She struck an alluring pose to emphasize her point.

Tom, who was now fully awake, felt as if his brain was short circuiting. "How would I know . . . I was half asleep."

"Of course you knew." Jessica unpinned her French twist, her hair cascading down around her shoulders. "Don't tease, Tom. I had a bad night," she pouted. "No one would dance with me."

"I'm sorry if you had a bad time," Tom said dryly.

"I don't know what I did wrong. I look good, don't I?"

Tom's eyes quickly scanned her body, then darted away in embarrassment. "Of course you do. You look great."

Jessica touched her throat demurely. "If you had gone to the gala, would you have danced with me?"

Tom nodded reluctantly. "Yes."

"I was hoping you'd say that," Jessica said with a seductive smile. "Because the whole time I was there, I couldn't think of anyone else but you."

Tom's knees began to shake. *Jessica wants you* . . . that's what Danny had said. Even though Tom didn't want to believe it could be true, he was starting to think that Danny might be right.

"That's nice," he said.

Jessica ran her fingers through her hair. "It would've been a lot nicer if we could've slow danced together." She kicked off her heels. "Just you and me."

The smart thing to do is to run out of the room, Tom told himself. *Leave before things get complicated.* Although he knew it was the smartest solution, Tom couldn't go. He felt as though his body was anchored to the chair.

"Liz is your sister . . ." he argued weakly.

"I can't help it if I have feelings for you, Tom," Jessica said. She moved closer to him. "She has you, and I don't. If things were to change and I had you instead, she'd be left out in the cold. It seems unfair either way."

Tom let out a nervous laugh. "I don't get it," he said, backing away from her. "I thought you hated me."

Jessica stared at him intensely. "I know I've been awful, and I want to apologize," she said. "I guess I acted that way because I was angry I couldn't be with you. Will you ever forgive me?" She hovered over him.

Tom swallowed hard. He looked at the door, praying Elizabeth wouldn't come in. "Sure, I forgive you."

235

"Whew!" Jessica breathed a sigh of relief. "That makes me feel a whole lot better." She peeled off her satin gloves and draped them over his shoulders. Tom felt as if his insides were disintegrating.

Jessica sat on his lap and ran her fingers through his hair. "Now," she said with a sexy grin. "How can I make it up to you?"

"That's a wineglass! You don't put water in a wineglass," Porter barked at Nancy. She stared at the crystal stemware in confusion. Porter impatiently picked up one of the four goblets in front of his place setting and held it in the air. "*This* is a water glass," he said pointedly. "When are you going to learn?"

Lila watched quietly from the other end of the long dining table. Nancy had poured water into her champagne flute, but Lila didn't care. A sharp, burning pain seethed in her bandaged wrist as she lifted the glass to her lips.

Porter cocked an angry brow at Nancy. "Next time you make hollandaise sauce, I suggest you serve it *immediately*." His lip curled in disgust as he poured the congealed sauce over the platter of asparagus. "Or it will separate. It's not the sort of thing where you can start it, then just leave whenever you please. Fine cooking takes great care."

Nancy's face was flushed, but she said nothing.

A wave of sympathy washed over Lila. "Porter, maybe you shouldn't be so critical," she said diplomatically. "Nancy worked hard to cook for us. I

think it's a fine dinner." She took a bite of asparagus to prove it.

Nancy smiled gratefully before leaving the room.

Porter dismissed her with a wave of his hand.
"You *would* think this is good food," he said
haughtily.

"I just thought you were being too hard on her."

Porter slammed his fists on the table, making
his silverware bounce with a clatter. "I had Nancy
make this dinner especially for you. Forgive me if I
want everything to be perfect."

Lila set down her knife and fork. "Porter,
everything doesn't have to be perfect."

Porter threw down his napkin. "And obviously
it hasn't been, or else you wouldn't have tried to
kill yourself last night."

His words hung in the air.

Lila touched her bandages. "I told you—it was
an accident."

"If you weren't trying to slash your wrists, then
what exactly *were* you doing?" he demanded.
"Were you trying to break the window open so
you could jump out?"

"No," Lila insisted. Her heart ached as she remembered how Bruce had driven away before she
could stop him. "I'm not sure what happened."

"That was quite a spectacle you made of yourself
last night," Porter said. His ice blue eyes glared at
her across the table. "I've ordered all new bedding
for you. It should arrive sometime this afternoon. I
have to do hospital rounds again tonight, and I hope

you'll have the decency not to destroy your room," he said roughly. "Or yourself, for that matter."

Lila looked down at her plate. "You're going out again?" she asked quietly.

"I don't have a choice—this is my career," Porter said defensively. "I have patients who need me."

"*I* need you."

Porter leaned back in his chair. "I'm with you all day long, except for a few hours at night. Nancy's here—you're never alone." His eyes narrowed. "To be honest, I need a few hours away. You're really draining me, Lila."

Lila trembled. Nightfall was eight hours away. The seconds ticked down in her brain like a time bomb. As soon as Porter left, the thundering footsteps would return. Her head throbbed with exhaustion. She couldn't take it anymore.

"Take me to the hospital with you," Lila blurted impulsively.

Porter shook his head. "And what am I supposed to do with you while I'm doing my rounds? We both know I can't leave you alone in the hospital. You'll start stealing the patients' belongings."

Lila looked away in shame. Tears glistened in her eyes. The last thing she wanted was to become a burden to him. She wished she didn't depend on him so much, but he was all she had.

"Why don't you let a few of my friends come over?" she pleaded. "I just need someone to talk to."

"You have to understand something, Lila,"

Porter said intensely. "The only way you're going to get well is if you make a clean break from your past. You can't move forward if you allow yourself to be continually dragged down by the people who used to be part of your life." He took a long drink of water. "I think we both know how much going to the gala set you back."

A tear rolled silently down Lila's cheek. The thought of never seeing her friends filled her with an overwhelming sense of loss. She stared sadly at her wounded arms. *Will I ever be happy again?*

"Thanks for holding me back at the mansion last night," Bruce said to Elizabeth as he leaned against the headboard of his bed, gripping a football in his hands. "I was so wound up, I probably would've wrecked the whole thing." He extended his arm, holding the ball firmly, as if he were about to execute a pass. He pulled back and repeated the imaginary throw continuously, perfecting his form.

"No need to thank me," Elizabeth said, taking a seat at his desk. "I thought we were going to be arrested for assault. I wasn't in the mood to spend the night in jail."

"It's just that I hate not knowing what to do." Bruce shook his head. "I feel like we've hit a huge brick wall."

If only life was more like football, he mused. On the football field there were rarely any surprises that Bruce wasn't prepared for. He could make decisions in a split second with a great deal

239

of accuracy. On the field he was confident and bold and never indecisive.

Elizabeth leaned her elbows on Bruce's desk. "Being in love with her doesn't help matters. Emotions can mess everything up to the point where you can't even see straight."

Bruce smiled at her. "That's why I need your help. You have a good head on your shoulders."

The sun had set, and Bruce's room was getting dark. He turned on the overhead light. Bruce squeezed the football furiously as he remembered the arrogant face of David Carrier as he walked into the gala last night with Lila on his arm.

"What do you suppose that bozo wants with Lila?" Bruce wondered aloud. "Obviously he's not in love with her. If he was, he wouldn't lie to her about his identity."

"You're getting better at this detective stuff all the time," Elizabeth said good-naturedly. She opened the manila folder containing the newspaper articles and spread them across his desktop.

Bruce rubbed his chin pensively. "The answer to the mystery lies somewhere in the breakup of Chester Cage and David Carrier."

"I still think it had something to do with Katherine. Maybe Carrier was obsessed with her," Elizabeth said.

"It has to be more than that," Bruce said. Deep down in his gut he knew that there had to be more to the story.

"What does David Carrier want?" Elizabeth murmured.

As soon as the words escaped her lips, Bruce knew the answer.

"I think I've got it. . . ." Bruce picked up one of the articles. His mind was spinning as the pieces of the puzzle began falling into place.

Elizabeth looked at him anxiously. "Bruce, what is it?"

"David Carrier wanted Katherine's diamond," he said in triumph.

"Okay," Elizabeth answered cautiously. "Follow through on your reasoning."

Bruce began to pace the floor of his room. "Carrier befriended Katherine when she received the diamond, hoping that if they became close, he'd have an opportunity to steal it. Chester must've sensed that Carrier's intentions weren't honorable and cut off his relationship with him. When Chester died, Carrier probably tried to renew his relationship with Katherine in another attempt to steal the diamond. But Katherine died, and since Lila was the heir to the estate, Carrier moved in on her."

"That's all well and good," Elizabeth answered. "But you forgot one important detail. The diamond was never recovered at the scene of the crime. The murderer has it."

Bruce massaged his temples. He felt his brain cruising a mile a minute. "You're *assuming* the murderer has it. What if the jewel is hidden somewhere? What if the murderer never found it?"

"So if the murderer didn't find the diamond, Carrier is trying to take a crack at it," Elizabeth reasoned. "But how would he know whether or not the murderer found it?"

Elizabeth's words rang out in the silence of the room. Bruce stopped in his tracks. *I guess that means only one thing*, he thought. A chill ran down his spine as the final clue fell into place. *David Carrier is the murderer.*

Bruce grabbed the keys to his Jeep and ran out the door.

Chapter
Eighteen

_____

"Don't leave me alone."

Tears streaked down Lila's face as she watched Porter's white Mustang pull out of the driveway. She had cried so much in the past few weeks, she didn't believe it was possible to cry any more. But the tears flowed freely from her burning eyes. Lila imagined that she would spend the rest of her life like this, crying and watching out her window, waiting for Porter to come home.

Lila couldn't stand another night of this. It was like being stretched out on a torturer's rack, pulled to the limit. The sound of one more footstep was all it would take to snap her in two.

Lila pulled a rocking chair near the window and waited in the dark. The silence was heavy, weighing on her like impending doom. Any minute now, the noises would begin.

"He'll be back soon," Lila mumbled to herself.

She folded her arms across her chest and rocked back and forth. The anxiety was starting up again, a hot, tingling sensation in her spine.

"One . . . two . . . three . . ." Lila focused all her energy on trying not to fall apart. For the moment, counting was the only thing that seemed to work.

"Ten . . . eleven . . . twelve."

Lila looked out the window to see the head-lights of a car turn on. The vehicle was speeding up the driveway. In the faint glow of the garage light she could make out the shape and color. It was a red Jeep.

Bruce had come back.

"Bruce is here!" she said excitedly, bounding out of the chair. Lila checked her reflection in the mirror. Suddenly she stopped. "What is he doing here?" she thought out loud. "Does he want to see me or get even with Porter?

We both know how much the gala set you back. Porter's voice echoed in her mind. *If you want to get well, you need to make a clean break from your past.*

Porter was right. Everything seemed to be falling apart since the gala, and it was all because she didn't listen to his advice. She never should've gone out. She wasn't well enough yet. Now Porter was at his wits' end with her. And Lila was going out of her mind.

Lila smoothed down her hair. Even though she knew her friends were bad for her, she still missed them. She had hardly had an opportunity to talk to them, to tell them about her new life. Although she had a beautiful house and Porter to take care of her, it all seemed empty and unreal without being able to share it with anyone.

Thump! Lila's eyes darted toward the ceiling in a frenzy. *Thump!* The footsteps were starting again. The sound seemed to be coming at her from all sides, squeezing and suffocating her. She had to talk to someone before she went out of her mind. Lila clasped her hands to her ears and ran out into the hallway.

"Nancy! Where are you?" Lila glanced toward the front door at the bottom of the stairs. Bruce hadn't made it to the door yet, but he'd be there any second.

Nancy was dusting the grandfather clock in the corner. "What now?"

Lila skipped down the stairs, trying to seem casual.

"Nancy," she said quickly, with an authoritative tone. "Go make me a pot of tea, please."

Nancy dropped the feather duster at her side. Her hands rested on her hips in defiance. "I'm busy. Have you forgotten where the kitchen is?"

Lila held her trembling hands behind her back. Bruce would knock on the door at any moment. She didn't have time for a showdown. "Please, Nancy. Just do this for me," Lila begged. "I never ask you for anything."

Nancy waited a beat or two for effect, then turned her sneering face toward the kitchen and stomped down the hallway.

*   *   *

Bruce reached for the brass door knocker, but the door opened before he could touch it. Automatically he wedged his boot in the door, expecting the maid to slam it shut the minute she saw him. But the maid wasn't the one who answered the door.

"Lila!" he shouted. Bruce breathed in sharply, caught off guard by Lila's delicate but sallow complexion and her strange, glassy eyes.

"Shhhh!" Lila's eyes were filled with alarm. She brought her forefinger to her lips to silence him. "Follow me," she said, turning and heading up the stairs.

Bruce trailed behind, taking the steps two at a time. He scarcely had a moment to take in the decor. Everything had been fixed and polished. The enormous brass chandelier hanging in the front hall cast a warm glow of light on the carpeted stairs. It was all so different from the way it had been on the day of the quake. Obviously David Carrier had gone to great lengths to convince Lila that he wanted to build a life with her.

Lila brought him into her room and closed the door behind them.

"I'm so glad to see you," she whispered. She walked around in tight circles. Her movements were jerky and unpredictable. "Porter's gone to the hospital and I don't want to be alone."

Bruce shifted from one foot to the other, trying to make eye contact, but Lila continued to move around. The second her eyes rested on his, they dashed off to another part of the room.

246

"How have you been?" he asked.

Lila's lips moved to form the words, and Bruce waited patiently to hear what she had to say. The next moment a sound came from the attic, and Lila's face twitched in what seemed to be fright.

Bruce held her by the upper arms to hold her still. "Concentrate, Lila," he said in a firm voice. "Tell me what's going on with you."

Lila's eyes moved from side to side. "I'm losing my mind, Bruce," she said, her voice trembling. "I keep forgetting things . . . I take things without even realizing it—" She stopped, her eyes darkening. "There are strange sounds in my head. I hear footsteps and wind chimes. . . . You have to help me, Bruce. I can't take it anymore."

Bruce gave Lila's shoulders a gentle shake, trying to break her from her trance. "You're not crazy, Lila," he said reassuringly. "I hear them too."

Lila stopped moving. "You do?"

"Of course—I can hear the sound right now. I heard it when I came in the room."

"No one else has heard it," she said gravely. Her breathing began to slow down. She looked up. "It's coming from the attic. That's where all Aunt Katherine's things are. She's angry at me— that's the only reason I can come up with. She's haunting me."

Bruce made Lila sit down on the edge of the bed. "First of all, Lila, you're not crazy. Second, I can assure you that your aunt is not haunting you. There's a reasonable explanation for all of this."

247

Bruce brushed back a strand of her hair. He gazed down at her. "But I don't think you're going to like the answer."

"Let's celebrate," Elizabeth said happily as she plopped down on the couch beside Tom.

"What for?" Tom asked abruptly. He turned around so that he faced Elizabeth and his back was to Jessica, who was sorting through the clothes in her closet.

"Because you and Jessica have finally made up," Elizabeth answered. She leaned against his shoulder. "I never thought you two could get along."

Jessica held a purple slip dress against her body and admired her reflection in the mirror. "I didn't think we could either. But I guess I had the wrong idea about Tom," Jessica said. She turned around, still holding the dress against her. "What do you think of this dress, Tom?"

Tom didn't answer.

"Tom?"

Elizabeth nudged him in the ribs. "Tom—my sister is talking to you," she murmured.

Tom sighed and turned around.

Jessica smiled broadly. "So what do you think?"

Tom swallowed nervously. "It's nice."

"Do you think it would look better with black satin gloves or without?" she asked playfully.

Tom quickly turned his head away. "Without, I guess."

Jessica hung the dress back in the closet. "Liz,

248

this is what I love about your boyfriend. He gives great advice."

Elizabeth gave Tom a proud pat on the shoulder. "I know—I'm pretty lucky."

Tom felt a wave of nausea sweep over him. He felt Jessica's eyes boring through the back of his head.

"Take last night, for example," Jessica said, moving to the front of the couch. "I came home from the gala feeling kind of depressed and unattractive, and good old Tom was here to cheer me up."

"That's my guy," Elizabeth said.

Jessica moved closer. "He's like a brother to me," she said. Wrapping her arms around his neck, she gave him a hug and sat on the other side of him.

Tom sat stiffly, inching away from her.

Elizabeth's eyes were misty. "I can't tell you how great it is to see you guys being so friendly to each other," she said thickly. "Let's go to Julio's Pizzeria to celebrate."

If ever Tom understood how a circus animal felt, it was at that very moment. He was caged on both sides, unable to escape. Elizabeth watched him with expectation, certain that he'd never let her down. On the other side was Jessica, leering at him with her catlike eyes. She was armed and ready to make him jump through hoops if she saw fit.

"I'm in," Jessica said, putting her arm around Tom's shoulders.

Tom shook off Jessica's arm and stood up. "You'll . . . uh, have to go without me," he stammered. "I have some things to do."

"We can wait," Jessica said.

"No," Tom answered quickly. "Just go ahead." He leaned over and gave Elizabeth a kiss on the forehead, then bolted out the door.

"What's wrong with him?" Elizabeth asked quizzically as she watched Tom leave.

Jessica pouted her lips slyly. "I guess he doesn't like pizza."

Thud. The footsteps continued in the attic. Lila flinched every time she heard a noise. "Are you sure it's not my aunt haunting me?"

"Positive—and I can prove it." Bruce scanned the room. "Where does Porter keep his papers?"

"In the study across the hall," Lila said reluctantly. "But you can't go in there. No one can go in there." Her eyes were wide with fright.

Bruce walked out of Lila's room and into the hall. Lila ran ahead and leaned her body against the door.

"You can't go in—" Lila whispered. She blocked the entrance with her arms.

Bruce gripped the doorknob. "Lila, you're not crazy, and I'm going to show you why. But the only way I can do that is if you let me into Porter's study."

Nervously Lila lowered her arms and stepped aside. Bruce walked into the room. He clicked on the overhead light and closed the door. Lila cowered in the corner.

250

Bruce eyed the rolltop desk against the wall. Its cover was pulled down, and he had no doubt that it was locked.

"I have something important to tell you, so listen carefully." Bruce rested his hands lightly on her shoulders and waited until Lila made eye contact with him before continuing. "Porter isn't who you think he is. His real name is David Carrier."

Lila pulled away, backing up against the wall. "What are you trying to do?"

"I'm telling you the truth," Bruce said earnestly. "Give me a minute and I'll show you."

Bruce reached into the pocket of his jeans and pulled out a penknife. He jammed the blade into the desk lock and jimmied it. The lock was solid. Bruce threw the knife on the ground and kicked the lock with the heel of his boot, breaking open the desk cover.

Bruce opened every drawer and shuffled through the stacks of papers. *There must be something here to link Porter to David Carrier,* he thought. At last, in the back corner of the desk, he uncovered a letter that had been written to Katherine. The signature at the bottom of the page belonged to David Carrier.

"Here," Bruce said, handing Lila the letter. "Take a look at this."

Lila scanned the piece of paper. "I've seen this before. I found this in the kitchen one morning," she said, her eyebrows furrowed. "But it still doesn't prove anything. Just because Porter kept

251

this doesn't mean he's who you say he is."

"There's more." Bruce took the cuff link out of his pocket. "This is one of the cuff links he wore to the gala."

Lila held the cuff link delicately in the palm of her hand, as if she thought it would break. Her face wrinkled in confusion. "I don't know . . ."

Bruce exhaled as he ran his fingers through his hair impatiently. "Just trust me, Lila. Porter isn't who he says he is."

Lila turned her back on him. "Even if you're right, so what? What does any of this have to do with the noises in the attic?"

Bruce pressed his fingertips against his throbbing temples. "Porter is in the attic right now— that's why you hear footsteps up there," he said deliberately. "I bet you never hear anything when he's around, do you?"

Lila's mouth turned up in an amused grin. "That's an interesting theory, Bruce. But why on earth would Porter spend so much time in that dusty old attic without telling me?"

"Because he's searching for your aunt's diamond. David Carrier was a close friend of your aunt's who became greedy. He wanted the diamond more than anything. Carrier tried to intimidate Katherine, but she wouldn't tell him where it was." Bruce spoke slowly so that every word seeped in. "When she didn't cooperate, he murdered her."

Lila's ashen face took on a paler hue. "That can't be right—you must be mistaken."

252

"Maybe I am," Bruce said. "But if I'm not, you're in a lot of danger. Come with me right now. I'll get you out of here."

Lila closed her eyes and shook her head. "You're wrong. I just know it. Porter would never do anything like that."

Bruce reached for her hand. "You can't stay here. It's too dangerous."

Lila shrank back. "How dare you come into my house and make such horrible accusations, then expect me to run off with you?"

"Why would I lie to you?" Bruce asked. "Don't you believe me?"

"I don't know what to believe anymore," Lila said bitterly.

The door to the study opened. They both turned around to see Nancy holding a tray and glaring at them menacingly. "What's going on here?" she demanded.

Bruce was about to answer when Lila stepped forward. "He's just a friend, Nancy. He's on his way out."

Nancy shot Bruce an evil look. "Didn't I tell you I was going to call the cops if you came in here?"

Bruce's jaw tensed. "Go ahead—call them. I don't care."

Lila fell to the floor at Nancy's feet. "Just let him go," she sobbed. "Promise me you won't tell Porter about this."

"And why should I help you out?" Nancy snapped.

Bruce took a step toward Nancy. "If you have

an ounce of compassion in your body, you'll keep your mouth shut. Porter doesn't need to know."

"Oh, yeah?" Nancy laughed. "We'll just see about that."

Porter took a carpet knife and sliced open the brocade upholstery of an overstuffed chair. He reached in and yanked out handfuls of stuffing, throwing it onto the floor. Once all the stuffing was emptied out of the chair, he peered inside the chair's springs and examined it carefully.

"Nothing," Porter grunted in anger. He heaved the chair against the wall.

On the night of Katherine's death, he'd made an offer to her that he didn't think she'd refuse.

"Why don't we sell that diamond of yours and spend the rest of our lives on some exotic island," he'd suggested, stroking her cheek with his fingertips. "After all, half of it belongs to me."

She had been stubborn. Too stubborn for her own good. "No. Chester bought it for me for our anniversary."

"He bought it with my money," he'd said. "Half of everything you own belongs to me. If I want that diamond, I have every right to take it."

"You'll never find it," Katherine had said.

At first he didn't believe her. But after spending weeks searching the attic, Porter realized that Katherine was better at hiding her precious jewel than he had given her credit for. He had been through the attic from top to bottom. The only thing left to do was tear everything apart, looking for secret hiding places. If the final search didn't turn up anything, Porter could be reasonably sure that the diamond wasn't in the house at all.

"Maybe she was buried with it," he thought aloud. Porter wiped the sweat off his brow. He'd dig up her grave if he had to.

"Tell me where it is," he'd said.

Katherine had looked at him defiantly. "Never. It belongs to me."

His temper had flared. "You'd better do as I say."

"Don't you dare threaten me," she'd said. "Get out of my house."

"It's my house too. Don't you forget it." Anger had exploded inside him. He'd lunged for her.

Porter took the knife and slashed at a pillow. The attic was hot and dry, and the dust burned his throat. He had spent too many nights up here already, and it was beginning to push him to the breaking point. He tore open the cloth and ran his fingers through the filler. No matter what happened, this was going to be his last night in the attic. He'd search every single item thoroughly, even if it took until morning. If he didn't find it, he'd spend tomorrow night in the graveyard. By then, hopefully, he'd have the precious jewel in his possession.

Throwing the pillow and carpet knife aside, Porter grabbed a heavy crowbar and walked over to an antique bureau. He pulled out the first drawer. It was filled with letters and a few photographs. Porter dumped the contents onto the floor, then proceeded to break apart the drawer with the crowbar. He pried open the joints with mad satisfaction, thinking about how wonderful his life would be once he got his hands on the diamond.

Katherine had reached into the cupboard and grabbed a stack of plates, throwing them at him. The plates had smashed against the tile floor of the kitchen.

"Stop it!" he'd screamed at her. "Tell me where it is."

She'd thrown a crystal goblet at him. "Get out!"

Hot fury had bubbled in his veins. He'd drawn back a powerful fist and aimed it squarely at her. Katherine had ducked, and his hand had knocked out the pane of glass in the cupboard door.

He'd been planning the whole scheme for so long that he couldn't believe it was finally within his grasp. A buyer was set up in Switzerland, waiting to purchase the diamond. The money from the sale would go directly into a Swiss bank account. Porter would leave the country as soon as possible and live the rest of his life in perfect comfort somewhere in the Alps. It was a perfect plan.

The only possible wrinkle in his scheme was that stupid little girl downstairs. At first, Porter thought he'd be stuck with Lila for a long time. But with a few well-placed words and a missing object or two, it didn't take long for her to go off the deep end. Porter smiled proudly to himself. The night of the gala had been a stroke of pure genius. She had really flipped out. The wounds on her wrist from the broken window glass was just the kind of evidence he needed to have her committed to the state mental hospital. Nancy would be the perfect witness.

Once Lila's committed, I'm home free!

Even if she said anything against him, no one would believe her. After all, she was insane.

His hands had clenched her slender, graceful throat. "Tell me, Katherine," he'd said, his rage burning out of control. "Where is my diamond?"

"I'll never tell," she'd said, looking him squarely in the eye. "And you'll never find it."

Suddenly he'd snapped. His strong fingers closed over Katherine's throat, tighter, tighter. "I'm giving you one last chance."

Katherine hadn't said a word—she'd just continued to stare in defiance.

"Good-bye, then," he'd said, squeezing her throat with all his strength. He'd squeezed and squeezed for several minutes, until he'd seen the life go out of her eyes.

Porter picked up the splintered wood and threw it on the pile near the wall. He opened the next bureau drawer and dumped everything inside it onto the floor.

Porter dropped the drawer near his feet and peered down at the pile of old photos on the floor. At the very top of the pile was a picture of Katherine, in one of her tacky aprons. Porter adjusted the light attached to his hat and studied the picture. The apron was decorated extravagantly with appliqués and silver piping that spelled the words *Queen of the Kitchen*. His eyes settled on the center of the apron.

"Oh, my," he muttered under his breath. It

was the clue he'd been looking for.

Porter tossed the crowbar to the side and lunged for the trunk near the open attic window. Hastily he lifted the trunk lid, searching for the apron in the picture. When he'd been searching earlier, Porter had only reached into the pockets of the aprons. He didn't bother taking a closer look.

At last he found the horribly glittering apron and laid it delicately across the trunk.

"Katherine, you are a darling," he said happily to her picture. "Or should I say *were*." The apron was so tacky he never would've dreamed of finding the diamond here. But there it was, hanging from a pin, smack in the middle of the apron. It had been in plain sight the whole time. Katherine definitely knew what she'd been doing. All that time she had been wearing a priceless jewel on her apron, and everyone thought it was a cheap decoration.

"And now it's back with its rightful owner," he said aloud.

Porter laughed wickedly as he unpinned the gorgeous gem and slipped it into the pocket of his coveralls. He sighed with delight, relishing the moment. His search was finally over.

But there's still one more nuisance to take care of, he thought, *and she's waiting for me downstairs.* If they left right away, Porter could have Lila committed early tomorrow morning.

Reaching for the crowbar, Porter walked to the attic door. "I hope you're enjoying yourself, Lila," he said happily. "Because it's your last night of freedom."

Chapter Nineteen

Lila watched as Nancy stormed out of the study.

"Don't worry about her," Bruce said, helping Lila to her feet. "She won't do anything."

Lila's nerves were on edge. "Oh, yes, she will, and she'll take great pleasure in it, too."

The attic had suddenly become quiet. Bruce lifted his eyes toward the ceiling.

"You can't stay." Lila looked up anxiously. "If what you said is right, Porter could be back any minute." She ushered him out the door and turned off the light. "You'd better go."

"Why don't you come with me?" Bruce's brown eyes pleaded with her. "I'll take you away from this mess."

Lila wiped away her tears, directing nervous glances toward the front door. She imagined the profound look of disappointment on Porter's face if he walked in and saw her talking to Bruce. He'd never forgive her.

What should I do? Lila wondered. The decision weighed heavily on her. Bruce was looking at her with those sweet eyes of his, making everything sound so easy. *Just walk away from here,* he'd said, as if it were as simple as snapping her fingers. But what would she be going back to?

Porter had warned her that Bruce and her friends might try to turn her against him. He'd said they might try anything to get her back— even making up lies about him. *Be strong,* Porter had said. *Resist them. Don't believe in their lies.*

"I don't know," Lila said hesitatingly.

Bruce eyed the door. "There isn't any time to be indecisive, Lila. Either you're with me or you're not." He gazed at her intensely, as if he were trying to penetrate her mind. "This is your only chance. I'm not coming back. If you decide you don't want to be with me, you're on your own."

Lila winced. It all sounded so final. She held his gaze for several seconds, then turned away. "I'm sorry, Bruce. You have to go."

Defeat broke over Bruce's face. He tipped up her chin and kissed her softly on the mouth. "Good-bye, then," he said hoarsely.

Lila choked back a sob as Bruce walked out the door. And out of her life forever.

Bruce eased the Jeep out of the driveway, then parked it across the street. He turned off the headlights and waited in the darkness. The lamp was still on in Lila's room, making it easy for him to see the faint outline of her form near the window. She was probably waiting for David Carrier to come home.

Bruce tiredly covered his face with his hands. It would have been so much easier if Lila had just agreed to leave that jerk and left with him instead. Carrier might have taken off if he sensed they were on his trail, but at least Lila would be safe.

Bruce felt a sharp, stinging pain in his torso at the thought of her in that house with a maniac. Doubts nagged at his brain as he wondered if maybe he shouldn't have given up so easily. If he had talked to her just a bit more, she might have changed her mind.

I should've been more persuasive.

Bruce wanted to kick himself for leaving without her. But there had been so much pressure. Carrier could have come back at any minute. Besides, Bruce thought that when he told Lila he'd never come back, she'd go along with him. He never dreamed she'd say no. At that point he was so desperate to get her out of the house, he would have said anything.

Even if it was a lie.

Oh, Lila, Bruce thought as he gazed at her bedroom window. *Carrier's got his hooks in you even deeper than I thought.* It would take a bit more maneuvering—a bit more planning—but Bruce would see that the slimeball was brought to justice.

Bruce picked up his cellular phone and dialed the number of the police station.

"Detective Desmond—this is Bruce."

"I've been waiting for your call. What took so long?" the detective answered.

"She wouldn't come with me," Bruce said. He stared ahead at the dark mountain road. "Carrier was messing around in the attic the whole time. He should be back any minute now. I'm parked across the street, and I haven't seen his Mustang yet."

"Sit tight. I'll dispatch a few squad cars immediately," the detective said. "When Carrier pulls into the driveway, we'll be waiting for him."

Snap!

Lila heard the clean crack of splitting wood. She ran into the hallway to see what was happening. The boards nailed to the attic door splintered, and the door to the attic burst open.

Lila covered her eyes. "Leave me alone!" she screamed. Whatever was in the attic, it was coming after her.

Porter descended the attic stairs, wearing dirty blue coveralls. His face was twisted into a strange smile. He didn't say a word.

Lila dropped her arms to her sides. *Bruce was right,* she thought. *Porter was in the attic the whole time.* But that still didn't mean anything. He could have been up there for any number of reasons. She stepped aside to let him walk by.

"I thought you were at the hospital," Lila said meekly.

Silently Porter walked past her and opened the door to his study, his mouth still frozen in an eerie expression. He clicked on the light and suddenly stopped in the doorway. His body went rigid as he

262

looked at the broken lock on his rolltop desk.

"I didn't do that—" Lila blurted.

Porter turned and glared at her. His eyes were like chips of ice. "Who did it, then?" he demanded.

What should I say? Lila trembled. She didn't want to take the brunt of his anger—she had already upset him so many times. It would be much easier if she blamed it all on Bruce.

"It was Bruce," Lila started, her voice quivering. "He forced his way into the house. He was saying all kinds of crazy things, and then he wrecked your desk." She looked down at the floor. "I tried to stop him."

Porter dashed out into the hall, his hair flying about wildly. "Nancy—get up here now!" he growled.

Nancy, who must have been listening to the conversation nearby, came running in only a few seconds later. "What is it?"

Porter pointed to his desk. "Lila says that a man by the name of Bruce Patman was here tonight. She says he forced his way in here and destroyed my desk. Is this correct?"

Nancy looked at Lila with pity. "No, it's not."

A cold shiver ran through Lila's body.

"What part isn't correct?" he asked.

"The whole thing, sir."

Porter watched Lila carefully out of the corner of his eyes. "Are you saying that Mr. Patman wasn't even here?"

Nancy nodded. "That's right."

"She's lying!" Lila shrieked. She sank to her

knees, pulling Nancy's wrist. "Tell him the truth, Nancy," Lila begged. "You saw us in here. . . ."

"I don't know what she's talking about," Nancy said flatly to Porter. "She must be hallucinating again."

Porter gave Nancy a dismissive wave. "Thank you, that will be all," he said. "You can pack up your things and leave—I won't be needing your services anymore."

Nancy stared at him in disbelief. "But I—"

"Go!" Porter shouted. Without a moment's hesitation, Nancy scurried out of the room.

Lila rocked back and forth, her gaze distant. "I'm not making it up. He really *was* here."

"Shut up!" Porter yelled. "I'm sick of your lies." He grabbed Lila roughly by the forearm and yanked her to her feet.

Lila howled in pain. "It's the truth!"

"You have no idea what the truth is. Your sense of reality is totally warped," he said in an ominous voice. "Do you know what I think? I think you're *insane*."

"Stop it!" Lila covered her ears.

But Porter continued. He put his face right next to hers, so that she felt his breath when he spoke. "I think you'll never get well. You'd be better off spending the rest of your life in a mental hospital."

"No!" Lila sobbed.

Porter held her in a cold stare. "That wouldn't be very nice, now, would it?"

Lila shook violently. She tried to pull away, but Porter held her in his iron grip.

"Maybe I should just kill you and save you

from a life of misery," he said with a sneer.

A scream of sheer terror rose to Lila's throat, but the sound was muffled by Porter's thick hand covering her mouth. He dragged her out into the hall, then into her bedroom. With a kick he slammed the door behind them.

"You'll never get away with this!" Lila screamed as she struggled against him. She twisted and turned her body wildly, kicking and pulling to break free.

"Why not?" he said with a ghastly laugh. "I've done it before." Porter held Lila out at arm's length, barely straining from her effort. In an instant he released his hold on her wrists, then clamped his strong hands around Lila's pale throat.

Lila's lungs burned for air. "Let . . . go . . . of . . . me . . ." she said hoarsely as Porter's thumbs pressed harder against her throat.

"You sure put up a good fight." Porter smiled with psychotic pleasure as Lila dug her fingernails into the bony knuckles of his hands. "Just like your aunt." He squeezed tighter.

Gurgling noises escaped from Lila's throat. An excruciating pain consumed her as Porter's thick fingers crushed her windpipe. He stared at her with morbid fascination, as if he savored every terrifying second.

I don't want to die . . . Lila's head became fuzzy. She stopped digging into his hands—her fingernails were bloodied, trying to release his grip. The room tilted sideways, spinning in circles like the earth on its axis.

Then everything went black.

Chapter Twenty

"He should be driving up any minute now." Bruce stood next to Detective Desmond's unmarked squad car and watched the policemen taking their positions. Their cars were parked off the road, in the shadowy, tree-lined edge of the property. Bruce only knew where they were because of the glare of the headlights as they'd driven up. As soon as they turned off the lights the cars disappeared into the darkness.

Detective Desmond reached for the holster under his jacket. "I'm setting up my men in strategic points. There will be a few at the entrance of the driveway, some near the garage. I have one or two waiting in the bushes. There are two squad cars at the bottom of the hill in case he slips by us."

Bruce leaned against the squad car. "Carrier's a smart guy. I wouldn't be surprised if he figured out how to get past everyone."

"He won't escape," the detective said. He

unwrapped a toothpick and put it in his mouth. "I won't let him."

The only thing left to do was wait.

The sky was clear, and the full moon cast a surreal glow on the mountain. Hundreds of feet below, the restless ocean churned against rocky cliffs. The air was still and expectant, as if the earth were holding its breath.

Bruce's heart thumped loudly in his chest. His muscles were tense and knotted as he waited anxiously for the bright yellow beams of Carrier's headlights. But they were nowhere in sight.

Detective Desmond took the toothpick out of his mouth and snapped it in two. "Are you sure he was behind the house?"

"Absolutely," Bruce said. "He had nowhere else to go."

"I don't like this." The detective rubbed his forehead. "My gut tells me that Carrier's figured us out. He must've had an alternate escape plan."

Bruce shook his head. "There *is* no alternative. The only way down the mountain is this road—unless he took a helicopter. And I haven't heard one."

"There are a million ways he could have escaped," Desmond said with authority. "He could have just hiked through the woods on foot." The detective stomped the ground angrily. "I'll be damned if this one gets away." He reached into his car through the open window and radioed the station.

"I want an APB out on David Carrier . . ." he said into his handset.

Suddenly the front-porch light came on. Nancy came running out, her arms waving wildly. "Somebody—help!"

Bruce was about to go running up the driveway when Detective Desmond's strong arm blocked him. "Don't go in," the detective said. "It could mess up the plan."

"Hurry!" Nancy cried.

"I have to," Bruce answered. His heart raced. "Lila could be in danger."

"I'm telling you, it's a bad idea."

Bruce pushed past him. "I'm just going to check it out. Make sure she's safe."

The detective looked at him warily. "I'll send one of my men—"

"Forget it," Bruce said firmly. "I'm going in. If I need any help, I'll turn the light in Lila's room on and off a few times." Before the detective could protest, Bruce ran up the drive.

When he reached the front porch, he saw the wild look in Nancy's eyes. She covered her mouth with a shaky hand. "He said the whole thing would be quick and easy. We were going to go to Europe with the money." Tears streamed down her face. "If I had known that someone was going to get hurt—"

"Where is she?" Bruce shouted.

"Upstairs," she cried. "Be careful! He's crazy!"

Bruce burst through the front door and flew up the stairs. He didn't need to know the details. Just the look on Nancy's face was enough to tell him that Lila was in trouble. He bounded through the hallway and kicked open the door to her room.

"Oh, no!" Bruce exclaimed.

Startled, David Carrier turned around. Lila was lying on the floor, her body pale and lifeless. Carrier was still shaking her violently, his hands squeezing her throat. When he saw Bruce in the doorway, he dropped Lila and stood up.

Bruce's blood began to boil with rage. "What have you done to her?" he thundered.

Carrier just stared at him, his eyes cold and calculating.

Bruce looked down at Lila's frail body. He recoiled in horror as he touched her bony wrist. She was cold.

"My poor, sweet Lila . . ." Anguish surged within him. Bruce picked her up in his arms, her head rolling against his chest as he moved. He kissed her blue lips tenderly.

This is all my fault. I never should've left her here, he thought with pain in his heart. Everything that had happened in the last several weeks was his fault. If only he had been there on the day of the quake, none of this would have happened. One simple mistake, and suddenly their lives had spun out of control. And now Lila was dead and it was all his fault.

Bruce buried his head in her hair and cried. "I'm so sorry, Lila," he whispered to her with overwhelming sadness. "I loved you more than anything else in the world."

* * *

David Carrier watched the melodramatic scene unfolding in front of him.

How pathetic, he thought as he backed away from Bruce and moved toward the door. *A dead psycho and a dim-witted frat boy—what a perfect pair.*

His eyes focused on the back of Bruce's head to make sure that he didn't turn around. David inched slowly out of the doorway and into the hall. He touched the pocket of his coveralls and felt the smooth, round shape of the diamond. *It won't be long now,* he thought with pleasure.

Running up the attic stairs, he smiled to himself. Silver moonbeams illuminated the dusty floor. He was only seconds away from freedom and a life of supreme luxury. It all awaited him, just beyond the attic door. David imagined the snow-covered caps of the Alps. His little chalet in the mountains, with nothing around for miles. And now that he'd gotten rid of Nancy, it was going to be all his.

He threw open the attic window. The fire escape ladder was to the right of the window. Once he reached the ground, it was only a short run to the car. Then he'd be home free.

David lifted the window sash as high as it could possibly go, then reached out for the rusty fire escape with both hands. When his fingers were secure around the iron bar, he started to pull himself out of the window.

A pair of strong hands suddenly grabbed him by the legs and pulled him back inside. David's upper torso landed hard on the wooden floor.

"Where do you think you're going?" Bruce demanded. His eyes flared with anger.

"Ugh!" Shooting pain spread through David's lower back. He grabbed at Bruce's legs, trying to pull him down. Bruce shook free of David's grip. He kicked him in the side. "Cheap shot." David moaned in pain.

"That was something I should've done a long time ago," Bruce said.

David struggled to his feet. His head felt light. Looking Bruce squarely in the eye, he swung his arm and punched him powerfully in the stomach. Bruce sank to his knees.

David let out a grisly laugh. "How'd you like that one?" He landed another punch, then another, gaining momentum with each swing. Blood trickled from Bruce's nose and lip. Bruce doubled over, coughing.

"You stupid fool." David touched the jewel to make sure it was still there. "You should've just minded your own business."

"Why did you do it?" Bruce wheezed, trying to get to his feet.

"Because it's the most exquisite thing I've ever seen," David answered. "I value it beyond anything else."

Bruce leaned against the old trunk. He winced with each breath. "Obviously you don't value human life."

David flashed him a diabolical grin. "Not yours, anyway." He lunged toward Bruce and clutched at his throat.

Bruce had no time to react. David dragged him forcefully toward the window. He pushed him backward so that Bruce's head and upper body were leaning out the window. Bruce's eyes bulged in terror.

"Which would you prefer?" David said, his face glowing wickedly in the moonlight. "Being strangled or falling to your death?"

Tom sat in the back corner of the coffeehouse, reading the newspaper and drinking his third cup of decaf. *If only Jessica wasn't in her room all the time,* he thought miserably. Having to avoid her at all costs was quickly becoming the biggest priority in his life. Tom couldn't wait until tomorrow, when he'd finally be back in his old room.

"I've been looking everywhere for you," a sultry voice said.

Tom looked up from his paper, his stomach dissolving. Jessica pulled a chair up to the small wooden table so that she was sitting as close to him as possible. She was wearing one of the shortest skirts he'd ever seen.

"Why are you hiding out here?" Jessica asked. She flagged down the waitress and asked her for a café au lait. "I miss you," she said with a pout.

Tom pretended to read the headlines, but his head was swimming. "I just wanted to get out of the room, that's all."

Jessica pressed herself against him and read over his shoulder. "Well, I hope it isn't because of little old me," she breathed.

Oh, no, of course not, Tom thought sarcastically.

Jessica covered the newspaper with her hand. "I think we need to talk," she said.

Tom shifted in his chair uncomfortably. "Fire away."

The waitress set a tiny white cup of coffee in front of Jessica. She took a sip, then crossed her legs seductively. "I just wanted you to know that I'm not upset about what happened the other night."

"What are you talking about?" Tom said, trying desperately not to stare at her legs.

"You know—the night of the gala," Jessica explained, squeezing his biceps. "I wanted to tell you that I understand why you didn't act on my advances."

Tom looked up. "You do?"

Jessica smiled. "Of course. I know you're shy—but that's okay. I realize it has nothing to do with the way you really feel about me."

Tom sighed and looked at her uneasily. He took a drink from his coffee cup. He glanced around the room, hoping that no one he knew was watching.

Jessica rubbed the back of his neck. "But what I wanted to know is—when are you going to tell Elizabeth about us?"

Tom choked on his coffee, spraying it all over his paper.

Jessica quickly picked up a napkin and wiped his face. "Don't be upset, honey," she cooed. "If you want, we can tell her together."

               *   *   *

The thick, black fog that hung over Lila's head began to clear. She slowly opened her eyes. Taking a deep breath, she filled her grateful lungs with cool air. She reached up and touched her throat, wincing from the pain. Even though Porter was nowhere in sight, she could still feel the crushing power of his fingers around her neck.

Boom!

A heavy, pounding noise came from the attic. Lila stood up, steadying herself against the bed. *Porter's trying to escape,* she thought dizzily. *I can't let him.* Lila stumbled out of the room, wheezing as the air reached her lungs. She climbed the staircase slowly, supporting her weight against the banister. *I have to stop him.*

When she reached the attic door, Lila froze in horror. "Bruce!" she screamed. Porter had Bruce by the neck and was trying to push him out the window. Bruce's legs were kicking in the air.

Porter's eyes widened with surprise. "Get out of here!" he yelled at her. "Now!"

Bruce twisted fiercely—nearly half of his body was out the window.

You've got to do something fast, Lila told herself. *He's going to kill Bruce.* Adrenaline coursed through her veins, clearing her mind and her vision. She scanned the attic, looking for something to help him. Tearing through boxes, Lila at last came upon the perfect weapon.

Bruce gasped for air. "Ahhhh!" he cried out in

terror as his body started to slide backward.

Lila stepped forward, holding her aunt Katherine's marble rolling pin with both hands, high above her head. With one swift move she brought it down right on the top of Porter's head.

Instantly he released his grip and slumped to the floor.

_____

Chapter Twenty-one

Bruce looped the rope around the back of the chair and tied it in a square knot. "That should hold him until I get the police," he said.

Lila dropped the rolling pin at her feet. Her hands were trembling. "Are you sure you're all right?"

"Yeah, I'm fine," Bruce said casually, though his expression said otherwise.

Carrier lifted his head groggily and his eyes fluttered open.

"Where is it?" Bruce demanded, staring into his glassy eyes.

"Why should I tell you?" Carrier muttered, in a daze.

Bruce pulled the rope tighter across Carrier's chest. "Because there are five squad cars parked outside, and they're all waiting for you."

Carrier sneered in defeat. "It's in the top pocket."

Bruce reached in and took the jewel. In the

bright moonlight of the attic, it shone like a star. "It's beautiful," Bruce said, running his fingers over the smooth surface. "But it's not worth killing for."

"What would you know?" Carrier snapped back.

Bruce raised his hand as if to hit Carrier but thought better of it. "You're not worth it," he said, lowering his hand. He slipped the diamond into his jacket pocket and turned to Lila. "Let's get the detective and have him take this slimeball away."

Lila didn't move. "You go. I'll stay here."

"No," Bruce said forcefully. "You're coming with me."

"Don't tell me what to do, Bruce," Lila shot back. She looked at Carrier. "I'd like a few minutes alone with him."

"Listen to what you're saying . . . this man's a murderer—a lunatic."

Lila took a step toward Carrier. "Three minutes—that's all I ask."

Lines formed over Bruce's brow. "If that's what you want," he said worriedly. "But be careful. Don't fall back under his spell."

"We're finally alone," David said. His blue eyes closed slightly and he flashed her a dimpled grin. "Thanks for getting rid of him."

Lila rested her hands on her hips. "Why did you do it?" she asked.

"Do what?" he said hypnotically. "I didn't do anything."

Lila frowned. "You didn't?"

277

David shook his head. "Be a sweet girl and untie me. These ropes are digging into my wrists."

Lila looked blankly at him.

David stared deeply into her eyes. "This is serious, Lila. They're coming after me," he said. There was the slightest hint of anxiety in his tone. "I saved your life—now you can save mine."

Lila looked around. "What do you want me to do?" she whispered.

David smiled. "I think there's a carpet knife in the old trunk. You can cut the rope with it."

Lila's gaze was distant, confused. She looked like a child who was lost in the woods. "I can't do anything like that," she said in a soft voice. "I'm insane, remember? You told me I was."

"You're not crazy," he blurted. "I was just saying that."

Lila's eyes narrowed. "You were making that up?"

David swallowed nervously. "Of course . . . It was a kind of psychological . . . test . . . to see if you had fully recovered from the accident. . . . You can judge a person's mental abilities by how they respond to such a statement."

"Is that so?" Lila said. "And how did I do?"

"Very well," he said boldly. "You're in perfect health." His eyes darted to the trunk. "Don't forget, the carpet knife is in there."

"Yes, course." Lila laughed with relief. She opened the lid drawer. Inside were embroidered pillowcases, folded in neat squares. Sitting right on top of the linens was the locket Porter had given her the day they first moved in together.

"Look at this!" Lila said excitedly. "It's my locket. All this time I thought I had lost it. I wonder how it ended up in here."

"How wonderful," David said, anxiously looking at the attic door. "As soon as we get out of here, we can have it fixed."

Lila shook her head in amazement. "And I thought it was gone forever."

"Remember the day I gave that to you?" he said wistfully.

Lila nodded. It had been the perfect day. They had just moved into their new house. Everything in their lives had been filled with hope and promise for the future. Lila couldn't remember a time when she had been so blissfully happy.

Porter's soft blue eyes engaged hers. His face glowed angelically in the light of the moon. "We could have that back again."

Lila's eyes brimmed with hope. "Do you really think so?" she whispered.

"Absolutely," he said with a sexy smile. "Just think how wonderful it would be if we could have a fresh start—"

"That sounds nice."

"And we could move far away from here, where no one knows us. We could leave behind all these terrible complications."

Lila moved closer. She hovered above him. "I'd like that."

David parted his lips slightly and gazed at her. "All you have to do is untie me."

Lila looked at the shiny gold locket in the palm of her hand. She squeezed it in her fingers.

"Do you know what I'm hoping for?" she said coyly.

David grinned in expectation. "What is it, my love?"

Lila's smile shrank into a venomous glare. She drew back her arm and hurled the locket, hitting Porter in the face.

"I hope you spend the rest of your miserable life rotting in a prison cell."

"This place looks even better than it did before the quake," Elizabeth said, admiring Tom and Danny's new room.

Tom dropped a box of books on the floor near his bed. "Danny thought it'd be nice to give the walls a new coat of paint. I think he was right—it really brightened the place up."

Jessica plopped down on his bed, running her hands over Tom's new bedspread. "It's kind of funny. I didn't want you around at all at first, and now I hate to see you go."

Tom cringed. For the past hour, every time Jessica opened her mouth to say something, Tom broke out in a cold sweat. Every word she spoke had the possibility of wrecking his relationship with Elizabeth.

"I'm sure you'll be much happier without me,"

Tom said, moving to the farthest point away from Jessica.

Elizabeth stacked a few books on the shelf. "You can always come visit."

Jessica blew Tom a kiss. His face turned red and his palms were damp. *Why is she torturing me like this?* Tom desperately wished that there was a trapdoor under the floor of his room where he could fall through and disappear forever.

"Tom has something to tell you, Liz," Jessica said with a wide grin. "Go ahead, Tom. Tell her."

Tom scowled, baring his teeth at her.

"Tell me what?" Elizabeth asked.

Tom cleared his throat. "Jessica's just trying to be funny, that's all."

Jessica rolled her eyes. "He's *so* shy." She turned to him. "Why are you so shy? Tell her."

Tom's knees weakened. "I—"

"Tom and I had a little chat in the coffee-house," Jessica interrupted. She stared right at him. Elizabeth's back was turned as she continued to fill the bookshelves on the wall.

Tom panicked. He waved frantically at Jessica, begging her not to tell Elizabeth. He hopped around silently, like an overenthusiastic mime.

"So what did you talk about?" Elizabeth asked.

Jessica tossed her hair over her shoulder. "Tom said he was very grateful to stay with us and that you were the best girlfriend a guy could ever want."

Tom froze.

"Did you really say that?" Elizabeth asked.

Tom shook his head adamantly. "No way—" Suddenly Jessica's actual words penetrated his brain. "I mean, yes . . . of course I did." His body felt as limp as a wet dishrag.

Elizabeth threw her arms around Tom's neck. "That's the sweetest thing I ever heard."

Tom smiled happily, holding Elizabeth in his arms. He looked over her shoulder to see Jessica tiptoeing toward the door.

"I guess I'll leave you two alone now," Jessica said as she gave Tom a wink. "Gotcha," she whispered as she slipped out the door.

Lila, Bruce, and Nancy watched the flashing blue and red lights of the squad cars as they descended the hill. As the lights pulsed, Lila saw David's outline in the backseat, his angelic blond curls falling around his shoulders. Lila wrapped her arms around Bruce's waist, warding off the chill that seeped into her bones.

"I can't believe this night," Nancy said, crushing her last cigarette into the driveway gravel. She picked up her suitcase. "I can't believe I let myself get involved with a maniac."

"Can we give you a lift somewhere?" Bruce said.

Nancy shook her head. "That's okay. I have some friends nearby."

Lila touched her arm affectionately. "Thank you for helping me—I might've died if it hadn't been for you."

Nancy pulled on a thin cardigan over her

cropped shirt. "I had to do something. I was probably going to be next." She grabbed the suitcase strap and wheeled it behind her. "Good-bye."

"Bye." Lila waved. "Don't call if you need a reference," she muttered under her breath.

Bruce pulled Lila close to him. It felt wonderful to be in his arms again. Lila rested her head against his chest. Bruce sighed contentedly. "I never thought I'd get you back."

"I never thought you would either," Lila said jokingly. She looked up at him, her eyes glistening. "Thanks for coming for me tonight. I'm so sorry for everything I've put you through."

"I'm just glad you're okay." Bruce held her tight.

Lila wiped away a tear. "How could I have been so stupid? I can't believe I let him do that to me."

"There's no sense beating yourself up about it," Bruce said tenderly. "Carrier came into your life when you were very vulnerable. I just wish I had been there for you more."

"You were there—I just didn't know it." Lila pressed her cheek against his. "Do you think we could get things back the way they were, Bruce? Do you think you could love me again?"

Bruce tipped Lila's chin and pressed his soft lips against hers. Pulling away, he looked deeply into her eyes. "I never stopped, Lila. I never stopped."

We hope you enjoyed reading this book. If you would like to receive further information about available titles in the Bantam series, just write to the address below, with your name and address:

KIM PRIOR
Bantam Books
61–63 Uxbridge Road
London W5 5SA

If you live in Australia or New Zealand and would like more information about the series, please write to:

SALLY PORTER
Transworld Publishers (Australia) Pty Ltd
15–25 Helles Avenue
Moorebank
NSW 2170
AUSTRALIA

KIRI MARTIN
Transworld Publishers (NZ) Ltd
3 William Pickering Drive
Albany
Auckland
NEW ZEALAND